August Unknown

AVA BRADLEY

Ava Bradley

ISBN-13:978-0615714950
ISBN-10: 0615714951

Pink Pixel Publishing
Edited by Faith Williams, The Atwater Group

This book is a work of fiction. The names, characters, places, and occurrences are products of the writer's imagination or are used fictitiously. Any resemblance to actual incidents is entirely coincidental.

To the real Jeffrey in my life; proofreader extraordinaire and all around super fungi.

Author's Foreword:

When I originally wrote this foreword, I had just received back edits from my mother, an experienced sailor who fact-checked my boating references. The honeymoon sailing trip mentioned in this book was one she and my father took on their 95-foot ketch *Sea Venture*. I sent her the whole manuscript, but she only read the parts I'd marked for her. She returned it with a note saying she couldn't wait to read the whole book when it came out in print. Sadly, she never got the chance, as she passed away shortly before *August Unknown's* release. I'd like to take this opportunity to recognize her contribution. I miss you, Mom!

Now on to the nitty-gritty. For those of you familiar with Newport, Oregon, I ask that you suspend your disbelief just a teeny bit. While I conducted extensive research on the beautiful town, I have changed the names of streets, hospitals, and shops for fiction's sake. The house with the view of Yaquina Head in which the Barthlow family lives is real. I stumbled upon it on a real estate website and fell in love. In fact, the house is part of what inspired this story. As a born and raised California girl, there is something mysterious about the rocky Western coastline that enthralls me, and I find lighthouses, with their noble and haunting purpose, absolutely spellbinding. I couldn't help but wonder what might happen in a sleepy little coastal town on a stormy night after the power goes out, when two wounded souls find each other in the dark...

Chapter One

The ocean roared in her ears. Waves crashed over her head from all sides, stinging her eyes and choking her with mouthful after mouthful of salty water.

Numbing cold dulled her senses. She fought against the water pulling her down, but struggling only made it worse. In the darkness, she couldn't tell which way was up.

She strained to make out the flashes of light rushing across her vision. A buoy? A lighthouse? Deep rumbling followed. It was lightning, and dangerously close. A sudden pummeling of rain smacked the water around her like an eruption of stadium applause.

"Help me!"

She was hurt. The sharp stinging at her hairline burned more intensely with each wave that swept over her aching head. Lightning flashed again, brighter and longer this time, revealing the depth of the empty darkness surrounding her.

"Help. Somebody, please."

She closed her eyes to squeeze out the salty burn. She stopped fighting, letting the ferocious pull of the sea drag her under as she clung to the hope her lifejacket would bring her up again.

The sharp pain in her head receded to a dull thump. She was being battered by the pounding surge of the ocean, but the roar in her ears had faded. It almost seemed they were filled with cotton.

Hypothermia. The idea was terrifying, and...*not so bad.*

She closed her mouth against the bitter salty water, no longer calling out. She didn't know who she was calling to. The icy harshness of her surroundings drifted away and soft, velvety black draped over her awareness.

Her feet hit something. Before she realized what had happened, the surge tossed her onto a rock-hard beach. Her arm twisted painfully under her body. She felt as though she'd plunged from a third-story window.

A wave followed, crashing over her with ruthless force. Gravel churned around her as she was pushed farther out of the ocean's grip.

Her body weighed a ton, but the relief was intense. She lay there, gasping out silent thanks, floating at the edge of nothingness.

Another wave crashed over her, jarring her awake. Darkness surrounded her. It was night, and still storming. As awareness clawed its way back, she became aware of fat raindrops hitting her.

She forced brittle arms to push herself upright. Pain throbbed in her icy, numb fingers as she fumbled with the clips on her lifejacket. When it finally came free, she dropped it behind her and looked around.

There were buildings in the inky distance. She squinted through the rain. Not a single light shone, but a strange glow in the clouds bathed the beach in a surreal luminosity.

What is this, an abandoned compound of some sort?

She struggled to stand, only to collapse on her

hands and knees again. The beach was rough, mostly stones and coarse sand. Pebbles stuck to her palms.

A wave of nausea struck, and mouthfuls of ocean came up, salty and bitter with bile. She heaved again and again until all that remained in her stomach was gnawing emptiness.

She stood and wobbled precariously, but this time remained on her feet. She trembled uncontrollably, and each impossible step jarred her battered body. Her bones felt like toothpicks about to snap. She was so weak the gusting wind made her stagger back a step.

The shapes on the horizon were fuzzy, but she was too tired to focus. She just had to get there, that was all she knew.

Shelter. Warmth. *Safety.*

What had a moment ago been fat raindrops suddenly turned to torrential sheets of sharp, icy slivers, knifing into the top of her tender head. Lancing pain came alive again, strangely familiar, but she couldn't remember what caused it.

In the back of her mind, she suspected she was in a ghost town, headed for ramshackle buildings, but she didn't care. She had to get out of this rain and the chilling wind. She wanted to close her eyes so badly, to sleep, just for a little while. Sleep.

◆ ◆ ◆

Jocelyn grew bored with the remote control to the compact disc changer and turned off the music.

"Why does Grandma live at the Mirthful Mermaid?"

Geoffrey Barthlow maneuvered his BMW carefully along the dark road. As they traveled down the coastal highway from the summer house, the power had winked out, making the town below literally vanish before their eyes. He'd never been on the ocean road in darkness like this. Even with fog lamps and his high beams, the driving rain made it nearly impossible to see. It sounded like gravel hitting the car.

"The restaurant is her home," he answered as he slowed to negotiate a curve. "She's lived there for thirty-five years." Gusts of wind pounded them, but the car held the road beautifully.

"That's five times as old as me."

"You're right."

His niece was such a precocious child. He loved spending time with her. His sister accused him of spoiling Jocelyn, but with no kids of his own and none in the foreseeable future, he did it with gusto, and refused to be made feel guilty for it.

"Grandpa says it's a dive."

Geoffrey laughed. Actually, his father called it much worse, but never to Jocelyn's ears. As the founder and CEO of one of the top-ten most successful hotel chains in the country, his father hated being reminded of his humble roots almost as much as Gran Millie hated being reminded she wasn't Jocelyn's grandmother, but great-grandmother.

"This is cool. It looks like *The Fog*." Jocelyn stretched up taller in her seat to peer out the passenger window.

Thick, charcoal darkness like Geoffrey had never seen blocked out the ocean. It seemed the storm sat directly on the surface of the water. At the edge of the road, the world disappeared.

"I have to stop letting you watch those horror movies."

"Why?" She looked at him, bewilderment filling her pixie face. "I'm not scared."

Geoffrey thought back to the costume she'd fashioned last year for Halloween. She'd traded two Miley Cyrus CDs for an old Girl Scout's uniform. Without help from anyone, Jocelyn had then used red dye and craft putty to make herself into a dead Girl Scout. His sister had been horrified.

"Your mother is still mad at me for letting you watch *The Bludgeoning*. She wasn't happy about that Halloween costume." He could only imagine what she'd come up with this year.

"It was just a joke," Jocelyn said, twisting to peer out the window again. "Grown-ups are so serious all the time."

"Well, don't tell her, but I liked it."

She flashed him that magical smile that reminded him life was beautiful. "You rock, Uncle G." Her expression dimmed. "Do you think my mom and dad will be divorced by Christmas?"

She surprised him with that one, completely out of the blue. At the same time, he'd known she would ask something like that, sooner or later.

He slowed the car for another sharp bend and considered his answer. "Your parents are just working out some issues." As soon as he'd said it, he regretted it. *Working out some issues?* Jocelyn was seven; she wasn't stupid.

"They're separated. Amy Knoeller said that's just what they call it before the divorce becomes legal." Jocelyn settled in the deep leather seat and stared at her shoes. "Her parents are divorced. She has to live in two different houses."

"Your parents are *not* getting a divorce," Geoffrey said firmly, even as he wondered himself. Leah and Marc would work things out; they had to.

This whole family can't be unlucky in love, could we? Does the Barthlow curse plague us all?

"Are you ever gonna get married again, Uncle Geoffrey?"

Like a flash of lightning, the painful memories he'd worked so hard to bury came alive again, as bright and clear as if the accident that killed Christina happened only yesterday. A vision appeared in front of him, fuzzy in the sheeting rain, a ghost haunting the highway that had killed her.

The specter of death stared back at him, shadowed, frightened eyes caught in the ghostly glare of his headlights. *Christina.*

Jocelyn's ear-piercing scream filled the car, bouncing off the glass to pummel him from all directions. Too late, Geoffrey realized this was not the ghost of his dead wife, but another mysterious figure in white, very much alive.

And he was about to run her down.

Chapter Two

Geoffrey's heart surged into his throat and stuck there. He swerved and hit the brakes. The BMW slid sideways, and then fishtailed. A sickening thump filled the car and Jocelyn screamed again. They careened across the road, and then back to the right side and through a thick clump of salt grass before crashing against a wooden sand rail. Both air bags deployed, and immediately deflated.

A stomach-turning moment of confusion passed where nothing seemed real, as though what had just happened was part of a bad dream. Geoffrey released his seatbelt and turned toward his niece. Jocelyn had a bloody nose.

"Are you all right, sweetheart?"

Her eyes were wide with horror. "We hit a girl."

Geoffrey turned off the engine and looked out the back window. With the front end pitched downhill, all he could see was black sky.

"Stay here." He opened the door. His senses came back to life as the shrieking storm slapped him in the face, cold and furious.

"Uncle Geoffrey—"

He paused. The howling wind drove needle-like slivers of icy rain into the side of his face. "It'll be okay." Sickening déjà vu turned his insides to liquid.

He ran up the sandy incline to the asphalt. A glimpse of white in the salt grass on the other side of the road was gruesome proof this wasn't a waking nightmare, but horribly real.

The *whump* of the passenger door closing registered dimly.

"Jocelyn, stay back."

Jocelyn climbed over the ruined fence and stopped by the corner of the car. Silhouetted by the red glow of the taillights, she looked like a phantom.

"Is she dead?"

"Stay there!"

Geoffrey held his breath, praying for movement where the body lay on the sandy shoulder. Beyond the dunes, the town was still invisible. For all he knew, it had vanished. The night had turned terrifyingly unreal.

The woman lay crumpled on her side, her face hidden under a mass of long, wet hair. One arm protruded from beneath her body, the fingers of her limp hand slightly curled. Her delicate wrist was exposed where her blue and white striped sweater had inched up her arm. Blood spattered the band of white.

Geoffrey knelt and felt for a pulse. Her skin was so cold that for a horrifying moment he thought she *was* dead. Then he found it: a dull throb, weak, but steady. He held his breath, making sure.

She wore white jeans and white sneakers. The reflective clothing had saved her life.

Jocelyn lingered near the car, gripping her hands together in front of her heart. Already the rain had soaked her. Strangely, Geoffrey didn't feel cold or wet himself.

His hand went to his hip. His phone's holster wasn't

there. He'd dropped it in the center console when he'd gotten in the car.

"Get my phone from the car," he shouted through the wind. Without a word, Jocelyn disappeared around the passenger side.

He brushed the hair from the woman's face. Dirt and blood matted a nasty gash at her hairline. Driving raindrops hit her, making the blood dance grotesquely. His stomach flip-flopped. Geoffrey swallowed back a suddenly watery mouth.

Her eyelids fluttered and she moaned.

"It's all right. You're going to be all right," he said in a shaking voice. It felt like a lie.

She gave no indication she heard.

"The battery is dead!" Jocelyn's thin voice carried back through the storm.

What else could go wrong? Geoffrey knew he shouldn't move her, but he couldn't leave her lying in the sand. As gently as he could, he turned her onto her back and hefted her into his arms. The movement caused her to cry out.

He saw her face for the first time as her long hair fell away. Her lips parted, so pale they were nearly blue. Long, dark lashes, wet and clumped, fanned across deathly pale skin.

"Open the back door," he told Jocelyn. She raced around the car and pulled it open.

"Is she gonna be okay? Uncle G?"

"Yes," he said in a firm voice, trying to convince himself as much as Jocelyn. He slid the woman across the back seat and secured her with the center belt. "We need to take her to the hospital. I want you to ride in back with her. Can you do that?"

"Uh huh." Jocelyn slipped into the seat by the woman's feet and secured her own seatbelt without being reminded.

For a frightening moment the car stuck in the sand, its tires spinning uselessly. Then they caught and the BMW shot backward onto the blacktop. One headlight had been smashed on the fence.

He drove faster than he should along the dark road, worried by every second that ticked by. Numbness fought to take hold, pulling him back into that nightmarish, alternate reality.

"How are you doing, Lyn-Lyn? You okay, sugar plum?" He didn't dare take his eyes from the road to glance in the rearview mirror. He could sense Jocelyn leaning forward, her damp golden hair shining in his peripheral vision like the last ray of hope on this God-forsaken night.

"'kay," came the shaky reply.

"How's your nose? Are you still bleeding?"

"My nose is bleeding?"

The wind threw a gigantic palm frond into the side of the car.

"What was that?" Jocelyn wailed.

"Nothing, honey, just a branch. We're almost there." With only one headlight, the night was impossibly dark, and Geoffrey had trouble focusing. In his mind's eye, he kept seeing the white-clad figure mixing hellishly with visions of his past.

Once inside the city limits, they were no longer the last people on earth. The hunched shape he recognized as Russ Pearson from the library ran along the sidewalk, collar pulled up around his ears. As they raced past Newell Street, he glimpsed the flashing red and blue lights of a police car at the end of the street.

All the traffic lights were out. The danger of driving through blackened intersections at this speed was not lost on Geoffrey, but he had only minutes to save her.

I won't let you die, Christina.

Panic welled in his chest until he wanted to shout and pound the steering wheel with his fist.

A gust of wind buffeted the car. Geoffrey tightened his grip on the wheel, fighting to keep the BMW in his own lane. Finally, the glowing red sign of Pacific Communities Hospital Emergency loomed in the darkness, a reassuring beacon in an otherwise deathly-dark town. The building was dimly lit, running on emergency generators, but even those pale lights were intensely comforting.

Geoffrey hit the horn twice before he jumped out and ran to the emergency call button outside the door. Jocelyn slipped out of the back seat just as two orderlies ran out with a stretcher, followed by Dr. Carlson.

"What happened?"

"She was in the road; all the lights were out. I tried to swerve around her but the roads were slick. God, it all happened so fast...I knew I shouldn't move her but my phone was dead and I didn't know what else to do."

"Geoffrey." Dr. Carlson placed a hand on his arm. "You did the right thing." He and the orderlies crowded in the BMW's rear door to examine his unconscious passenger. They lifted the woman onto the stretcher and hurried her into the emergency room.

As if the storm realized it had lost its grip on its mysterious victim, the rain turned to a drizzle and a sudden lull in the wind turned the night eerily still.

Jocelyn waited in the hospital entry's glass foyer

while Geoffrey parked the car. She watched him run across the parking lot, her expression solemn. Though a preemie by two touch-and-go months, she had always been a fearless little girl, smarter and stronger than most kids her age. But tonight, she looked small and sick like she had when she was an infant. Geoffrey hoisted her onto his hip and took her to the registration desk.

"She was hit in the face when the airbag went off. Can someone take a look at her nose?"

The nurse's brows drew together. "Toddlers aren't supposed to ride in the front seat. They can be seriously hurt or even killed when an airbag deploys."

"I'm not a toddler," Jocelyn shrieked. "I'm almost eight."

Geoffrey's guilt deepened. He silently berated himself for even taking her with him on a night like this.

With her lips pinched together in a tight line, the nurse stood and rounded her desk. "Come on, sweetie, let's put you in examination four."

"No." Her lower lip jutted. "I'm okay, Uncle G. I just want the lady to be all right."

"No arguments. Your mother will never forgive me if I don't get you checked out."

The nurse held out her hand. "Don't-cha want a lollipop?"

"I'm too old for lollipops," Jocelyn mumbled. She scrunched her face into an exaggerated pout, but allowed herself to be led away.

Geoffrey lingered in the wide entrance to the ER. After what seemed like hours, Dr. Carlson emerged from the first bed. Geoffrey caught a glimpse of pale white skin before he pulled the curtain back again.

"How is she?" He fell into step with the doctor.

"Hard to tell. Have you called your brother-in-law?"

Geoffrey's heart dropped into his stomach. "Good God, you don't think she's going to die, do you?"

"No-no-no. Her vitals are strong, but her arm is broken and she's got a nasty bump on the head. You never can tell with head injuries like this. But regardless of the severity, all accidents need to be reported to the sheriff. You know that."

Geoffrey let out his breath and nodded. "Of course."

Dr. Carlson stopped at the registration desk. "Any idea who she is?"

"I've never seen her before. Thank God she was wearing white, or I wouldn't have seen her at all." He ran a hand through his hair. "Jesus. I was driving so slowly."

Dr. Carlson placed a hand on his shoulder. "It was an accident. The lights are out all over town."

As if to mock him, the main lights buzzed and the hospital brightened as the power came back on.

Geoffrey shook his head. "I couldn't bear knowing I killed another human being—"

"You haven't killed anybody. I've ordered a CAT scan to be sure, but other than the broken arm, it looks like those are her only injuries. That, and exposure to the elements. She's hypothermic. We've got her on heat coils right now. Where did you say this happened?"

"Outside town on the coastal highway, near the old fisheries."

Hypothermia? How long had she been outside in the storm? No wonder her skin felt like ice. Had she started walking toward town when the power went out?

Jocelyn burst from the examination room and ran

down the hall. Geoffrey picked her up and settled her on his hip.

"All fixed?" He forced a smile while inside, the contents of his stomach felt like month-old milk.

She nodded, happily sucking on a lollipop. She pulled it out of her mouth and stuck out a green tongue.

"Lovely. Come on, let's go call Uncle Mike."

"And Gran Millie, too?"

He nodded, feeling the weight of this horrible night settling over his bones. "And Gran Millie, too."

◆ ◆ ◆

Geoffrey glanced at the SUV's dashboard clock. Eight fifteen a.m. He was probably wasting his time. Visiting hours weren't until ten, and he wasn't even a relative.

After finally arriving home at midnight last night, he'd tossed and turned until he got up around four a.m. and tried to do some work. He couldn't get the accident, or the poor woman, out of his mind.

Over and over, he'd rehashed the scenario until he was convinced he could have avoided it a hundred different ways if he'd just reacted a little faster. If he'd been paying attention a little harder. If he'd had both hands on the wheel. If he'd been driving a little slower.

He'd nearly killed a person. She might even have died since they left the hospital last night. Dr. Carlson hadn't yet established how serious her head injury was.

A dramatic sigh emanated from the back seat of his father's SUV. "Why do I hafta ride back here?" Jocelyn demanded.

"I told you," Geoffrey answered without taking his eyes from the road. "It isn't safe for you to ride in the front seat if there's a passenger-side airbag."

She'd been dressed and watching cartoons in the living room when he'd tried to sneak past at eight. There had been no escaping her then, and Geoffrey never could say no to Jocelyn.

"I hope she'll let me sign her cast."

More reminders of the damage he'd done. Jocelyn had no idea the emotional turmoil he was going through.

"You can ask once, but don't pester. Okay?"

"I don't pester!"

"That's right, what was I thinking?" he teased. The effort took everything out of him, and sounded phony.

"Uncle G!" Jocelyn's giggle fluttered from the back seat like flower petals on the wind. God bless that little angel.

Though occasionally a fluffy white cloud with a dark center passed in front of the rising sun, the bright morning held little evidence of the viciousness that had passed through last night. Broken tree limbs lay in the rain-soaked streets, but otherwise, Newport had fared well.

He parked the car in the hospital's main lot and took Jocelyn's hand. He slowed his pace to match hers as she stared morbidly at the double glass doors of the main entrance.

"I hate hospitals," Jocelyn said softly. She had been unusually quiet all morning. Maybe she was more upset about the accident than he'd realized.

"Well, you were in them a lot when you were a baby."

"They stink."

Thankfully the attending nurse was not the same woman who last night had looked at him like he was the worst adult in history to let a child sit in the front seat of a car with airbags.

"We're here to see the young woman brought in last night." He swallowed past a sore lump of guilt. "The car accident victim."

"I'm sorry, visiting hours are ten until seven. Are you a family member?"

Dr. Carlson emerged from the office area. His face was etched with fatigue. "It's all right, Helen. I'll take them in."

Geoffrey picked up Jocelyn and followed him down the hall. "Tough night?"

"There were four separate car accidents and Roberta Norton slipped on her front stoop and shattered her elbow. Two broken arms in one night. I thought I moved to a small town to avoid all this."

"The first storm of winter always sends people slipping and sliding all over the place." As soon as he'd said it, Geoffrey's chest tightened. Christina's accident had happened just as the first rain of the season sprinkled over Newport in early October of last year.

Dr. Carlson hoisted Jocelyn onto his hip. "Hiya, Pumpkin. How's that nose?"

"Fat," she said with a frown. "I look ugly."

"The swelling will go away soon." He chuckled. "And you could never look ugly." He stopped at the elevator banks and hit the call button. "We moved your Jane Doe upstairs last night."

"How is she?" Geoffrey asked, even though he was almost afraid to hear the answer.

"We set the arm and stitched up her head. She came to for a while, but she's confused."

"So she's not in a coma," Geoffrey said over a sigh of

relief.

"No, nothing quite so serious. There was nothing in the CT to cause concern."

Dr. Carlson set Jocelyn down. They stepped out of the elevator and he gestured to the first room with his clipboard. "She's right in there, first bed." He set off in the other direction. "Come and see me before you leave so I can take a closer look at that pretty little nose."

Nervous tension coiled in his belly as Geoffrey looked at the open doorway. If they'd let her sleep, she couldn't be hurt too badly, could she? He didn't think people were allowed to sleep if they had a serious head injury.

Jocelyn took his hand and led him inside. The woman shared the room with two other patients, both elderly women who appeared to be sleeping. He sat in the guest chair and pulled Jocelyn into his lap. She leaned her head back on his chest and watched the woman with him.

Impossibly long eyelashes made crescents across her cheekbones as she dozed with lips slightly parted. He found it strange he'd noticed those lashes last night through all the chaos. Afterward, he thought he might have imagined them. Now, in the light of day, he saw they were more amazing than he'd first thought.

He'd suspected her hair was light, but last night when it had been soaking wet, he couldn't really tell. He'd had other things on his mind, like mind-altering fear. He never imagined it was such a magnificent, shimmering blond. It sprawled across the pillow beneath her head, long enough to reach her elbows.

"She's pretty," Jocelyn whispered.

She's more than pretty, Geoffrey thought. Though

frighteningly pale, her skin was clear and smooth. She looked a little green against the white bandage at her forehead, but when healthy and smiling, this woman was stunning—he would bet money on it. She appeared to be of Nordic descent, with high cheekbones and a narrow nose.

Her left arm rested above the sheets. A fiberglass cast covered the bend in her elbow and reached to the knuckles on her hand. Slender, delicate fingers curled around its edge. He remembered how she'd cried out when he'd moved her.

Geoffrey scrubbed a hand over his face. He'd done everything wrong last night.

She breathed a soft sigh and her lids fluttered, and then opened. Brilliant blue eyes that glittered like aquamarine gemstones locked with his, making Geoffrey's blood race. He held his breath, no idea what in the world he would say to her.

◆ ◆ ◆

A thin whisper brought her from the edge of a dream. Opaque light filtered through her closed lids. It was day, she realized as she came fully awake.

Antiseptic smells stung her nostrils. *This is a hospital.* In the back of her mind, she knew she was hurt. Her entire body was weak, sore. Battered.

Bass drums pounded in her head. She opened her eyes and the room came into view, fuzzy at first, then growing clearer like steam clearing from a window.

A man she didn't recognize sat in the chair beside her bed, an adorable little girl with curly blond hair in his lap.

She had never seen either of them before.

Confusion barreled over her, only to be replaced

instantly by fear. Dread. Worry. Confusion again. An underlying terror something horrible had happened.

The little girl sat upright and her face brightened. The man urged her off his lap. He had the same hair, only thicker and with darker undertones.

"Go get Dr. Carlson," he told her.

The little girl scampered off. Once in the hallway, she shrieked, "Dr. Carlson!" and the man in the chair winced.

"Sorry," he whispered.

He stood and stepped closer, bringing along a crushing fear. She couldn't breathe.

"Hi." He smiled, but his eyes held worry.

She swallowed, tried to speak. Her throat was dry and sore. She glanced up, looking for a call button. Something to bring help—safety. Her pulse raced. She was in danger. But from what?

More importantly, from *whom*?

Her confusion grew thicker, along with the solid pain throbbing in her head.

The little girl returned, tugging the hand of a man in a white coat.

"Well, good morning. How's my favorite patient today?"

Goodness, did she know this man? He smiled kindly, but it did little to appease her fear.

"What happened?"

"You were hit by a car last night, but you're going to be just fine."

She glanced to the other man. He smiled sheepishly. "I'm the guy who hit you."

"Where am I?"

"This is Pacific Communities Hospital in Newport,

Oregon," the doctor told her.

She tried to move. A spike of pain went off like a siren, racing down her arm and ending in the tips of all five fingers. She sucked in a breath as nausea rolled in her stomach. "Ouch!"

A new level of fear rushed in with dizzying force. Her left arm was in a cast. She held her breath and pinched her eyes shut, willing the pain away.

"Here, have some water." The doctor poured from a carafe into a paper cup and brought it to her lips. Refreshing coolness slid down her throat, and slowly the blaring pain faded.

"How badly am I hurt?" She dreaded the answer. Strangely, her fear was worse than the pain.

"You have a broken radius, right here, and a hairline fracture of the olecranon. That's here." He pointed to his own arm to demonstrate the locations. "Nothing required pinning, thank goodness, and both should heal better than new. There was a deep laceration at your hairline, but I did a marvelous job stitching you up, if I do say so myself."

A nurse stepped through the doorway. "Dr. Carlson, you're needed in recovery two."

"I'll be right along," he told her. He moved closer and gave her a pitying smile that sent her worry climbing. "Do you remember anything from last night? Can you tell us what you were doing out on the highway during the storm?"

The storm...the storm... She clawed through the darkness filling her mind, but nothing would come.

She shook her head.

"Don't try too hard. This is normal for head injury patients." He patted her knee. "But I do need to get you checked and listed. Nurse Barnes will help you fill out the paperwork."

All at once, the uncertain fear she'd been feeling was replaced by terror a thousand times brighter.

Everyone stared back at her, suddenly quiet.

"Don't worry," the younger man said, stepping forward. "I intend to pay for all your hospital costs, any rehabilitation you need, and fully compensate your for your pain and suffering. This whole thing was my fault, and I'm prepared to make amends."

He didn't understand. None of them did.

The nurse took the clipboard from Dr. Carlson. "Let's start with your name, and date of birth."

She choked on a hot lump of misery. The room fell into silence again. She stared from one to the next. Only the nurse seemed to have realized something was terribly wrong. She leaned forward, the concern evident in her face. "Are you from Newport?"

Hot tears stung her eyes as the frightening realization hit. "I don't know where I'm from. I don't know who I am!"

Chapter Three

Geoffrey knew he was staring, but he couldn't believe what she'd just said. *Amnesia?* It was unbelievable, the thing daytime soap operas were made of.

His heart wrenched as the woman burst into sobs. She bit back a cry of pain as she jostled her broken arm, and then settled one hand over her eyes as she cried.

"Now, now," Dr. Carlson said, patting her knee. "Don't worry. As I said, it's normal to be confused after a head injury. It's understandable that you wouldn't remember the events immediately after a head injury, and sometimes what happened before is foggy, too."

How much worse could this get? Geoffrey believed he'd only caused physical injuries that would eventually heal, but he never imagined he'd crippled her mentally and emotionally, too.

If it was the last thing he did, he would make this right. He only wished he knew how.

Nurse Barnes pulled a handful of tissues from a box on the bedside table and helped the woman blow her nose.

"I know this is frightening for you," Dr. Carlson said. "Let me assure you, you're in one of the best medical facilities Oregon has to offer, and we'll do everything in our power to get you reunited with your family."

Dr. Carlson's words crushed the rising protectiveness Geoffrey had just experienced. Did she have a husband who would pulverize him when he learned what had happened?

He glanced at the fingers curled around the edge of her cast. Did he imagine it, or was that a tan line circling her wedding ring finger?

Again, unbidden and unwelcome, gruesome emotions came rushing in. After Christina's death, he'd wanted to destroy whatever person or thing got in front of him.

The woman's sobs frightened Jocelyn. His niece's eyes were wide and shiny with tears.

"First of all, let's get you something for the pain that will help you relax." Dr. Carlson tried to sound upbeat. "You heard what Geoffrey said—he's picking up your tab, so you might as well indulge in the best."

The woman glanced from Dr. Carlson to him with wariness all over her face. She didn't know him from Adam.

While the doctor listed off a regimen for the woman, Geoffrey bent down and reached for Jocelyn. "Maybe we better get you home."

"No!" Jocelyn grasped both hands around the plastic rail at the side of the bed. "I wanna stay. I was in the car, too, you know. It was my fault just as much as yours."

His guilt tripled. Before he could find the terms to argue that a seven-year-old would understand, Jocelyn turned back to the woman and took a sideways step to the head of the bed.

"My name is Jocelyn Tanner." She stepped onto the lower bar of the guard rail and pulled herself up so she could see better. "I live with Uncle Geoffrey and

Grandpa Duke because my mommy and daddy are getting a divorce. Last night we had a really big storm and Uncle Geoffrey and me were going to get my Gran Millie. She lives at the wharf on top of the Mirthful Mermaid. We thought she would be safer if she came home with us because our house is on a hill and the wharf shops always get flooded in really bad storms. We didn't mean to hit you."

Geoffrey wanted to pull her away, but Jocelyn had captured the woman's attention, and stopped her tears.

She gave a hesitant nod. "I know you didn't mean to do it on purpose."

"Twelve years ago a real bad storm came and washed a bunch of people out to sea. That was before I was born, but my grandpa says it was real bad."

The woman's gaze drifted away, as if Jocelyn had jogged something in her memory.

"I'm seven," Jocelyn continued. "But I'm small for my age 'cause I was born too soon and I got sick a lot when I was a baby."

"Well you sure grew up..." the woman sniffled, "to be very pretty."

"No I didn't!" Jocelyn shrieked adamantly. A hint of a smile trembled on the woman's lips.

The nurse returned with a paper cup containing two pills. She handed them to the woman and poured her another cup of water.

"Thank you," she said in a thin voice.

All Geoffrey could do was stand there, staring like an idiot. His oldest brother Justin would have something witty to say, making everyone in the room chuckle. All David would have to do was flash one of his charming smiles to make the tension dissipate. Geoffrey was usually the one to cause that tension, and today was no different. Actually, this was the worst it had ever been, but still classically Geoffrey.

Running a woman down with his car would certainly be the coup de grace to his social life.

She swallowed the pills and turned back to Jocelyn. "How do you manage to grow all that hair?"

"I hate my hair," Jocelyn returned shrilly. "I wish it was soft like yours." She reached out and touched a lock of the girl's platinum hair where it fanned over her shoulder.

"I'm sorry," Geoffrey said. "Come on, Jocelyn." He pried her off the bed frame and stood her on the floor.

"Don't go, please," the woman said, stopping him. "I don't want to be alone."

He felt as if someone had opened a faucet and let warm water trickle over him. Geoffrey shifted from one foot to the other, searching for something to say to end the aching silence. He wasn't witty or charming, and knew he should probably keep his mouth shut.

But common sense had never been his strong point, either.

"I'm Geoffrey Barthlow. Geoffrey with a G." *G, for Geek.* "I meant what I said. I intend to pay for your hospital bills, and whatever else you need."

"Thank you." She blinked slowly and her eyelids drooped.

"Is there anything I can get you?" He moved closer, setting a hand on the railing. This much closer to her, he realized an entirely new level of beauty. She had the perfect features of a movie star. As her gaze drifted to something across the room, he studied her flawless complexion and the unique flecks of gray in her pale blue irises. All at once, he felt like an intruder. He stepped back again.

"A toothbrush would be nice." Already the painkillers had softened her voice.

"Let's continue on this paperwork before you drift off again." Nurse Barnes took her clipboard and sat in the guest chair. "For now we'll call you Jane Doe."

The woman's eyes flashed open. "No, please. I don't like that."

Nurse Barnes pursed her lips and leaned back in the chair. "What would you have us call you, then?"

"We could call her August," Jocelyn suggested. Everyone looked at her, and her cheeks turned pink. "What? I have a friend named April and a friend named June. August is a name, too, you know."

"But it's not her name, honey," Geoffrey said. Jocelyn was acting like she needed a nap. She'd probably slept as fitfully as he had last night.

"How do you know?" she argued. "She was born in August. It might be her name."

Another silence reigned. Even the woman's attention was caught.

"Your birthstone," Jocelyn explained. She touched a fingertip to the patina stone in the delicate gold ring the woman wore on her right hand. "Peridot is my birthstone, too."

"August." She yawned. "I like that better than Jane Doe."

"August it is, then," Nurse Barnes said. "August Unknown."

◆ ◆ ◆

Geoffrey returned to the hospital that afternoon with a new toothbrush, a plush velvet robe, and a cheerful floral arrangement of yellow daisies.

August was awake and staring across the room at the window. Afternoon light flooded through, bright and warm. She turned and saw him as he entered. Her eyes were red and puffy, and she tucked away a damp tissue.

"Hi," he said stupidly.

He suspected he was imagining it, but her smile seemed genuine when she saw the flowers. "Hi. Geoffrey, right? With a G."

He groaned silently and heat rushed into his face.

But her smile only grew. "Are those for me?"

"Actually, they're for her." He gestured to the sleeping woman in the next bed. "I thought she'd like them."

August actually laughed. "I'm sure she'll love them." She tried to hide her bashful smile. It made her absolutely enchanting.

"Do you think she'll like this? I know how those hospital gowns are drafty in back."

He opened the gift box and held up the royal blue robe. When she saw it, her face filled with amazement. "So generous. I think her husband will get jealous."

Husband. The word hit him like a punch in the gut. *What about your husband, August?*

Since leaving this morning with Jocelyn, mysterious August Unknown had filled his every thought.

He'd gone out to talk to his brother-in-law at the sheriff's office, and then to visit his grandmother at the Mirthful Mermaid.

He'd hoped Gran Millie would say just the right thing to ease his conscience, but he should have known she'd be angry instead. She wasn't a child who couldn't take care of herself in a little storm, and if he'd stayed at home where he should have been, this wouldn't have happened. By the time he'd left, his guilt was burning hot and bright.

He'd driven home through Newport, intending to get some work done in his home office for a while, but had only made it as far as *Le'gante Boutique* for the robe before turning around to come back. He'd thought about the flowers on the way, and stopped at *Everlasting*, the exclusive florist who'd done his sister's wedding. He didn't want to show up with hospital gift-shop flowers.

Now he felt ridiculous. How could he be such a fool? He glanced to the door, wondering if an angry husband would come bursting through, eyes blazing, clawed hands reaching for Geoffrey's throat.

"Actually, I did get you something." He set the toothbrush on the food tray jutting over the bed.

"You know just what a girl wants." Her expression grew somber. "This is all very nice, but you really shouldn't go to so much trouble."

He moved closer and placed his hand on the dull beige railing. "You've been crying again."

She glanced away. Those summer-sky blue eyes paled as they caught the sunlight flooding the room. They held such sadness he felt himself shriveling up inside.

"I'm frustrated," she said. "Frustrated that I can't remember a thing. Frustrated that I can't use my left arm. Frustrated that I have to lie here in this bed, not knowing what happened to me, or why." August made a fist with her right hand and hit it against the mattress. She winced in pain and closed her eyes.

"Do you want me to get the doctor to give you something?"

She shook her head. "I don't like what they gave me. It makes me feel dopey."

"I can talk to him about something different—"

"No. The pain makes me feel more alive." She sighed and relaxed the scowl in her brow. "I'm sorry. I'm having a hard time dealing with the fact I can't remember my own name."

He nodded and glanced down, fighting for something to say to help ease her grief. He couldn't think of a single thing. There was nothing that could lessen what he'd done.

"What's this you're writing?"

She turned the paper toward him. "They sent a psychologist up to see me. She suggested I write letters and numbers to see if they go anywhere, like a phone number or zip code."

"The police can run a sequence of numbers to see if they match a street address," he told her. "The sheriff is my brother-in-law. I'll ask him to give your case special attention."

He looked up to find her watching him. "Do these look like anything you use here?" she asked.

Geoffrey didn't have the heart to crush the hopeful look in her eyes. Newport's zip codes started with a nine, and most of the area codes started with a five. The woman in the next bed moaned in her sleep, sparing him.

"I spoke to Dr. Carlson about moving you to a private room," he told her. "I'll take care of the costs."

"It's not necessary. They're letting me go in two days. They'd let me go tomorrow if I could remember where I live."

"I thought you'd be more comfortable in a private

room." In his heart he knew it was irrational—she was only being polite—but he felt as though he'd just been rejected.

"I need to stay with people," she explained. "Mrs. Thornton and I were talking after you left this morning, and I remembered little things. Nothing I could put my finger on, but crumbs were there."

She gave that pitiable smile he'd seen too many times before. The *I just like you as a friend* look.

The guilt that had been growing in him felt like steadily rising water. Now it felt like it was about to go over his head. "I can't begin to imagine what you're going through. I want to do whatever I can to help you. This is all my fault—"

"Stop saying that." She placed her hand over his where he held the rail. He looked down to see her slender fingers curling around the knuckles of his hand. When he looked up and met her eyes, she drew it away. A cold spot was left where she'd touched him.

Her eyes clouded over with something dark. "I'm not so sure it's true. What was I doing there in the first place?"

He didn't know what to say to that.

"You said it happened near vacant fisheries," she pressed. "What was I doing out on a dark road in the middle of nowhere, after ten o'clock at night, in a storm?"

"Are you saying you think there might have been foul play involved?"

She closed her eyes and pressed two fingers to the bridge of her nose. "I don't know what I'm saying. But I have a strange feeling I can't get past." She leveled a determined gaze on him. "Why hasn't anyone reported me missing?"

"I may have the answer to that." Officer Gaffney stood in the doorway holding a folder. Geoffrey knew his brother-in-law well enough to recognize the solemn look on his face as bad news.

◆ ◆ ◆

The sight of a uniformed officer made August's heart kick against her ribs. Geoffrey seemed to recognize the man. He stepped around the bed and offered a handshake to Geoffrey.

"Heard you had a bit of an accident last night. What in damnation were you doing out in a storm like that?"

"I was after Gran. Jocelyn wanted her to come home with us."

"I think Leah's better off not knowing Jocelyn was in the car with you," the officer warned.

Geoffrey held up both hands. "She won't hear it from me."

"You must be Geoffrey's brother-in-law." August hoped the sheriff was here as a friend to Geoffrey and not on some grim, official business.

"This is Mike Gaffney, Sheriff's Department Investigator. Mike is married to my sister, Paige."

The officer gently shook her good hand. "Dr. Carlson tells me you took a nasty bump on the head and can't remember much."

August nodded, fighting a sudden stinging of tears. She took a deep breath.

"Don't you worry. I've seen it before and it always passes. I'm sure it'll all come back." He craned his neck to look at the paper on the meal tray. "I see Dr. Lohman gave you a homework assignment."

"She's been writing numbers in case something

comes out naturally, like a phone number or address," Geoffrey told him.

"May I?" Officer Mike picked up the paper. "These don't look like local prefixes or area codes, but I'll run them through my database." He folded it up and placed it in his pocket. "Is there anything at all you can tell me, even something simple, like a hobby that interests you, or a favorite food?"

August's frustration came barreling back. "Favorite food? How in the world is that going to help?"

Officer Mike twitched his bushy mustache. "You might be surprised."

"Sure," she snapped. "I like the white clam chowder better than the red."

The men glanced at each other.

"I'm sorry," she said quickly. "I know you're just trying to help." She sighed. "Actually, I like them both."

Geoffrey smiled and August couldn't help but smile too. There was something comfortable about his face that made her feel safe. Though he was a virtual stranger, she was glad he was here with her during the officer's questioning. All day, a dark and frightening presence had been lingering in the shadows of her mind, and in a strange way she couldn't quite identify, the officer's appearance made it worse.

Good God, I wasn't a criminal, was I? She shuddered before she could stop herself. The nagging ache in her arm spiked.

"I've been trying to picture a house, but I can't see anything," she told them. "I have to have lived somewhere, didn't I? I feel like I'm reaching through a dark doorway for something to grab onto, but there's nothing there."

A long moment of silence hung in the air. Dr. Lohman had explained there was no cure for amnesia. No one knew how to help her. She was desperately alone.

Officer Gaffney laid a manila folder on the tray. "Last night a sailboat sank off the coast, near Astoria."

As though someone had opened a furnace, a blast of heat struck August. Behind the two men, the room drifted away.

"Three people up on deck trying to keep her afloat were washed overboard. There was one survivor, an older woman who didn't know how to use the radio. The Coast Guard found the boat adrift, partially submerged this morning."

"And the three people?" She hardly found the strength to ask.

"The bodies of two men were found this morning. A woman matching your description is still missing."

The room began to spin. August's stomach churned.

Officer Gaffney flipped open the folder and sorted through until he found an eight-by-ten photo of a young woman with shoulder-length blond hair. "According to the grandmother, this photo is quite old."

"That isn't August," Geoffrey said.

She breathed out her fear in a whoosh, relieved and at the same time strangely disappointed.

"August?" Officer Gaffney passed a quizzical glance from one to the other.

"I didn't like the name Jane Doe. I was born in August—at least we think so. Jocelyn figured it out." She held up her right hand. "My birthstone ring is a peridot."

"Well, Miss August, I can't say this is bad news. It's never pleasant to notify someone they've lost a relative."

"I'm glad it isn't me, too." She chewed her lower lip, trying to force back tears. Though the two dead men weren't related to her, the tragic news still made her ill.

"There is something I remember," she volunteered hesitantly. "Though I don't know how it will help you."

They both looked at her with expectant expressions. She let her gaze drift over the photo of the missing woman. "This morning when I looked at myself in the mirror, I wasn't surprised to see what I looked like. I recognized myself."

"That's a good sign," Officer Gaffney told her. "You'll probably recognize other people and things you know, too. It's just a matter of time, and getting you up and out of this bed."

"When you're released, I'll be happy to take you wherever you want to go." Geoffrey smiled sheepishly. "If you trust my driving."

"That might not be necessary," Officer Gaffney told them. "I'm going to take a thumbprint and run it through the Department of Motor Vehicles. There's a good chance we'll know your real name before you'll need to."

Worry sat like a lead ball in her stomach, but August allowed him to take her print. She didn't know why, but the thought of discovering her identity before she remembered what happened to her sent needles of ice prickling up her spine.

Chapter Four

August toyed with her food—a strange concoction that was supposed to be stew—until it was so congealed the mystery chunks no longer slid easily across the plastic dish.

She couldn't get over the uneasiness that had started her insides quivering when the sheriff said he was going to run her thumbprint through the DMV database. In the back of her mind, fear lingered. Was she a criminal on the run? A frightened wife fleeing an abusive husband? She looked down at the faint tan line on her wedding finger.

"Not hungry?"

She looked up to find Geoffrey in the doorway. She hardly knew him, but already the sight of him gave her a thrill. His comfortable smile and timid charm almost seemed to ease her aches and pains.

He was handsome in a unique way. The things she liked about him weren't the typical things she suspected women observed in attractive men. He had a nice physique and the toned body of a man who exercised, but she admired the kindness in his smile that reached all the way to his eyes, and the graceful lines of his strong hands. He possessed the same thick blond curls Jocelyn did, and probably found them just as unruly. His brows and the clipped beard he kept trimmed into neat lines were darker brown which, contrasting with his blond hair, gave him a sun-bleached, surfer look. His eyes were a rich, cocoa brown that made her want to smile when he gazed at her warmly. The mint green polo shirt and faded denim jeans he wore today added to the casual flair of a man who was confident of his looks.

He grinned as he entered the room, pulling a paper bag from behind his back as if it were a surprise. "You look a lot better."

"I feel a lot better, thanks to the toothbrush you brought me yesterday."

He set the bag down on the tray table. Stenciled in turquoise blue, a smiling mermaid sat on a rock encircled by the words "The Mirthful Mermaid." The logo didn't bring even a hint of recognition.

He shifted her unfinished meal tray to the small clothing cabinet and removed a paper to-go bowl from the bag, which he set on the utility tray jutting over the bed. "Boston clam chowder. I like the white better, too."

The delicious scent of seasoned chowder and fresh sourdough bread rose around her, wiping away the stringent hospital odors. Her stomach rumbled with renewed hunger.

"You're so nice to me." She used her good arm to push herself up taller. "You don't have to worry. I'm not going to sue you. Unless I find out my father is a lawyer."

He froze, plastic spoon in hand.

"That was a joke."

Geoffrey relaxed, chuckling. "You had me going there for a minute."

"Really, you shouldn't feel you have to spend so

much time here. Your family must miss you."

He shook his head. "It's just me and Jocelyn up at the house. My father went back to Portland last week. Mike and Paige live up in Agate."

"What about you?" she asked in a hesitant voice. "No wife?"

A somber shadow passed over his features. "My wife passed away last year."

"Oh, I'm sorry." She suddenly felt pathetic. She realized how much worse her situation could be, and understood she had a lot to be thankful for.

Geoffrey served up a spoonful of chowder. She closed her eyes and let him feed her, savoring the creamy broth on her tongue. "Wow, that's good. I may not have my memory, but I'm pretty sure that's the best I've ever had."

"It's my grandmother Millie's secret recipe. She owns a restaurant. That's where we were headed when..."

"That's what Jocelyn said. Where is that, in Portland?"

"Yep." He nodded as he spooned up another mouthful. "I drove all the way to Portland to get you clam chowder."

"Don't tease me," she scolded. "I have no idea where I am. I'll believe anything."

He stopped and took on a humble expression. "I'm sorry. I keep forgetting. I can't begin to imagine what you're going through."

"It helps to talk to people. Tell me more about your family. Are you originally from Oregon?" The question wasn't so much to help jog her memory, but to learn more about her handsome visitor-protector.

"Actually, we're from right here in Newport. The Mirthful Mermaid has been in our family for seventy years. My grandmother has run it for thirty-five."

"It sounds like quite a landmark. I'll have to go see it. Maybe it will help spark my memory." She accepted another mouthful of chowder. "Mmmm. Anything to get another bowl of this."

"Does that mean it's okay for me to come back?"

"I'd like that. But I meant what I said. You have to stop blaming yourself." She leaned back against the pillow. "Until I know why I was out there, the whole thing is just one strange mystery."

Geoffrey set the spoon down and August could tell he was looking for the right words. When he looked up, his warm brown eyes were like melted chocolate. "Are you still worried someone tried to hurt you?"

The seriousness of his question slithered across her skin like the slow, oily traverse of a snake. "I don't know. But I'm almost afraid of what your brother-in-law is going to find." She forced a smile that felt thin. "You haven't heard of any bank robberies in the news, have you?"

He laughed as he picked up the spoon again. "That's another joke, right?"

"I honestly don't know." She swallowed another mouthful. The delicious chowder brought renewed strength with every spoonful. "I don't feel like bank robber material."

"It may seem hard to believe now, but sometimes people panic when they get caught in bad weather. Maybe your car broke down. You were probably just trying to get home and didn't expect a car to be coming around the bend." Geoffrey dropped the spoon in the empty container and bundled it all up in the paper bag. "Mike went to question the late season stragglers in the Chalets today. I'll bet you're traveling with a sweet old aunt who's just frantic about you."

It was too good to hope for. "You really think so?"

The second of hesitation before he opened his mouth to reply told her he didn't.

"Don't placate me." She leaned back and frowned. "I'm not made of glass. I can handle the truth—I just wish I could remember it."

"You will."

"But until I do, I don't know who I can trust."

His expression changed then. She felt guilty for even implying as much after all he'd done, but in truth, she couldn't rule anyone out.

"I'm sorry, but I don't even know you. All I have is your story that I stepped in front of your car."

"I understand."

He took a step back. She'd insulted him.

"Wait, I'm sorry, Geoffrey. I don't think you tried to hurt me." She patted the mattress by her hip. "Please, come back and sit."

He returned a half smile and sat at the edge of the bed. She met his eyes and held them, content to stare into their warm depths. She had nothing to fear from this man; she knew it in the deepest part of herself.

But someone *had* tried to hurt her, of that she was also certain.

"Something bad happened to me," she finally said. It was hard to find her voice. "Maybe your brother-in-law should suspend the search until I remember exactly what happened that night."

◆ ◆ ◆

Geoffrey saw Dr. Carlson as he signed the visitor's roster Friday morning. "How is she this morning, Doc?"

"No better, no worse," the doctor said. "But it's only been four days. I don't expect a miraculous recovery, and neither should you."

"She can't stay here indefinitely. What's going to happen to her tomorrow when you check her out?"

Dr. Carlson slipped his pen into his pocket and made his way over. "Any number of things. There's a women's shelter in Corvallis where she can stay without charge for seven days. If she needs a place longer than that, they'll put her in a temporary job or she can do administrative work to earn her stay. August seems like a pretty smart cookie. I don't think it'll be a problem."

There was no chance Geoffrey was going to let her stay in some shabby women's shelter. Not if someone might be after her.

"You can't just kick her out onto the street," he told his longtime friend.

If someone did want to bring August harm, turning her out on her own would be turning her into a sitting duck. She wasn't safe until she remembered what had happened to her, and if someone had indeed tried to hurt her, who that person was.

"I'm sorry, Geoffrey, once she's healthy enough to leave, we can't make her stay."

"So you're just going to turn her loose tomorrow."

"If her family were here, I'd discharge her today." The doctor's brows inched up his forehead. "Care to share your thoughts?"

"What if I take her to the summer house? Would you release her into my care today?" Even as he asked the question, Geoffrey knew August would refuse. She didn't know him, and would probably see the gesture as pathetic and desperate.

"Are you sure you want to get involved in this? You've already done all you're expected to in paying her bill."

"Why not? Everyone's gone back to Portland. It'll just be me, Jocelyn, and Leah when she returns next Tuesday. It's no imposition, and it's better than some shelter full of strangers."

Dr. Carlson considered him for a minute. "Well, if she agrees, I can't see why not. She can continue her appointments with Dr. Lohman if she stays nearby."

A rush of triumph cooled the hot tension that had wound Geoffrey up tight these past few days. Somehow, he believed protecting August would make up for his failing Christina. He knew that was irrational, but at the same time he couldn't live with himself if something happened to August simply because he didn't lend his help.

The sliding doors opened and Officer Mike walked through, hat in his hand. "Good morning."

Geoffrey's heart gave a strong kick against his ribs. His brother-in-law would only be here if he had found something. Maybe August wouldn't need his hospitality, after all. A tiny, selfish part of him hoped that wasn't the case.

I'm scum.

"Good morning, Mike," Dr. Carlson greeted him. "Have you learned anything about our mysterious guest?"

"I'd like to see her, if I may."

"We were just headed there now."

August emerged from the bathroom as they entered

the room. Her platinum hair spilled over the royal blue robe. Freshly washed, it shimmered in the morning sun. Renewed vitality colored her cheeks. Dr. Carlson had replaced the bandage at her head with a smaller one which was nearly obscured by her wispy bangs.

"This looks official." Her expression grew somber as her gaze found and held Mike. "Is something wrong?"

"Not at all," Mike assured her. "I came by to tell you we were unable to identify you by your thumbprint. I wanted to relay the news in person."

Her shoulders dropped. Geoffrey relaxed with a sigh of relief. At least they hadn't found she was a criminal on the run. He doubted she was, but it would be just his luck to have a woman like August literally dropped in front of him—only to find out she was a fugitive.

"I had a feeling that scar on the pad of your thumb would be a problem."

Eyes downcast, August climbed back onto her bed. She rubbed her thumb against her first two fingers.

"It's a fairly new scar, at least it looks to me." Mike glanced at Dr. Carlson. "The doc can say for sure. What that tells me is you're probably not yet twenty-six. In Oregon, you're required to renew your driver's license in person at the DMV, at which time you would have updated your fingerprint. Of course, if you live in California or Washington, that theory flies out the window because you'd be able to renew online if your driving record is clean."

She glanced at her thumb.

"But you don't look much older than twenty-six to me." Mike cleared his throat. "One of my officers questioned the remaining renters in the cottages near where you were found. No one is missing anybody."

"So I just fell out of the sky."

An uncomfortable silence stretched.

"How about some good news?" Dr. Carlson cut in, trying to sound cheerful. "Geoffrey has offered the guest room at his house. If you accept, I can release you today."

She glanced up with a wary expression. "That's very generous, but you've already done too much for me."

Geoffrey shifted uncomfortably from one foot to the other, embarrassed by being rejected in front of an audience.

"The other alternative is the woman's shelter in Corvallis," Dr. Carlson went on. "But in that case you'll be released into your own care, and I can't authorize that until tomorrow."

August's blue eyes were as pale as the sky as she watched the doctor, chewing her lower lip.

"It's just me and Jocelyn rattling around in that big house," Geoffrey told her. "I'm sure she would love to have you if you change your mind."

"You've been absolutely wonderful to me, Geoffrey." She hesitated. "But I can't go home with a strange man I don't know. You could be an axe murderer or something."

Dr. Carlson chuckled, then fell silent when he realized no one else was laughing. Geoffrey thought back to their private conversation yesterday when she'd gently accused him of sinister involvement in her accident.

"I can vouch for him," Officer Mike said with a playful punch to his shoulder. "His axe collection is purely for display."

August wouldn't meet his eyes. She didn't like being pressured, Geoffrey could tell. "She said 'no,' guys. Let's not make her feel uncomfortable about it."

"All right, then." Dr. Carlson pushed his glasses up his nose. "I'll make arrangements with the shelter to expect you tomorrow. It's called New Start Foundation." He turned to go.

"Wait." August sighed. "Can you vouch for him, too?"

"My wife delivered all six of the Barthlow children, and Jocelyn." The doctor hesitated in the doorway and gave her a wink. "But I've never seen the axe collection, so I can't say for sure what he does with it."

Hope lodged in Geoffrey's throat as a long second ticked by.

"Hold off on that call," August said slowly. "I'll take Geoffrey up on his offer. Hopefully my memory will come back within a few days and I'll be out of his hair quickly."

Geoffrey's mood soared, even as he called himself a fool for it. Still, it would be nice having her pretty smile in his world for a few more days, and he would take any opportunity to make up for turning her life upside down.

Dr. Carlson scribbled on his clipboard. "One call, held off. I'll send up a nurse to discharge you."

When the doctor left them alone, Mike went to the cubby where her clothes were neatly folded. "Is this what you were wearing the night of the accident?" He picked up her sweater.

She nodded.

Mike brought the bundle over and set it on the bed. He picked up one of her white canvas Keds. "Any of this look familiar?"

"None of it."

He thumbed through the layers. "They washed everything?"

She nodded again. "Why?"

"Brilliant." He scowled. "There may have been DNA evidence on them, or at least something that might indicate where you'd been that night. Like salt water, for instance. Geoffrey did find you on the beach road."

"I thought we'd already established that I didn't fall overboard."

Mike shook his head. "Not necessarily. For all we know, you went out in a boat alone without telling anybody."

"Doubtful. Any good sailor knows not to do that."

He regarded her curiously. "Do they?"

August glanced from Mike to him, and back. Geoffrey saw the confusion in her expression.

"It's common knowledge," she contended. "Just because I know that doesn't mean I'm a sailor. Even if I was, how would that help find out who I am?" She swung her legs over the side of the bed and picked up the clothes.

Mike sat in the leather chair beside the bed. "We'd have to do some investigating, but it might be a lead."

August stiffened. "What kind of investigating?"

Before Mike could answer, Geoffrey stepped in. "Maybe it would be best if you didn't."

His brother-in-law's expression hardened. "All right you two, what is it you're not telling me?"

August glanced at Geoffrey. He nodded. "It's okay. You can trust him."

She set her clothes down and turned, but her gaze fell. "What are my rights, Officer Gaffney?"

"First of all, call me Mike. If you're going to be a guest of my brother-in-law, I'm not only officially investigating your case, but I'm here as a favor to my family."

Immense gratitude swelled inside Geoffrey.

"Thank you, Mike," she said in a tiny voice.

His brow furrowed slightly. "And as your new friend, I'm wondering why you'd ask a question like that."

"Does there have to be an investigation at all? Can't I decide to stay missing?"

Mike's frown deepened into what Geoffrey recognized as his suspicious policeman's stare. "Why would you want to?"

"August and I were talking yesterday," he cut in. "She's afraid, because she can't remember what happened to her. Wouldn't you be?"

"I can't answer that. I'm sorry, August. I can't even begin to fathom what you're going through." Mike's frown melted away. "I know my family would be worried to death if I disappeared. I'd move heaven and earth to find them again."

"But what if you found yourself injured and you didn't remember how it happened? Wouldn't you suspect, even a tiny bit, that someone might have tried to hurt you?"

"Well now, I suppose maybe I would." He folded his arms across his chest. "Is there a reason you think someone did this to you on purpose?"

August sighed and paced away. "The truth is I have a bad feeling, but the harder I try to get a hold of it, the farther away it goes. But I can't escape it, either." When she turned back, her expression held defeat. "I'm almost embarrassed to admit it, and that alone tells me there's something to it."

"Can you be more specific?"

"I wish I could. But there is this—" She moved close to Mike and used her right hand to lift her broken arm. She gingerly splayed the fingers of her left hand. "I have a tan line on my wedding ring finger, but no ring."

Mike looked at her hand, and then glanced at him. The wariness Geoffrey found in his brother-in-law's eyes turned his blood to ice.

"Maybe I was running away, maybe I wasn't—I don't know," August said in a deadly serious voice. "But I do know that before I let anyone find me, I need to be sure I want to be found."

Chapter Five

The minute August stepped through the front door of Geoffrey's lavish beach home, she knew she was unaccustomed to this level of luxury.

The immense house sat alone on a narrow street on the beach side of the coastal highway, at least a half mile from any neighbors. It was built into the rough cliff face, staggered right down to the sand. The outside was painted a very pale blue that almost blended into the hazy sky. With a driveway that sloped downward, only part of the roof was visible from the street. A wood fence painted ocean blue, and expertly placed juniper, pine, and ice plant further aided its chameleon-like presence within its environment.

Several steps down from an elevated foyer, the spreading living room boasted an entire wall of windows looking out over the ocean. Plush leather couches and elegant accent pieces contrasted with the white pile carpet. Enormous abstract paintings in muted colors reached high into the vaulted ceiling on each side of the elegant room, complimenting the spreading view of the dunes and sea.

The sky had turned overcast before they'd left the hospital, and now a blanket of gray hung over the ocean, swallowing the line where sea met sky.

"You have a beautiful home." August felt out of

place, a little like Cinderella at the ball.

"It's my dad's," Geoffrey told her as he closed the door behind her. "The whole family uses it as a getaway. We all meet here for birthdays and holidays."

Geoffrey had a large, happy family who enjoyed celebrating together. Why did that seem foreign as well?

She followed him down the connecting hall to the right and into the massive, galley-style kitchen that opened to a formal dining room perched above the immense living room. The entire house was masterfully designed on staggering levels, worthy of a *House Beautiful* magazine spread.

A wrap-around deck appeared to stretch the entire ocean side of the house, the lower half of its railing covered with Plexiglas to ward off the cold Pacific winds.

August walked through the dining room to look out the windows. About two miles away, a gleaming white lighthouse tower stood on a jutting point.

"That's Yaquina Head, Oregon's tallest lighthouse. Does it look familiar to you?"

She shook her head. Nothing did. No part of the town they'd driven through, the lonely ocean road that had taken them to the house, or even the section of highway where their accident had occurred.

August slid into a bar stool at the kitchen's massive island as Geoffrey crossed the room and punched a button on the answering machine. His father left the first message, telling him he would be staying in Portland longer than planned. Then a second message about a banquet for the Northern Sierra Foundation benefit.

"It looks like it's just you, me, and Jocelyn until next

Tuesday."

August felt a guilty rush of relief. She wouldn't be required to meet any more of Geoffrey's family until she'd had a few days to settle. "Thank you for everything. I don't know what I'd do if it weren't for you."

"You wouldn't have a broken arm."

"Not necessarily."

He stood across from her at the island. "Has something come to you?"

"No, but I've been thinking about what might have happened. If someone was attacking me, trying to hit me over the head, maybe I threw my arm up in defense."

"Probably not. Dr. Carlson said it was a good thing I got you to the hospital right away before the bones started knitting in the wrong position. Besides, I heard an awful thump when the car hit you." He grimaced. "I'll never forget it."

She sighed and turned to stare out into the milky gray afternoon. The ocean seemed to be calling her, reaching for her. She felt precariously perched above it in this cliff-constructed home. "I wish I could remember something. Anything. It's so frustrating not knowing a thing about myself."

"It'll come to you. In the meantime, relax and enjoy a few days off. When you get your memory back, your life will be more hectic than you can imagine." He gave her that warm, comforting smile she already treasured so much. "And if you are a bank robber, this place is most definitely better than jail."

He laughed, but August barely managed a smile.

Geoffrey cleared his throat. "Sorry."

"No, I'm sorry. That was funny." She wondered what

lucky stars had aligned her with this sweet man who went so far out of his way to take care of her.

I don't deserve this. As quickly as she had the thought, she wondered why such a thing would enter her head. *I couldn't really be a criminal, could I?*

"Come on, I'll give you a tour of the house and show you your room."

The rest of the tri-level home was as impressive as the main level. The next floor down had another deck running the ocean side of the house, also with Plexiglas sheltering the lower half of the railing. As they moved through the halls, Geoffrey pointed out each room and told her who occupied it.

"This is Jocelyn's room," he said, stopping at an adorable room decorated like a 1950s soda shop in red, black, and white. "Leah and Jocelyn moved in when Leah and her husband separated. They live here year-round and Jocelyn attends the elementary school in Newport."

"It's a wonderful room for a child."

He checked his watch. "The carpool should be dropping her off soon. She'll be thrilled to see you. She took an instant liking to you."

"I like her, too." August stared into the room any child would love, but few were lucky enough to have.

Jocelyn had her own television set with an attached set of joysticks. A large fish tank boasted an exotic arrangement of salt-water fish. She even had her own personal computer. One entire wall was a floor-to-ceiling bookcase crammed with dolls and stuffed animals.

"Jocelyn was a preemie. She almost died at birth, and had us worried again when she was two and caught pneumonia. I guess as a result, we spoil her."

When she glanced at him, Geoffrey smiled. "I could read your mind."

She smiled back, instantly comforted by the kindness in his eyes. His was a face she could spend a lot of time gazing at. "Could you look a little further in there and tell me what *I* can't read?"

The more she saw of the luxurious house, the more August was sure she didn't live like this. She gawked at the expensive décor and fashionable design. It was so perfect it almost didn't seem lived in, more like a showplace than a home.

"This is the den," he said as they continued down the hall. "It's my office away from the office, so if you ever can't find me, chances are I'll be here."

Inside, the walls were covered with rich burgundy wallpaper. Bookcases filled with leather-bound books stretched across two sides. A sleek, impossibly thin laptop computer sat on a mahogany desk. Covering one wall, eight-by-ten photographs displayed luxury buildings. Like the rest of the house, floor-to-ceiling windows on the ocean side brought the surrounding nature into the room.

"Are you one of those people who bring your work home with you?" she asked him.

"My grandfather founded Palisades Hotels. I'm the vice president of operations at our West Coast headquarters in Portland." He shrugged. "It's all title, really. I can do the work from anywhere, and they don't miss me much when I'm gone."

"I'm sure that's not true." She moved inside and looked out the windows at the lighthouse on the point again. She didn't recognize it, but somehow knew she should.

"I have a loft in Portland, but with Leah and Richard separated, I spend more time here so I can help with Jocelyn," he told her. "I don't miss the daily grind. It's not as satisfying as I thought it would be when I was in school. But, you know, family legacy and all that."

She turned around. "University of Portland?"

He glanced away. "UC Berkeley, California." He said it as though it tasted sour in his mouth. "I have some work to do, but afterward you can try some more memory tests on the keyboard like you did with the pen and paper at the hospital. See if anything comes to you."

"I'm not even sure I know how to use a computer," she said, eyeing the laptop. "But I'll try anything."

"Your room is down the hall." Geoffrey stepped out of the doorway and waited for her to follow.

She started after him but stopped. "Do you have a blank notebook I could use? Maybe I should keep a diary of my intuitions." She didn't feel comfortable telling him the first thing she would write was how she was certain she didn't live in this kind of opulence.

Geoffrey retrieved a spiral-bound notebook and a pen from the office. He led her to the end of the hall to a pretty room decorated with blond pine furniture, and bed coverings matching the flowery wallpaper. Soft peach hues reminded her of summer, even though the gray sky outside threatened with another storm.

"It's lovely." She stood in the doorway, gingerly cradling the heavy cast with her good hand, almost afraid to venture in. Her arm had begun to throb again, and with it, her head.

"Better than the shelter, I'll bet." He moved to the window and fully opened the blinds. The cedar deck at this level met the sand dunes without a railing. It wound out of sight to the right. A fluffy juniper in a massive pot stood on the left side of the window, partially obstructing her view of the ocean. Beside that, ice plant covered the sandy hill that slanted toward the beach.

"The lower master-suite is on the far side on this level, but no one is there so you've got the deck all to yourself. You're welcome to use the hot tub if you like."

"Where's your room?"

He turned back and faced her. Opaque light filled the bedroom with a gentle glow. "Top floor, opposite side."

It sounded as though he wanted to assure her she had all the privacy she could possibly want, and that he'd stay far away from her. She wanted to tell him she appreciated it, but was afraid it would sound like she was hoping that was the case.

Already this arrangement felt like a bad idea.

He crossed the room to stand before her, silhouetted by the gray light filtering through the window. August studied his features in the dim light. His brown eyes were gentle, with a touch of sadness at their edges. She suspected this man wasn't only shy around women, but had a past as deep and mysterious as her own.

"Is your arm starting to hurt again?"

She nodded. "But not so badly I want another of those pills. They make me feel groggy."

She glanced past him to the ocean. A spike of fear raced to her heart at the sight of it. Somehow, she understood she shouldn't be dulling her senses. That unidentifiable threat hovering at the edge of her memory was always there, always just out of reach.

August suspected whatever dark, dreadful thing was following her, it was closer than she knew.

She glanced into Geoffrey's eyes and relief replaced the spike of fear. She placed her hand on his arm. A tingle of brilliant awareness raced through her fingers.

"I'm more grateful than you know. This is difficult for me, but you're making it easier."

His gaze slipped away, and then met hers again. "I'm glad I could help. I need to do this for you. I owe it."

His broad shoulders blocked out the light as he stood over her, taller than she'd first thought. Looking up at him, she saw it again: something haunted lingering in his eyes.

"Why do you feel indebted?"

Geoffrey moved past her and headed for the door.

"We're all indebted for something."

◆ ◆ ◆

August spent a few hours flipping through magazines in the living room. Some of the ads started to look familiar, but she suspected she'd merely convinced herself of that rather than really feeling it. She gave up when her head started throbbing and her stomach started grumbling in synch.

She found Geoffrey in his office, clacking away at the keyboard.

"How do you feel about peanut butter and jelly sandwiches?" she asked from the doorway.

"They're one of my favorite things." He looked up from behind the monitor. "Sorry. I disappeared, didn't I?"

She managed a smile. "Don't apologize. The last thing I want to do is disrupt your life."

He looked at his watch. "I have a conference call

with the Portland office in five minutes. It shouldn't last long. I'll be up soon. Make yourself at home."

She headed upstairs and poured herself a cup of water, but went onto the deck to wait for Geoffrey. She didn't feel comfortable rifling through the kitchen without him.

August sat at a patio table and stared out at the lighthouse in the distance. A biting wind blew over the deck railing, but the crisp, salty air helped clear her mind.

"Yaquina Head," Geoffrey had called it. The name didn't sound familiar, but something about it nagged at her. She watched the surge of light at its peak sparking against the sooty clouds, instinctively counting. Four seconds on. Four seconds off. Four seconds on. Twenty seconds off. The light's signature, she realized. Different from all others on the coast.

She made a fist with her right hand. *How do I know that?*

A clicking sound behind her gave her a start. A strange man leaned against the patio doorjamb, lighting a cigarette.

She shot to her feet, knocking over her chair.

Chapter Six

"Who are you?" August staggered backward. Fear choked off her breath and sent large black spots swirling in her vision.

She rapped the fiberglass elbow against the wooden railing and bit back a gasp as pain shot through her arm. Delicately she cradled her cast in her other hand.

"Seeing as you're sitting on my deck, in my house, drinking out of my father's favorite coffee mug, I should be asking you that question."

He took a long drag on the cigarette and slowly pulled it away from his lips, looking her up and down like a hungry dog eyeing a piece of meat.

"So who are you?" he pressed.

"I'm a friend of Geoffrey's."

"No kidding." He burst out a sarcastic chirp of laughter. "You look more like a friend of David's, or a friend of Justin's, but not a friend of Geoffrey's."

Something about the look in his eyes made her skin crawl. They were cold, yet guarded, and almost resentful.

"Does Geoffrey's friend have a name?"

"You still haven't told me yours."

"Touché." A sardonic smile touched his lips, but it didn't erase the antipathy from his face. "I'm Derek, Geoffrey's brother."

He was unkempt, but she knew it was in an intentional way, with too-long hair and a growth of stubble shadowing his jaw that he likely thought made him sexy. His baggy jeans sat low on his hips, and a scarred leather jacket hung off his shoulders. He leaned back against the doorframe in a James Dean slouch.

"Geoffrey didn't tell me he had a brother named Derek."

"No, he wouldn't." He sniffed indignantly and turned his gaze out to the sea as he took another draw from his cigarette. "I'm the prodigal son returned."

Nervous fear fluttered in her stomach. She wondered if she would have found him handsome before she lost her memory. His clothes were only made to look worn, and she somehow knew they were expensive. But despite the gritty fashion model look, there was something dark and unpleasant lying beneath the surface that she couldn't put her finger on.

"So what happened to your arm, friend of Geoffrey's?"

"I broke it."

"No kidding. Must have hurt like hell. Did they give you any painkillers for it?"

"What the hell are you doing here?" At the far right, Geoffrey's heavy footsteps marched up the wooden steps from a lower section of the deck. August felt a rush of relief, but still couldn't make herself relax. Derek's sudden appearance had sent her nerves jumping, reminding her how vulnerable she was. If her attacker found her again, she wouldn't realize it until it was too late.

My attacker. I was attacked. Admitting it to herself brought on a rush of nausea.

"Didn't know I needed your permission, bro."

"Since when would my permission mean anything to you?"

Derek took a drag on his cigarette and raked August with his gaze. The simple look told her the man was disrespectful to women. "I can see how you'd be upset."

Geoffrey moved close and rested his arm on the railing behind her. "Just surprised. I figured this was the last place you'd want to come back to."

"Yeah, well, I called Dad and he's cool with it, so ease up. I just want to chill out for a while. Why don't you do the same?" He repositioned his cigarette butt between two fingers, ready to flick it.

"Don't," Geoffrey warned. "Unless you want to hike down and hunt for it."

Derek made an exaggerated face and strode forward to put it out in the ashtray on the table. He then turned and headed back to the house. "Geoffrey." He flipped his hand in a mock salute. "Geoffrey's friend."

"August," she volunteered. "Nice to meet you, Derek."

Derek slid open the glass door leading to the kitchen and dining area. "Geoffrey, your friend August is a liar. But she's a babe, so I won't hold it against her."

"Be nice," Geoffrey growled, "if you're going to stay here."

He stopped. "Yeah, we all need to chill. No prob', G. I thought you were in Portland or I wouldn't have come. But I'm here now, so let's deal with it."

Deal with what? August wondered. There was definitely bad blood between them.

Jocelyn bounded through the dining area and through the opened patio door. "Derek!" She flung herself into his arms.

"Hey, munchkin." He picked her up and heaved her into the air, earning a squeal of delight, before he caught her weight and settled her back on her feet.

"I'm not a munchkin. I'm a pixie. I can do magic."

"Show me some?"

"Later." She looked over and saw August. "Hi, August. Are you gonna stay with us?"

August forced herself to smile. "Maybe for a few days."

"Awesome! I'll show you my room. I have a pet eel named Mr. McEely. He's a snowflake eel. What's for dinner, Uncle G?"

"I'm going to take you two gorgeous ladies out to dinner. How does that sound?"

"Hamburgers and French fries?"

Geoffrey glanced at August. "If that's okay with you?"

She was tired and her arm was aching like the devil, but she could tell Geoffrey wanted to put some distance between himself and his brother. "That sounds great."

"Jocelyn, you take August to meet Mr. McEely while I talk to Derek for a minute."

She allowed the little girl to lead her away while a dramatic pause hung in the air. She glanced back to see Derek step onto the deck and light another cigarette as Geoffrey waited for them to get out of earshot.

◆ ◆ ◆

"Listen. I'm going to tell you why August is here, and then I'm going to leave you alone so you can say whatever sarcastic thing that comes to mind to the only person who cares."

Derek made a dramatic, wide-open gesture with his

hands. "I'm not going to say anything sarcastic."

"Right." Geoffrey crossed the deck and leaned on the railing to look out across the sea, but left more than an arm's length between himself and Derek. "Jocelyn and I were in an accident."

"So it's not only me wrecking the family cars," Derek returned. "Yet I seem to be the only one catching shit about it."

"Yeah, well, we're still three to one, so the score's not even close," Geoffrey cut in. "And you were high when you did yours. Big difference."

That shut him up.

Geoffrey went over the events the night of the storm as sparsely as he could. The words ground against his teeth like gravel, but somehow he knew it would be better if it came from him. Get things straight, right from the start.

"Hey, whatever you need to do to get yourself a date, it's no business of mine."

"Now why on earth did I think you'd say something sarcastic?" He should have known better than to think Derek would cut him an inch of slack. "I'm so glad to see your attitude has improved."

"Yeah, whatever."

"Why did you come back here, Derek?"

"I told you. Just to chill."

"You mean to get clean?"

Derek turned away to stare at the sea, but didn't respond.

"You'd better get that way and stay that way, or I'll toss you out on your ass."

"You and what army?"

Geoffrey turned and delivered the icy glare he

couldn't keep off his face whenever he thought of Derek. *Derek and Christina.*

"I don't need an army, Derek." Geoffrey poked him in the shoulder and gave him a shove.

"Hey!" Derek swiped his hand away, but as Geoffrey expected, he backed down.

"But I haven't decided if it'll be more fun to call Mike, or kick your ass myself, if you even hint at giving me trouble."

As Geoffrey suspected, his brother had no retort to that. Derek and Mike would never be called friends. "August is here to recuperate and if you do anything to interfere with that—"

"You mean interfere with your putting the moves on her." Derek glanced sideways with narrowed eyes.

"I am not *putting the moves* on her," Geoffrey said firmly. "And neither are you. Got it?"

Derek took another puff from his cigarette as he scanned the water. He let it out in a slow breath. "I've got as much right to be here as you. If you don't like that, route your complaints to Dad."

Geoffrey took one step toward the patio door, but hesitated. "What have you ever done for this family? I have the key. This is my house. Mine and Leah's and Jocelyn's. We're trying to put our lives back together and we don't need you coming in and screwing it up again."

"Am I really the one who screwed it up the first time?" Derek stared into the distance, silent for a moment as he watched a circling gull. "You need to get over what happened," he finally said in a softer voice.

What was that Geoffrey heard? A hint of regret? Maybe a sliver of guilt? He could hardly believe Derek capable.

"I'll never get over what happened."

"That's your problem," Derek shot back, the harshness returned to his voice. "Life goes on."

Geoffrey shook his head. "Not for Christina, it doesn't."

◆ ◆ ◆

"This sucks. How long do I have to sit in back?"

Geoffrey didn't respond when Jocelyn whined from the back seat. He'd been silent through most of the drive back to town.

August glanced over her shoulder. "You have to be this tall to ride up front." She held her hand four inches over her head.

"No fair!" Jocelyn complained, but she giggled, too.

August tried to appear casual as she looked at Geoffrey. His expression was like granite. She didn't know him well enough to anticipate his thoughts.

He maneuvered the car around a bend. The Lexus SUV hugged the pavement with hardly a vibration inside.

Like the impressive house, August knew she wasn't used to such a luxurious vehicle. The engine hummed with a throaty power almost awe-inspiring, and she felt well-protected behind its heavy doors.

"Penny for your thoughts," she said.

He sighed. "Derek's timing couldn't have been better."

"I'm glad he's here," Jocelyn said from the back seat. "I missed him."

As they emerged from a rise in the coastline to see the town of Newport spreading before them, August's gaze landed on the crowded harbor nestled into the corner of the bay. Before she fully understood what she was thinking, the profiles of some of the boats fit into her mind like puzzle pieces falling into place. *Sloop. Catamaran. Bayliner.*

But instead of feeling happy that she recognized them, the sight of the marina brought crushing fear that squeezed off her breath.

If she walked onto its docks, would someone recognize her? She was sure she'd never seen this marina before, but was that because of their angle, driving in like this from above? Or had she been there and simply forgotten it with everything else she couldn't remember?

"We're here."

Geoffrey slowed the Lexus and pulled off the highway at the first row of buildings at the edge of town, opposite the harbor.

He angled the SUV into a parking spot in front of a large wooden building weathered by the unrelenting breath of the sea. Its large front windows looked over the harbor across the road. August recognized the symbol from the bag of soup he'd brought to the hospital.

The Mirthful Mermaid. "Your grandmother's place?"

"Yay!" Jocelyn squealed from the back seat. She released her seatbelt and bounded out of the car before Geoffrey could stop her.

He turned off the engine and swiveled in his seat. "I'm sorry if you're not up for this, but I know she'll want to meet you right away. She's protective over our family."

August's mouth soured at the thought. After meeting Derek, she *wasn't* up for it.

"Don't worry, her bark is worse than her bite."

"Oh, *great.*"

He grinned as he released his seatbelt. "Let me get the door for you."

Some of her anxiety faded. She let out a long breath as she watched him walk around the hood, knowing Geoffrey would never let his grandmother get too fierce with her.

The Mirthful Mermaid was as quaint as could be, its rough-hewn walls covered with seafaring treasures hanging in old-fashioned fishing nets. The dark interior created a sheltered feel, cozy and safe. The bare floor squeaked underfoot, and heavy wooden furniture filled the open eating area. A long bar ran the length of the left side. Soft country music flowed out of the jukebox in the opposite corner. The place smelled of a delicious mixture of hearty food and the salty sea.

A silver-haired woman held Jocelyn in a bear hug. She set the little girl down and faced them as Geoffrey and August walked over.

"So, this is your mysterious guest."

August swallowed, trying not to cringe as the old woman looked her up and down.

"She looks tired." She scowled. "What are you thinking, bringing her out the day she's released from the hospital?"

Geoffrey cleared his throat. August suspected he was trying to gently put into words that they had left because Derek showed up.

"I had a craving for some more of the New England clam chowder he tempted me with in the hospital," August said first. "Even though I don't have my memory, I'm certain I've never tasted any so delicious."

"Ah! I like her already. Come, sit over here where nobody will jostle that arm. Does it hurt, girl?" She reached out, urging August under her arm. "I broke my index finger once. It was the darnedest thing—I couldn't blow my nose worth a damn until it healed."

She pulled out a heavy wooden chair for August.

"Thank you, Mrs. Barthlow."

"You call me Millie, and as things progress we'll see about you calling me Gran Millie, but do one thing for sure and leave that Mrs. stuff behind, y'hear?"

August smiled. "Thanks, Millie."

Geoffrey watched her with a quirky grin playing at his lips.

She stood back and placed her hands on her hips. "Soup isn't enough. You're too thin. What do you like to eat, sweetheart?"

"Anything I can manage with one hand."

"Then you'll be wanting my famous pasta with red pepper cream sauce. I'll have Roberto prepare it with corkscrew, so you can eat it easily."

"I want a cheeseburger," Jocelyn said. "And cheese fries."

"You're a cheese-head." She bent down and mussed Jocelyn's hair, and then kissed the top of her head. "For you, grandson?"

"I'll have the pasta, too." He cleared his throat again. "And we should probably take an order to go. Derek's up at the house."

"Well, for heaven's sake, why didn't you bring him along?"

"Er, he was tired."

"Stoned is more like it. Is that boy gonna clean up his act?"

Geoffrey leaned back in his chair. "He'd better, or you'll find him knocking on *your* door. He's all out of second chances with me."

"Lord knows you've given him more than he deserves." Millie's voice softened. "How are you holding up?"

Geoffrey's uncomfortable gaze flicked over August. Now she was sure of it: there was bad blood between them, and not just because of childhood bickering.

"I won't lie to you, Gran, I don't like him being here. But he's my brother and I can't turn him away."

"Sure you can." She placed her fists back on her hips after another twirl of the towel in her hand. "Send him on down here and I'll give him the room upstairs. He can wash dishes to earn his board."

Jocelyn giggled. "Yeah, right."

Even Geoffrey laughed.

"That pretty boy needs a taste of the real world. Life isn't about prancing around in front of a camera. Besides, if he keeps up the drinkin' and smokin' like he does, it'll ruin his looks faster than a skinned apple left out in the sun. Then what'll he do?"

She turned and started away while shaking her head.

"Derek is a model?" August asked.

Geoffrey glanced away. "Something like that."

"He does Gucci ads," Jocelyn volunteered. She seemed oblivious of the thick tension swirling around Geoffrey at the mere mention of his brother's name.

A waiter appeared with glasses of water and a basket of French bread. August drank down two Tylenol with the icy water.

"This, I remember," she said as she plucked a slice

of bread from the basket. "Seaside eateries always have the greatest sourdough bread." She was grateful for a reason to change the subject. She didn't like seeing Geoffrey so uncomfortable.

Geoffrey's gaze snapped over. "Do you like crab?"

She pictured sweet, moist chunks of freshly cooked crabmeat. "I do," she said. "That was a test, wasn't it?"

He nodded. "It appears to have worked. Has anything else come to you?"

She shook her head. "Nothing." She saw Jocelyn buttering a piece of bread and slid her bread plate over. "Would you help me butter mine, please?"

Thankfully Jocelyn chattered about her day at school through most of the meal. Millie's famous red pepper cream sauce was everything she'd promised, including spicy. It was the first meal she'd eaten outside the hospital, August realized. The first real meal she ever remembered eating. With her stomach pleasantly full and two Tylenol taking effect, August felt better than she had in days.

She glanced across the room and saw a heavyset man at another table. His unwavering gaze was sinister, pinning her with such precise intent August knew without a doubt the reprieve she'd discovered in the hospital was over.

The man wiped his mouth, dropped his napkin, and leaned over to remove his wallet from his back pocket, all the while staring at her.

August's blood went cold. The man rose and headed for their table. He was huge, taller than she'd first anticipated because he was so round around the middle. Her heart was pounding so fast she could hear it in her eardrums. She picked up her glass and took a long, cool drink.

Something about the man was dangerous in a specific way. His stare had been too deliberate, too knowing. The closer he got, the greater her fear grew.

He turned his gaze as he moved past the table. "See ya, Millie. Jenny."

"Bye, Joe," Millie responded.

"Say hi to Althea for me!" the young woman behind the bar said as he left.

August tingled from head to toe as she let out the breath she'd been holding.

I imagined the whole thing. God, what is wrong with me?

Had she also imagined the suspicion there was something dangerous about the docks? Did the boats really look familiar, or had she merely recognized them the same as a person might recognize a Maserati or Lamborghini, even if they had only seen one in a picture?

"You okay?" Geoffrey eyed her. "You look a little pale."

She swallowed. Was it possible she'd been ill before Geoffrey hit her? Her heart continued its frantic pace as she wondered if she could be...*unbalanced.*

These were paranoid delusions, which might have plagued her before the accident. The idea made her sick. Could she even be so messed up as to have multiple personality disorder? That would certainly explain the gigantic blackout that was her past. She shrugged the thought away and focused on the question he'd asked.

"It's hard lugging this cast around. Even though it's fiberglass, after a while it gets heavy." She didn't want to tell him the body sling caused more pain than it helped ease.

He nodded. "I can imagine. Is your arm starting to hurt again?"

"A little," she lied. It hurt a lot. Though the pain had dulled thanks to the Tylenol, her shoulder and back were stiff and her fingers throbbed, hot and swollen.

The idea she might have a mental illness sent chills up and down her spine. Maybe she suffered from panic attacks. They were innocent enough, and many people got them. Maybe that was what she was feeling now, caused by everything that had happened. Maybe this was her first panic attack; that would explain why she didn't understand what was happening.

"Can I sign your cast? I write real good," Jocelyn said.

"Sure. Maybe you could even draw a flower to brighten it up." She hoped her voice wasn't shaking. Slowly her heart rate returned to normal, but she was left feeling quivery and light-headed.

"How was the pasta?" Millie asked as she set a paper bag on the table.

"Wonderful as always," Geoffrey said. "What's the damage?"

"You know your money is no good here."

"I also know the rule is we can eat, but we have to pay if we bring our friends." He grinned at August. "Ever since I was a kid."

"How long has the Mirthful Mermaid been here?" she asked Millie.

"She was built in 1917, and rebuilt again in 1945 after a fire. She's been in our family seventy years."

"So if I were from the area, I would know this is a landmark." The very idea caused her spirits to sink. It was so frustrating not knowing a thing about her past. Was she from Oregon? If not, what had brought her here?

"Don't let it worry you." Geoffrey rose and moved around the table to help her out of her chair. "It's only been a few days. I'll bet after your appointment with Dr. Lohman tomorrow, you'll feel a lot better."

The young woman behind the bar looked up as they started toward the door.

"Hey there, Geoffrey. Hiya, Jocelyn."

Geoffrey stopped. "Hello, Jenny. I'm surprised to see you here. When's your last day?"

"Not until next week. Who's your friend?" The girl gave August a friendly smile.

"This is August. August, Jenny."

August noticed the oversized sweatshirt with UOP emblazoned in bright white letters. "Nice to meet you. Are you going back to school?"

Jenny laughed. "No, I'm pregnant. I'm going to have a baby!"

She stepped around the end of the bar and displayed her rounded belly.

August hardly saw her. It was as if she'd left the room, transported back to the storm three nights ago.

I'm pregnant...I'm pregnant...

She was arguing with someone, but all she could see was darkness, sheets of torrential rain, and the flashes of red that were her anger.

"August?" Jenny's smile faded.

"I'm pregnant." The words slipped over her lips.

"What?" Geoffrey and Millie exclaimed in unison.

"Not me," she clarified quickly. The memory drifted away, and August felt like she was waking up from a trance.

"I remembered something. Someone else recently told me she was pregnant, but I don't remember who. I think it was the night of the storm."

Chapter Seven

Morning sunlight streamed through the window over the kitchen sink and landed on a spot of linoleum that had faded to nearly white. It was almost too bright to bear. The rest of the floor was dingy yellow with faded pink flowers, a gaudy pattern from the seventies that should have been torn out years ago.

They had been planning to live here together. Though the house was only marginally larger than the bungalow Emily's parents had left her, she'd said she liked this one, at the edge of the water, better. She'd never made a single complaint about his father's neglect of its décor.

Colin looked at the half-empty coffee cup between his hands, refusing to acknowledge the ringing phone. His father hurried in, but stopped when he saw that the call was intentionally being ignored. He stepped closer to peer at the digital face on the unit, as though he needed confirmation of who was calling.

"You have to talk to them, Colin."

Colin knew who it was, even without looking at the display. They'd been calling his cell nonstop, too. He glanced to the white square on the floor again, something satisfying in the way it stung his eyes.

"They have a right to bury their daughter."

He squeezed the cup. The cold coffee quivered

under his grip. "There's no body."

The phone abruptly stopped ringing, leaving heavy silence behind. The same silence had been in his head lately, an emptiness that Emily's beautiful smile and happy voice had once filled.

"They're going to plan the funeral without you—"

He surged to his feet, shoving his chair backward. "She might still be alive! Why are they in such a hurry to write her off?"

Graham shook his head. "You know as well as I do..."

Colin hurled the cup across the room, spraying its remaining contents. It crashed against a cabinet and shattered.

"Don't say it." He pointed his finger. "Don't. She was wearing a lifejacket."

"Colin." His father gave him a pitying look that Colin wanted to punch right off his pathetic mug. "It's been over a week."

"I don't care." Colin whirled away and stalked out of the tiny kitchen. "No funeral!"

◆ ◆ ◆

August awoke aching with longing as the dream slipped into the foggy recesses of her mind. It had been a dream, but also a memory, she was sure of it. The first she'd had in over a week.

She flipped the covers off and bolted out of bed, cradling her cast. The notebook Geoffrey had loaned her sat on the desk, opened to her last entry. She wrote as quickly as she could, but even still, parts of it were already gone.

Drive-up sock hop, or root beer parlor. Convertible— Mustang, or Maverick. Sunny day.

She was in an older car of some kind, a four-seater,

with five other people. She crowded into the back seat with two others, sitting on the left behind the driver. They were all laughing, having a great time. It was a bright spring day, yet she couldn't see any of the other faces in her dream. The only face she saw was her own, glimpsed in the driver's side mirror as she leaned over and let the wind catch her hair.

August sat back and tapped her pen against her lips. This wasn't a recent memory, she felt certain. This had been a while ago, when she was younger. In high school, perhaps. She looked back at the page. As the memory continued fading, her sparse notes took on a hopeless air of meaninglessness. They were just a collection of words.

But they had come from somewhere.

Excitement and depression battled inside her. She thought of Geoffrey, and her mood brightened. He would want to know about the dream, or memory. Whatever it had been.

Over the past week, she'd grown attached to the sweet man who had given so much of himself to helping her. He seemed genuinely happy for her accomplishments, and listened with great concern when her mood turned fragile. She enjoyed watching him in the kitchen when he cooked for her and Jocelyn, and loved the evenings playing board games with them and helping Jocelyn with her homework. Geoffrey was great with her, and August could tell the little girl adored him.

When she finished dressing and emerged from her bedroom, she found the house strangely quiet. As she passed the spacious living room with its gigantic windows, she saw the morning was bright and clear. The sea stretched out forever, glittering with the morning sun. Diamond-like shimmers trailed across the water, leading directly to her, and August wished she could go out onto the water. While the ocean still caused a thrill of fear, at least there she could be sure she was alone, truly free of the dark evil following her like a phantom.

The sound of a cupboard dropping shut drew her to the kitchen. "Geoffrey?"

Derek stopped rifling through the cabinets, a guilty look on his face. "Not here. He's on carpool duty this morning. Gotta drive Squirt to school."

She cradled her cast with her good hand, hugging her arms around herself. So far, Geoffrey's brother had made himself scarce, and she'd hardly exchanged two words with him. The sudden realization she was alone in the house with him made her stomach tighten.

"Oh." She turned to go. "Excuse me."

"There's coffee."

She turned back.

"Don't worry, I'm under threat of life and limb to leave you alone."

She considered him for a long moment. He looked harmless enough, no longer wearing the suspicion he had when they'd first met.

"Did you find a tea bag in your exploration?"

"Yep." He pulled open one of the closer cabinets. "That and coffee is about the strongest thing they've got in this house."

He set a box of Darjeeling on the counter. "Have a seat. I'll put the kettle on."

"Thank you." She sat at the small eat-in table, still not sure if she was comfortable in his presence.

He turned on the stove and then hopped up to sit on

the counter. "Did you really fall out of the sky and land on my brother's car?"

"Seems that way."

"'Cause.. he's not exactly poor." Derek grinned. "I wouldn't blame you if this was some scheme to marry a rich dude."

August tried to keep her expression passive, even though the words sparked her irritation. "I'm afraid not."

"Naw. You don't look like you'd need to scheme I bet you could have any guy you want, with a face like yours."

"That sounded like a compliment."

"I'm not as rotten as G would have you believe." He leaned both hands on the edge of the counter and eyed her. "What's it like not having your memory? Like, do you know if you're really a blond? I guess you would, if the carpets match the drapes. Know what I mean?"

"Yeah, I know what you mean."

He chuckled sheepishly. "You really don't even remember your name? That seems so impossible."

"I wish it were." She stood from the table and moved to the bar overlooking the sunken living room. The ocean stretched before her, as wide and empty as her memories. "It's frustrating. Lonely. Scary. But I can't help but wonder if there's something I don't want to remember."

"I know how that feels. I can tell you, there's definitely stuff in my past I don't want to remember."

His voice had taken a far-away essence. She glanced over her shoulder, wanting to ask but knowing it was wrong to pry. Was he talking about the incident that had caused him to be at such odds with his brother?

The teapot whistled. Derek jumped down off the counter and flipped off the burner. August moved back into the kitchen and pulled open the last cabinet. It was filled with plates.

"Where do you keep the coffee mugs?" she asked, closing it.

"Here," Derek said.

A flash of white sailed toward her face. She screamed and threw up her good arm, desperate to block the blow heading straight for her head. Her cast rapped against the counter as she staggered back. Bright agony shot through her arm, so sharp and intense, a curtain of red filled her vision. She fell backward and landed on her tailbone.

◆ ◆ ◆

Geoffrey flipped off Jocelyn's bouncy music and drove the distance back to the house in silence. He'd spent another rough night battling the turbulent thoughts his mysterious guest brought alive. He hadn't experienced emotions like this since before Christina died.

Dammit, why did Derek have to come back now? Geoffrey couldn't lie to himself: his brother's return fueled half of it.

Throughout Derek's chaotic career as a model and his heaviest drug use, Geoffrey had always tried to help, always been able to forgive. But then to learn about him and Christina, to hear from her own lips...His feelings had done a complete reversal. He could never forgive his brother.

It was Derek's fault Christina died. She'd been getting better; she'd actually been happy in those last few months before Derek had come home that first time—or was it the second?—to dry out.

August brought out all the protective feelings all over again. He knew she wasn't Christina, that helping her wouldn't undo what had happened a year ago. But a part of him knew he had failed his wife, and Geoffrey wouldn't make the same mistake twice. He couldn't possibly turn his back on this helpless young woman with unknown terror in her past.

And yet there was more to it, Geoffrey realized. He knew she had her own life. It was only a matter of time before she remembered it, and returned to it. But a part of him clung to a sliver of hope, a smidgeon of selfish need.

In these few days, Geoffrey had already learned she was the sweetest, most delightful young woman he'd ever met.

August was unlike any other woman, both in her unique and stunning beauty, and in the gentle charm that radiated from every part of her. When she spoke, her voice rang with a soft and joyous tone. When she smiled, her eyes almost appeared to twinkle. She was a woman who had known happiness, but had also known pain. Not for a second did he doubt the unseen danger her sixth sense was trying to reveal to her.

He turned the car in to the driveway and pulled to a stop under the oleander tree where he always parked. He turned off the engine and sat in the car.

Some terrible event might have happened to her, but August displayed none of the characteristics he would expect of a battered wife. She was too easygoing, too free with her smiles and her trust.

But what about the tan line?

Geoffrey shook his head. What was he thinking,

clinging to a feeble hope that life here might be better than her old life? That she might be convinced to stay? He had nothing to offer her but a nice house to live in.

He was as plain as taupe wallpaper. He'd always drifted behind his brothers, who outshined and out-performed everything he did. In high school, girls had only befriended him for the chance to get close to football star Justin, or water polo champion David.

Thankfully, being three years older than Derek, he no longer faced that problem by the time his younger brother was a freshman in high school, but the steady stream of girls following Derek home always made Geoffrey slightly jealous. Derek attracted the prettiest girls. Girls like August.

He opened the door and slid out of the car in time to hear a scream inside the house.

He hardly realized his feet were carrying him at a dead run until he was through the front door and barreling into the kitchen.

August sprawled on the floor, bracing herself with her good arm. Derek loomed over her. He glanced up as Geoffrey flew at him.

"Get away from her!" He grabbed his brother by his t-shirt and shoved him off his feet. Derek staggered down the steps into the living room and tumbled over the couch.

"Whoa, bro! What the hell?"

"I should have known. I tell you one thing—to stay away from her—and you do exactly the opposite."

"Geoffrey!" August's shrill cry brought him back to the here and now. For a moment, déjà vu had taken hold, bringing him back to that tragic autumn day.

"Nothing happened, really!"

"Don't make excuses for him." Geoffrey turned back and advanced with several threatening steps toward his brother. Derek scrambled to his feet and darted away "I want you out! You've used up all this family's patience."

"You mean *your* patience." Wearing a scathing scowl, Derek straightened his t-shirt and stalked past, giving a wide berth. "Dude, chill. I'm going."

Once his brother was out of sight, Geoffrey let cut the breath he hadn't realized he was holding. He turned around and saw August was still sprawled on the floor.

"God, August, I'm so sorry." He rushed to help her to her feet.

"It's all right, I'm okay."

"What happened?" he demanded a little too harshly. He softened his tone. "Are you hurt?"

She swallowed and shook her head. The hand she braced on his arm trembled.

"I never should have left you alone."

"He scared me, that's all." She managed a tremulous smile. "It wasn't even him, really. I just saw his hand, coming at me."

The front door slammed hard enough to make the house shudder. Stomping footsteps crunched through the gravel on the drive.

"He didn't do anything. He was only getting a cup out of the cabinet."

Geoffrey blew out a heavy sigh. August's eyes were pleading. They welled with glossy tears she blinked away.

"Please, stop him. I know things are bad between you, but please, don't let me make them worse."

"It isn't you, August."

"This wouldn't have happened if I wasn't here."

He considered her for a long moment. "It's long overdue."

She glanced down. "I can't bear knowing whatever exists between you two escalated because of me. Please, don't make him leave."

A knifing jealousy sliced through Geoffrey's gut. But August wasn't like all the other girls. Her motivation wasn't selfish; it was simply her sweet nature to try to make things better between them. He reminded himself he had no right to feel jealous. August was free to make her own choice, even if it wasn't him.

Even if it was Derek.

He clenched his jaw. Her warm hand found his forearm. He looked down, and all the rage flowed out of him. He sighed, feeling deflated.

"Christ."

"Please?"

"All right." He ground it out.

"Good. That makes me feel better." August raised up on her toes and placed a quick kiss at his cheek.

All at once, warmth spread over his body like rivulets of bath water. "I'll have to remember that," he said with a chuckle.

August blushed and dipped her chin, hiding a bashful smile.

He turned and headed to the door, sparing her further embarrassment by saying something nerdy. His car keys were lying in the middle of the marble foyer where he'd tossed them on his way in.

He could hardly believe he was going after Derek. Over the past year, there wasn't a single day when he didn't wish his brother would stay in New York forever.

Geoffrey got behind the wheel and put the key in

the ignition. Now with a few deep breaths in him, he understood how August could feel this was her fault. She didn't understand the history between them, or know how truly bad things were. Though she was right in assuming that incident wouldn't have happened if she weren't here, she didn't realize that something else would have, sooner or later.

"Christ," he said again as he started the SUV.

Derek had made it all the way to the highway. He walked backward down the ocean road, duffel bag slung over his shoulder, one thumb stuck out. When he recognized Geoffrey coming, he turned around and kept hiking.

Geoffrey slowed the SUV and rolled down the window. "Get in."

"Naw, dude. You made the scene clear."

"Derek, Jesus! For once, can you act like an adult?"

He stopped and faced the open window. "August made you come after me, didn't she?"

Geoffrey ground his teeth. He stared through the windshield, mentally counting to ten. "Are we going to sit here arguing in the middle of the road, or are you going to get in?"

Derek managed one more scowl before he opened the passenger door and slid in. Geoffrey flipped a U-turn and headed back to the house.

"August doesn't want to be responsible for any additional friction in our family."

Derek gave a snort, but didn't add whatever sarcastic thing was on the tip of his tongue.

Geoffrey guessed his thoughts; the damage was already done. August could hardly be held responsible for the bad feelings between them.

"Look, I'm not moving in on your girl," Derek muttered.

"She isn't *my girl*."

He turned in to the driveway and brought the SUV to a stop under the oleander tree again. He shut off the motor and turned toward his brother. Derek wisely stayed put. He stared forward, as if afraid to turn and look at Geoffrey.

"August is hurt. Do you understand the situation? She needs a place to rest, heal, and feel safe. Can we pretend to be a normal family for the short time she's here?"

"Sure." Derek gave a flippant toss of one hand. "Whatever."

"Thank you." Geoffrey slipped out of the car and headed back toward the house without waiting for his brother.

◆　◆　◆

"It wasn't so much a dream as it was a memory," August told Geoffrey on the fifteen-minute drive to town. "I'm sure it was something I experienced. I was laughing and having fun with my friends, and this burger joint, or whatever it was, was a place we went often."

"But you couldn't see anyone else's faces?" He glanced over at her when the road straightened out.

"Not yet, but it was like they were right there, at the edge of my memory." The landscape opened up, showing a breathtaking view of the ocean. "Now I can't even remember much of it, but I wrote it down as soon as I woke up. It was one of those old-fashioned diners meant to look like a 1950s sock hop. Maybe Jocelyn's bedroom spurred the memory."

"I remember them. I don't think there are any left, though. There's never been one here. Do you want me to have Mike check on it while you're with Dr. Lohman?"

"Definitely." She looked over, memorizing his profile as he drove. From this view, she admired the length and thickness of his eyelashes. He had a straight, clean profile. "There's something else."

They passed the Mirthful Mermaid. Geoffrey stopped at the first red light leading into town and he swiveled toward her in the seat.

"The night we came down to dinner at the Mirthful Mermaid, I got scared when I saw the marina." She glanced out the passenger window and looked at it, now at a different angle as they were level with it. The same jolt of uncertain fear hit the pit of her stomach. "Like the person who...might be there."

"The person who what, August?"

She shook her head. "I don't know. I don't want to say 'the person who's after me,' or 'the person who's trying to hurt me,' because I'm not sure either is true. It's just this feeling I have."

The light turned green and he drove on.

"Right now your instincts are all you have. You need to trust them."

She reached across herself with her right hand and placed it on his forearm. "I knew you would understand." She smiled at him when he glanced over. "Thank you."

He swallowed, as though her touch made him uncomfortable. August worried she'd crossed a line she shouldn't have. She drew her hand away and adjusted herself more comfortably in the plush leather seat.

"You don't have to thank me, August. I told you I

would help you as much as you needed."

"No, I mean, thank you for being so nice to me."

He glanced over and returned her smile, a touch of pink in his cheeks. She wanted to kick herself. She *had* made him uncomfortable.

"I enjoy helping you. You're nice to be around."

The rest of the short ride was spent in silence. Geoffrey dropped her at the hospital's main doors, and then left to find his brother-in-law.

Though Dr. Lohman's office was plush, with comfy leather furniture and artistically textured paint in warm rust and beige, still the room had a sterile, laboratory-like feel.

"Hello, August. How's your arm today?" The doctor pulled two delicate china cups from a cabinet and made herbal tea from the hot water spigot of a watercooler.

Dr. Lohman was a pleasant enough woman who wore fashionable street clothes, but she was still a virtual stranger. August had to force herself to remember the doctor was trying to help, but something about seeing a psychiatrist seemed ridiculous. She felt guilty, knowing she was only pretending to believe the visit would help.

August read her observations from the notebook and relayed the incidents since the last time she'd seen her. "Geoffrey is having his brother-in-law, Sheriff Mike, check on the burger joints that look like a 1950s sock hop right now."

Dr. Lohman scribbled something in her notes. "You're the first amnesia case I've had," she said when she looked up. "Right now, I'd like to focus on the fear you're experiencing."

"Do you think it's real?"

"If you're feeling it, it's very real," she answered.

The uncomfortable tension in August's shoulders eased. It felt good to have another supporter in her corner, at the very least. Her guilt increased for having doubted the woman's profession.

"Most cases of amnesia aren't caused by the actual injury to the head, but by a trauma that the patient can't bear to remember."

"Like if my husband tried to hurt me."

The doctor nodded, though noncommittally. "It's possible. Do you think you were married?"

"I don't know. I do have the tan line." She looked down at her finger. Geoffrey's handsome face flashed across her mind's eye. In her heart, she hoped she wasn't married, that she had just moved her peridot ring from one hand to the other. The fingers on her left hand were still too swollen to test the theory.

"It's possible you've confused one type of memory for another: for instance, the memory of a movie you'd seen, or a story someone else told you."

"So you don't think it was really me with the other kids?"

"No, I'm not saying that," Dr. Lohman answered carefully. "It's promising that you remember your own reflection in the mirror. I'm just saying you shouldn't struggle too hard for things, let them come naturally. Amnesia is almost never a permanent condition."

By the time the hour wound down, August was feeling less confident about the fading dream.

Dr. Lohman scheduled her for another visit in two days, and August smiled and took the reminder card while secretly not sure if she would keep the appointment. At the very least, she owed Geoffrey to explore any means necessary, and the doctor did seem genuine about wanting to help.

Even if I am just one gigantic Guinea pig to her.

August headed to her physical therapy appointment on the second floor, hoping it would pass quickly, eager to see Geoffrey again. The exercises she could do with her arm were minimal due to the bend in the cast, so the therapist set her on a lifecycle.

By the time she returned to the waiting area in front of the hospital, her mind was the clearest it had been since the night of the accident.

Geoffrey pulled up in a black BMW sedan and reached over to push the door open for her. "You're looking rejuvenated."

"I'm feeling it," she said, sliding in next to him. "Though no clearer on the memories. This is your car?"

"Yep." He helped her draw the seatbelt before pulling out of the hospital's circular driveway. "Just got it back from the shop."

"Did I dent the bumper?"

He glanced over with alarm in his eyes.

August laughed. "I'm kidding. No, really, did I?"

"No, thank God. I wouldn't have kept it if you had." He clenched his jaw. "How did the appointments go?"

"The physical therapy was good. What did Mike have to say?"

"He's checking on the burger joints." He glanced over. "Dr. Lohman wasn't good?"

August sighed. Was she that easy to read? "I feel like a lab rat. Every time I ask her a question, she answers it with one for me."

Geoffrey pulled the car into the Mirthful Mermaid's parking lot. He turned off the engine and faced her.

"We talked awhile and did some more tests with numbers and names, but nothing much came of it." She sighed. "It's frustrating. It's like my memory has been wiped clean. I can't believe I don't even know my own name."

"Maybe it was really awful, like Grizelda, or Prunella."

She laughed. "Would I be less attractive if it was?"

He shook his head and his expression grew somber. Those deep brown eyes were as soft as velvet. "I don't think there's anything that could make you less attractive."

She blushed and turned her gaze out the front. So she hadn't imagined the tiny hints that he was growing attracted to her. That was okay, because she was growing attracted to him, too, and was sure she'd slipped tiny hints as well.

But what if I have a husband, she wanted to ask. *What if I'm running away? What if I did something really awful in my past, so horrible I can't even face it in my own memory?*

"You don't have to go back if you don't want to," he told her. After her last thought, his innocent words took on a deeper connotation.

But August knew he was talking about the therapist. She shrugged. If she didn't continue the sessions, it would almost be like quitting. "I'll try one more, how about that?"

"Deal." He offered his hand. August reached around with her right hand and accepted his shake.

He held her hand tenderly, and in his gentle grip August could feel the magnitude of his caring. Their relationship had changed. They'd gone from being two people who had been in an accident, to friends whose lives had been forever changed by the events. She would never forget him, she was sure of that.

"Hungry?"

She smiled. "Starved. I rode eight miles on the lifecycle."

The Mirthful Mermaid was crowded with lunch-hour patrons. Millie saw them and motioned to them to come to the bar. She popped open two bottles of beer and served them to two men in fishery uniforms, and then poured two glasses of water for Geoffrey and August and slipped a slice of lemon in each.

"Jenny's popping early. I'm on bar duty. Pull up a stool." She smiled and gave August a wink. August could see where the rest of the family, all the way down to Jocelyn, got their friendly eyes. "You must really like my chowder."

"Actually, that looks delicious," she said as one of the waiters served a crab salad sandwich on toasted sourdough slices to one of the patrons next to her. "And we already established I like crab."

"Two crab sandwiches, coming up." After Millie moved off, August swiveled her stool toward Geoffrey.

"I told Dr. Lohman about all the feelings I've been having, and I want to tell you, too."

Geoffrey set down his water glass and gave her his full attention. That was one of the things she loved about him. He really listened when she talked.

"I didn't tell you this before, but I had some incidents of fear. Maybe, technically, they were panic attacks. I'm not sure, because I've never had one before." She shrugged. "Or I don't remember if I did."

He leaned closer, concern filling his eyes. "Panic

attacks? August, when?"

"I told you about the sensation I had when we first drove past the marina. It also happened here, the other night. I got short of breath when I saw this scary man looking at me. He seemed so...purposeful. But now I realize I was probably triggered by the terror I felt when I saw the docks."

"Why didn't you say anything?" He touched her hand where her cast ended, gently curling his fingers around hers. She opened her grasp to receive his, and squeezed.

"I realized right away I'd imagined it, and I thought you would think it was ridiculous. Dr. Lohman said it was possible I had the panic attack because everything is so unfamiliar to me."

Geoffrey frowned. "Did she dismiss your fears?"

Now August felt guilty. She shouldn't have voiced her reservations about the doctor. "Not exactly. She thinks something bad happened to me, and my amnesia isn't so much from my head injury, but from a terrible incident I won't let myself remember. When I told her you were looking into the sock-hops, she said it was a good idea if I go to them."

His eyebrows rose. "And to the marina?"

She nodded. "What do you think?"

He took a deep breath, and August sensed he didn't want to answer. "Not to be like Dr. Lohman, but what do you think?"

"I'm not ready." She traced the wet spot on the bar left from her glass into a flower shape with her fingertip. "Not yet."

"Then I don't think it's a good idea."

Gran Millie sashayed toward them with two plates

in her hand. "Here you go, Millie's famous baked crab sandwiches and a side of our equally if not more famous coleslaw. Sweetheart, yours is cut into four pieces to make it easier on you."

"Thank you, Millie."

"That's Gran Millie to you, missy."

August blushed and cast a secret smile at Geoffrey. His wonderful family had made her feel so at home she wanted to cry. Even Derek didn't seem so bad anymore.

Millie served them tall glasses of iced tea with lemon, and brought a side of delicious three-bean salad in a tangy Italian dressing.

"Sorry I can't gab more," she said, rushing to pop open four bottles of beer. "I'm shorthanded without Jenny behind the bar."

"I'll send Derek down. He needs something to occupy his time."

His grandmother stopped and gave him what August suspected was the tried and true *don't-even-think-about-it* eye.

"No you won't. He's clumsy enough as it is. And the last thing I want to do is put a mouse to work in the cheese factory, if you get my drift." She hurried away to serve the beers.

"She has a point," Geoffrey said over a sigh. "I guess we're stuck with him."

August dug into her sandwich, wondering if he was ever going to divulge the history between them.

◆ ◆ ◆

She paused outside the brick building. Her stomach turned as those last six months at University of the Pacific came rushing back. She'd tried to put it out of her mind. That part of her life was over, and she would never sink that low again.

But even as she drove into this rat-hole part of town, it all came back like a relapse of some hideous disease.

When her dad got laid off and the money for college stopped, she'd tried to get work as an exotic dancer. The seedy manager of the place snorted, looked her up and down, and told her to come back after she "got new titties." The response had been the same at the three other "gentleman's clubs" that were within driving distance. No way was she getting breast augmentation, even if she could afford it. How would she explain it back home?

The only way she could stay in school was to go to work as an escort. And the only way she could stomach being an escort was to get high. Vince was the man who could always make that possible.

At least no one back home would know. The taint of those wretched experiences was on the inside.

And now it was all in the past. She was off that shit and would never go back on it. She could hardly believe she was standing outside Vince's run-down building again, even if all she sought was information.

She stepped over a sleeping drunk on the stairs, thinking he looked vaguely familiar, and started up the three flights to Vince's top-floor loft. She rapped the knocker on his door. One, two, pause, and a third time. The secret knock seemed ridiculous now that she was sober.

He opened the door. After a moment's surprise, he gave her a smarmy smile. "Thought I'd never see you again."

"Likewise." She pushed inside. "Not a social visit,

Vinnie. Don't get your shorts in a bind."

"Hey, no problem. Whatever you want, you know I'm always here." He snickered. "Though I wouldn't turn one down for old time's sake?"

Thankfully she had her back to him, and he couldn't see her grimace. She gagged at the memory of the many times she'd exchanged a blow job for a hit. Even though he spent most every day in this rat hole, he didn't bathe much.

She glanced at the messy coffee table. The assortment of glass paraphernalia made her mouth go dry. Too-familiar longing rolled through her, ending as prickling chills across her flesh. She swallowed her uncertainty through a dry throat. This was the point when recovering alcoholics called their sponsors.

She turned away. She didn't need a sponsor, or anyone else. She was strong. This was behind her.

"I only need information. You owe me a favor. When Carly and I got busted, I told her I'd kill her if she ratted you out."

"Yeah, I know."

She faced him. She'd never noticed, or never cared, what a crap hole this loft was. When she was in college, living in a dorm room with three other girls she despised, having a loft this size all to herself was her greatest fantasy.

Geez, did he ever clean? A dust bunny the size of a kitten sat on the floor in the corner by an old pizza box. Empty aluminum cans lay scattered about. Overfilled ashtrays made her want to gag.

"All I require is your time. I need information."

He eyed her, working a piece of candy in his mouth. "What sort of information?"

"Nothing you can't handle. I'm looking for a missing person."

"Why don't you try the police?"

She scowled. "Why do you think?"

He crossed the room and sat in front of his computer. The setup looked like an alien beast, with its tangle of wires stretching out behind it like monstrous veins. "Give me a lead."

She sat beside him on an old office stool. "Her name is Emily Atkinson. She went missing September ninth. Fell overboard near Hutchison's Island."

"So I'm looking for bodies washed up." His fingers tapped across the keyboard with surprising speed. "You'll want me to check the coroner's records for any unidentified women?"

"Will there be pictures?"

He tapped away. "Depends on where she is."

"I want you to look all the way down to Southern California."

He made a face. "That long in the water, won't be pretty." He leaned back in the office chair and swiveled back and forth as the computer ran its search.

She waited as irritation crawled up her spine. This loft, and its dark memories, made her itchy.

A fat orange cat walked into the room and plopped down on the floor. Did Vinnie ever get confused between it and all the dust clods?

The computer beeped and Vinnie righted his chair to face the screen. "All right, um, eight drownings in the past two weeks." His mouse clicked. "Five bodies so far recovered."

"That many?" She tried to sound concerned instead of perturbed. "That's terrible. Any of them have pictures?"

He shook his head, pushing the hard candy left and right across his mouth. "None. Can't say I'm disappointed. The sight of a stiff always makes me want to hurl."

"I need any incident on the ninth or tenth concerning a twenty-five-year-old blond woman. I'm looking for Jane Does."

The cat rose and ambled over to sniff her pant leg. Usually she hated cats, but reached down and scratched his head to be congenial.

"Jane Does, huh." Vinnie's fingers clacked away. Ghostly flashes of blue and orange moved over his face as the screen changed. "Hmmm. Also got a traffic fatality in Crescent City involving a pedestrian still unidentified, approximately thirty years of age."

She rose and peered over his shoulder. "No picture?"

"Nada. Hmmm, this one's interesting. Splatto."

"The short version, please."

"This one jumped off Yaquina Bay Bridge. Again, no photo available." He rolled his eyes. "*Thank God.*"

A jumper? Emily? Unlikely. "Probably not her. Give me the location anyway."

He wrote it down and continued. "Here's another unknown, blond woman is still missing after a boat sank off the coast of Agate. No picture or names released at request of the family."

At first she thought it would be the report on Emily, but then as "Agate" registered, her heart leaped. Could Emily have been picked up by someone? She chewed her lip to keep from smiling. That would be poetic justice; Emily rescued, only to get swamped.

"Here's another on the night of the ninth: a traffic accident victim with head-trauma, checked in to the hospital at eleven thirty p.m. Strange...this file's confidential.'

That one couldn't possibly be Emily. The bitch would still have been floating. She'd wager a month's pay Emily was the blond woman on the swamped boat. Still, she had to rule out every possibility, at least until her bloated corpse surfaced.

"Can't you hack the password?"

"That's just it—there's no password to bypass. The information simply isn't logged. Someone wants to keep this *off* the records."

Cold worry rushed into her gut. Was it possible Emily had been rescued and was biding her time as the authorities made their case?

"Where is she?"

"This report was first filed by Pacific Communities Hospital, Newport. It's a coastal town near Eugene—"

"I know where Newport is, thank you."

"But there's no police report to go with it. Probably a false alarm."

She'd learned long ago not to count on such luck. A coastal town, was it? Could it be Emily had made it ashore that far south? *Better check it out, just to be safe.*

"Write down what you can find. I'm going to check them all out." She opened her wallet and fished out some bills. "Will fifty bucks make you forget you saw me here today?"

He snatched the cash from her hand. "Saw who?"

Chapter Eight

Geoffrey and August came through the front door to find Derek sitting on the living room couch talking to a woman with shoulder-length, honey-blond hair. The sight of yet another stranger made August's shoulders tighten, but Geoffrey brightened instantly.

"Leah! I thought you weren't coming back until Tuesday."

She swiveled around and smiled, taking August in with a degree of guarded curiosity. At the same time, her friendly eyes and the warmth in her smile told August she didn't have anything to fear.

"I decided to come home early after Jocelyn told me the most amazing story."

"Uh oh."

"Don't worry. Heaven knows I've let her sit up front, too." She stood up and came around the couch. "But I had to see the mysterious woman for myself."

Her words held subtle warning, but her smile only increased. She extended her hand.

"I'm Leah Tanner. Derek tells me you've lost parts of your memory."

She shook the woman's hand. "I wish I could tell you my name. Dr. Carlson tells me I have hysterical retrograde amnesia."

"Hysterical amnesia? Isn't that just like him. I bet if

you were a man, it would have a strong, macho name."

August laughed, already enamored with Leah.

"I'm glad you're here." Geoffrey dropped his briefcase on the foyer table. "I was planning to take August for a drive down the coast tomorrow to see a chain of restaurants she thinks she remembers."

"Actually, Geoffrey dear, I'm here because I remembered the Sierra Foundation awards benefit is tomorrow night. You know I don't dare leave Jocelyn in Derek's care." She glanced over her shoulder with a sly look.

Derek smirked. "That's my loving sister."

Leah smirked right back. "Sweetheart, love has nothing to do with it."

Geoffrey put a hand to his forehead. "I completely forgot. I can skip it."

Leah's eyes grew wide. "Don't you dare! You've earned this award. There's no way I'm letting you skip out on it." She grabbed August by the right arm. "Talk some sense into him. I have a dress that'll be perfect for you."

"Oh no, I couldn't go." August choked down the sudden welling of dread. "I can't go to public events. Not yet."

"Nonsense. Didn't Dr. Carlson say you should be out seeing as much as you can?"

August glanced over at Derek, still slumped into a deep leather loveseat in the living room. He shrugged. "We're family—we talk."

"Now Leah, don't pressure her," Geoffrey said. "If she doesn't want to go, she can stay here with you and Jocelyn."

August had an instant to convey her gratitude in a

smile before Leah hauled her away. "We'll let her decide. In the meantime, I can show her the dress."

She suspected Leah wanted a private moment to talk more than she wanted to show her any dress. August didn't blame her. Even without her memory, she knew she'd be wary at finding a stranger in her home, too, especially if there were small children there.

"Derek told me what happened this morning," she said softly as they walked down the hall to the bedrooms. "I want to thank you for sending Geoffrey back out after him."

"Derek knew that?"

"He guessed as much. Geoffrey sure didn't do it on his own."

The woman's statements made her curiosity grow. What had happened between those two brothers to put them at such odds, when the rest of the family was closer than most?

August suddenly wondered how she knew that. Was the ache of longing squeezing at her heart because she was separated from her own loving family, or because the closeness she saw in the Barthlow house was truly a foreign thing?

"Derek didn't do anything, really." She allowed Leah to lead her into a beautiful room decorated with flowery striped wallpaper. "I couldn't let things get worse between them because of a misunderstanding."

"Sweetheart, things are bad enough already. You don't have to worry about causing anything." She slid open one of three mirrored doors to reveal an enormous closet filled with clothes. Instead of divulging more about Geoffrey and Derek, she rifled through her clothes. "Here we go. I'll never fit in this again."

She removed a tea-length silk dress in pale blue and held it in front of August. "This compliments your eyes beautifully. Of course you can't wear a bra with these little spaghetti straps. I have a strapless one you can borrow."

"It's beautiful, really, but I don't feel right—"

"Have you been wearing these clothes for an entire week?" She pulled the dress back and looked August up and down.

"I've been washing out my underwear at night," August said with a twinge of self-conscious heat in her cheeks. "And we do a load of laundry every other day."

"Well goodness, there's no reason to keep doing that." Leah turned back to the closet. "I need to take Jocelyn shopping for new clothes tomorrow. I'll pick you up some undies. Can't have you putting on damp drawers every morning."

"That's so nice of you, really." August sat on the edge of the bed. "But I don't want to be a bother."

"No bother at all." Leah started yanking clothes off their hangers and tossing them onto the bed. "There's so much crammed in here because I never throw anything away. I've been meaning to donate a lot of this stuff."

"I don't think..." August stammered, unsure how to put her situation to this woman who had obviously never been without money. "I'm not sure I could pay you back."

"Well, it's just some underwear for goodness' sakes, and maybe some comfy sweats to sit around in. Don't worry a bit. Geoffrey's picking up the tab, right? Wait a minute, I have some yoga clothes that'll fit you."

She turned and dug through the top drawer of her dresser. After pulling out a pair of black cotton pants and an oversized t-shirt, she went back to the closet. "Geez, I still have this? And this is from before Jocelyn was born. I'll never squeeze my rear end into these again..." A pair of jeans flew through the air, followed by a coral colored blouse and a pair of blue cotton slacks. "This one is too out of style for me to interview in."

August picked up the chic blue velvet jacket Leah'd flung at her. It was fabulous, and she loved the single glittery rhinestone button that fastened the front.

But something about accepting such generosity just felt wrong.

"Leah, this is all very nice, but I couldn't even get this on over my cast if I tried."

"Well, you won't be wearing that cast forever. Don't worry about it, hon. I'm a clothes horse. I have another closet full in my ex-husband's house. Actually, it'll be fun dressing you up. Jocelyn's too young to appreciate trendy clothes, and she's an incurable tomboy. Besides, it's nice to have another adult female around here to talk to."

"I understand this must be unnerving for you," August volunteered. "You need to feel Jocelyn is safe, and you shouldn't find a strange person here."

Leah smiled. "You're not strange. I liked you just from what Derek told me."

August took a deep breath, uneasy about what might have been said. "If you'd feel more comfortable, I can see about staying in the apartment above the Mirthful Mermaid."

"Don't even think about it. Derek says Jocelyn adores you. Besides, we need someone here to distract those two before they kill each other."

August glanced away.

"Sorry. Bad choice of words." Leah sat down on the bed near August and a moment of silence passed. "Did you think he was going to hit you?"

August thought back to the incident this morning, and the sudden shock of fear that had exploded in her.

"Truly, it happened too fast for me to think anything. But now that I'm in a calmer frame of mind, I realize it was the white cabinet that frightened me more than his hand. That's weird, isn't it?"

She finished with a soft chuckle, but Leah's face was deadly serious as she shook her head. "No, it isn't." She looked at August's fingers where they curled around the edge of her cast. "Did Geoffrey tell you what I do?"

August shook her head.

"I'm a psychologist specializing in marriage counseling. Not exactly as gritty as an abuse counselor, but I've seen my share of battered wives."

Leah was staring at the tan line on her wedding ring finger.

"That's what the consensus is, I gather." Already it appeared to be fading, but it was still there, like a brand. "That I'm running from my husband."

"What do you think?"

"Honestly? No, I don't think I was married. Even though I've lost my memory, if I had a husband, I would remember something about him. Or remember the feeling of being married, at least."

Leah gave her a sad smile. "It's a powerful feeling. Trust the marriage counselor who's going through the divorce."

◆ ◆ ◆

August twisted in bed, unable to get comfortable around the heavy cast. It was like sleeping with a log.

She didn't want to take one of the painkillers just to sleep. They left her mind too foggy, even the next day. She needed to be sharp...at *all* times.

Nighttime was the worst. Her tension rose as the sun fell, and the darkness harbored a thousand threatening shadows. She was almost happier not being able to sleep, and when she did, only sleeping lightly.

It had been another ring she'd had on her wedding finger, one that she had taken off for some reason. The peridot birthstone ring simply didn't fit on that hand. Not even after she'd soaked her hand in ice water until her fingers ached, and then tried to coax it on with liquid dish soap. It wouldn't pass over the second knuckle on her finger.

She sat up in bed. Beyond the curtains, the ocean called to her with its never-ending crash and surge. August rose and made her way to the giant sliding glass door. A full moon gilded the beach in silver.

Pieces of her memory were now clear, having come back so subtly she almost didn't realize it—just somehow knew they were there.

Walking across dark pavement, watching her steps carefully to keep from falling down. Pummeling rain stinging her eyes, making her sore head throb harder. Blinding headlights coming straight at her. She now remembered the accident that had brought them together. Her broken arm was from the car accident. Her head injury...

Everything else, anything further back, was still dark and murky, out of reach like an item submerged in a bucket of muck she didn't want to sink her hand into.

At least now she knew beyond any doubt that Geoffrey was not involved in whatever had happened to her. She had believed it already in her heart and in her gut, but now she had the memory of the accident to cast her trust in stone.

She smiled into the darkness as his handsome face floated across her mind's eye. He was the one thing in her fragile existence that gave her strength. She could hardly wait until morning, when sunlight chased away the darkness, to see him again.

He'd said he had a surprise for her. Her mood brightened. He was so sweet and kind, placing his life on hold to put her first. He'd tried to get out of his awards banquet to take her down south to the burger joints he'd researched. August was glad Leah was here to stand behind her, because she wasn't about to let him do that. If there was one thing about him she'd discovered in their brief time together, he was humble and shy when it came to his own qualities.

August made her way quietly through the dark house to warm a glass of milk in the microwave. It was only two thirty a.m.; she still had a good chance for a few solid hours of sleep.

She poured her milk, heated it for forty seconds and removed it from the microwave.

"I can't sleep either. Damn ocean keeps me awake all night."

She jumped, sloshing milk onto the counter.

"I wish you would stop sneaking up on me," she snapped at Derek. He sat in the living room in the darkness, a silhouette against the moonlit night. He raised a glass bottle and took a swig. A shiver of fear skittered over her spine. The clear liquid inside glistened, illuminated by the fat moon behind him.

"I didn't shneak anywhere. Been sitting here the

whole time."

"Geoffrey isn't going to like you drinking." She cringed inwardly, certain that was the wrong thing to say.

"Why donchoo run and tell him."

"I'm sure it will be obvious in the morning."

He laughed and leaned forward, squeaking across the plush leather couch. The finger he pointed at her swayed. "You're trying to remain neushral. That's commenbdible. But we're past fik-shing."

"Why?"

Because of Christina. She longed to know more, while at the same time, was terrified of what it would reveal.

Derek laughed again, but this time it was a pained, pathetic sound. He glanced sideways, staring into a dark corner of the room.

"Imagine this, Derek. Imagine you wake up one day and your family is gone. You'd look back on today and wished you *had* fixed it."

"He hates me. Can't be fixed."

"He doesn't hate you." Again, she was sorry she'd spoken too soon. She had no idea if that were true or not.

"You like him. Don't you?" His drunken gaze found her in the darkness. She couldn't exactly see his eyes as much as she could feel them on her.

"I do." A spike of longing pierced her heart as she said it. "Very much."

"You're good," he said. She wasn't quite sure what he meant until he said, "Good enough for him. A good person. Better than Christina. She didn't deserve him."

"That's enough, Derek." Geoffrey's gruff voice cut

through the darkness. He crossed the living room below the kitchen and snatched the bottle from his startled brother. Once in the kitchen, he poured the remains of the bottle into the sink and then faced her. "You probably shouldn't wander around the house late at night, as my brother obviously can't be trusted."

"I'm sorry I woke you," August said. "Just let me wipe up this milk."

Geoffrey flipped on the light switch, flooding the kitchen with too-bright light.

"Don't worry, bro," Derek slurred from the living room. "I don't think Auguss likes bad boys."

"She doesn't like drunk boys, either," August added for herself. A touch of a smile found Geoffrey's lips. It vanished as he turned around to face his brother.

"You aren't supposed to be drinking, Derek. That's why you're here, to clean up your act. Do I have to dump all the booze?"

"Drugs." Derek bobbed his head to enunciate his point. "I'm here to clean off drugs. A little drink helps take the edge off. Can't go cold, man. Not possible."

Geoffrey turned back to her and spoke in a soft voice. "Where are the painkillers Dr. Carlson gave you?"

"Put well away. Tomorrow, they go down the toilet."

Geoffrey rinsed out a sponge and wiped up the milk. He picked up her mug and swabbed the dribble of milk off the side before turning back to his brother. "You—go to bed."

"Can't sleep."

"I don't care! Go, before you do something stupid like fall off the balcony again."

"Aw man, I was twelve years old."

"And you were a whole lot smarter then than you are now. Move it, before my patience runs all the way out." Geoffrey pointed. Derek rose unsteadily to his feet and shuffled away.

Geoffrey waited a long minute before turning back to her.

"I'm sorry," August said again. "I couldn't sleep and I thought some warm milk would help. I didn't mean to wake you. I know you have a conference call in the morning."

"Don't apologize. I wish this house was safe for you to move around in without worrying about him."

"He doesn't bother me."

"What if Jocelyn got up and found him like that? She's only seven years old. She shouldn't have to see that. He could really upset her and she might never forget it."

"I know." She nodded and smiled. "Don't ask me how I know that, but I know you're right." Darting memories flitted around in her head. She hated to watch anyone pour a drink. Someone in her past was an alcoholic.

If only I could remember!

Geoffrey pushed both hands through his hair. "I've had it with him."

It must be the late hour and that she was punchy, because August couldn't stop herself from saying what she knew she shouldn't.

"Is it because he was drinking, or because he was talking about Christina?"

Geoffrey sighed and leaned back against the kitchen counter. "He knows how to push my buttons, no matter what he's saying or doing."

August sipped her milk, waiting for him to continue.

"Somehow he always seems to find a way to bring her up, even though he knows it's a sore subject for me."

She wanted to reach out and touch him, to say she knew that, to be the person he could talk to about it.

Irrational disappointment clawed at her edges. Without her memory, he was all she knew, but he had an entire life separate from her. She was only a brief detour for him.

Though her feelings for him had grown steadily with each day that passed, August wished Christina were still alive. She wished she could take Geoffrey's pain away and give him back the life she knew he deserved, even if it was one without her in it.

"He's my brother, and you were right when you said I don't hate him." His brow furrowed and his eyes were red-rimmed with sadness. "But a part of me wishes I never had to see him again, because I can't see his face without also seeing hers."

Chapter Nine

August didn't tell Geoffrey about her newly recovered memories of the night of the accident. She still wasn't certain she was on a boat that night; she only had her gut feeling. Regardless, she wasn't ready to share that with him, or even put it into words. With the reclaimed memory came a deeper level of fear she couldn't explain. So when he turned the SUV onto a narrow road toward the marina just before reaching town, she bristled.

"Um, Geoffrey—"

He glanced sideways and grinned. "Trust me."

She settled into the deep leather seat, her heart pounding painfully against her ribs.

With her suspicion she had been on a boat came an almost certain understanding someone had pushed her overboard, intending for her to die under the brutality of the stormy sea. Would he think her crazy if she said so?

She should trust him enough to tell him so, but a part of her was afraid. Why couldn't she shake the strange embarrassment that came with every shadowy memory?

Because someone I trusted did this to me, and I feel the fool for it.

Oblivious of her discomfort, Geoffrey glanced over,

still grinning like a mischievous little boy eager to spring a surprise.

"Still trust me?" He angled the car around the back side of the marina and up a winding road. This was the hill blocking the ocean from the highway on the outskirts of town.

"I think so." She swallowed to cover her quaking voice.

"You don't sound very convincing. I'm hurt." His tone was teasing, but August couldn't be convinced to smile.

"Sorry," she whispered. "Of course I trust you."

He pulled the car into a bank of parking spaces under a giant oak. This was a recreational park of some kind. Judging by a walking path leading up a small hill, it was a vista point.

Geoffrey reached into the back seat and removed an igloo bag. "Come on. I have something to show you."

They walked up the hill in silence. August breathed in the dry salt grass and fresh ocean breeze, determined to grasp whatever peaceful minutes she could. At the top of the rise, she discovered they were indeed on the hill high above the marina, looking out over a magnificent view of the ocean. Far to the left, the Mirthful Mermaid dominated the row of shops across from the marina, its turquoise blue mermaid logo identifiable in the gleaming sea-silvered wood even at this distance.

"I thought it might be easier to take a long-distance look."

The tension trickled out of her in cooling relief so intense she was nearly brought to tears. They sat on a wooden bench and Geoffrey opened the cooler bag between them. In it were two turkey sandwiches, two bags of potato chips, two cans of ginger ale, and a pair of binoculars.

Her heart swelled with something that couldn't entirely be called gratitude, and the sensations in her stomach turned warm and ticklish. Whatever it was, admiration wasn't a strong enough word to describe what she was feeling, deep down in the centermost part of her.

Or was the intensity of her emotions playing tricks on her mind? Was the natural progression of their friendship being mistaken for something more than it truly was?

She didn't think so. Geoffrey was a special man with a one-in-a-million heart. Love wouldn't be a long leap at all.

The idea both thrilled August, and terrified her. Until she knew about her past and the people in it, she had nothing to offer him.

He handed her the binoculars. "Tell me what you see."

August peered through. The marina bustled with people this Saturday morning, crowded with boat owners enjoying the unusually mild September day.

"Boats, people. Water."

"What kind of boats?"

"Well, there's a catamaran," she said, looking at a gigantic behemoth called *Issaquah*. "But everyone knows what a catamaran is."

Her nerves jumped. He was testing her. Why was she so afraid to confess her suspicions to Geoffrey? Because he would set his brother-in-law to investigating her more deeply, and they might actually find her past.

Before I'm ready to find it myself.

And that led to another question: why? *Because I'm not ready to go further with Geoffrey, or because I'm not ready to face a would-be killer?*

Both were terrifying prospects.

August set down the binoculars. She could trust him—he wouldn't do anything she didn't want him to do. But the sooner they found her past, the sooner her time with him would end.

The sooner the dangerous thing following her would catch up with her.

"Thank you for doing this. You're so good to me. I don't think I've ever been treated so nicely by anyone."

He stared back with those fathomless brown eyes she wanted to fall into. "It's my pleasure. You've helped me take my mind off..."

When he didn't continue, she asked, "Christina?"

He merely nodded and gazed out at the sea.

"Do I look like her?"

Geoffrey chuckled. "Not at all. She had Italian features. Dark brown eyes, olive skin, jet-black hair."

August realized she'd seen her portrait. "She's in the photo on the piano, with Jocelyn. She was beautiful."

He nodded. "She died last October, in a car accident."

Not even a year past. August reached across the igloo bag and placed her hand over the back of his. "I'm sorry."

She wanted to ask how it involved Derek, but knew she shouldn't expect him to reveal any more than he was comfortable telling her. The sadness in his eyes was now a thousand times brighter, and she regretted bringing it up.

She picked up the binoculars and scanned the marina again. Nothing jogged her memory. If she had been on a boat that night, it didn't mean she was a sailor. She could have been a passenger. She might have even been taken out by her attacker as a captive, her first time ever stepping aboard a boat.

"Does anything look familiar to you?" Geoffrey's voice was heavy, as though he'd swallowed down the sadness she'd seen rising in him moments ago. "The names of any of the boats? That ketch there?"

Her long-distance gaze flew to the twenty-five-foot double-masted vessel named *Ketch-ekan*. Did she know it was a ketch because of its play-on-words name, or because of its lines and rigging?

"You tell me. Which one is the ketch?"

"That's not fair," he said in a lighter voice. "I'm a sailor. One of those boats is mine."

She put the binoculars down. "I should have known that about you. You've got that 'Polo by Ralph Lauren' look about you."

He groaned. "Don't say that. Derek is the family model, not me."

"Derek looks more like the drummer of a grunge rock band. You're much more attractive."

"Me? Nah." He actually blushed. August found it charming.

"Yeah, you. Definitely." She peered through the binoculars. "Which one is yours?"

"Guess."

"My arm is getting tired."

"It's good exercise."

"You're merciless."

There were a few bigger vessels that would require

several hands to sail, but August wagered his family would own one of the smaller, beautifully restored sloops that one or two people could take on a casual afternoon outing.

"*Justin's Pride?* Isn't your older brother's name Justin?"

"Yep, but wrong. Purely coincidence."

"*Honeysuckle Rose?*"

"Nope."

"Right. You don't seem like a *Honeysuckle Rose* kind of guy. But I'll bet you like the Beatles?"

"Love 'em."

"*Penny Lane.*" She glanced at him and found him smiling back.

"What made you think so?"

She peered down again. "Its gleaming wooden deck. You seem like the type of person who would invest the care and time in something so beautiful."

Geoffrey said something, but she didn't hear. A black Labrador had trotted through her line of vision, making her breath catch. She scanned in front, and then behind the dog to find its owner. Before she could get a good look at the woman trailing behind the dog, she'd moved so that August could only see the back of her head and a mass of curly red hair.

She gripped the binoculars harder, following the woman. There was nothing out of the ordinary about her. She was of average build, wearing blue jeans and a t-shirt with a sweatshirt tied around her waist. She glanced sideways, giving August a fleeting glimpse of her profile, half hidden by dark sunglasses.

"August, what's wrong?"

Remembrance danced at the edge of her

subconscious. *Roger...Rodney...Rocky.* She knew a red-haired woman with a black Labrador named Rocky. Dread sank into the pit of her stomach. A sickening feeling accompanied the memory, but the reason, and the woman's face, remained a mystery.

She watched the woman stroll down the dock until the muscles in her arm burned from holding the heavy binoculars.

"Jesus, August, you're white as a sheet. What did you see down there?" He moved closer and reached for the binoculars. "Let me help you hold these."

"Never mind, she's gone." August dropped them in her lap.

"Who's gone?"

"The woman. I saw a woman with a dog."

"Someone you remember?"

"I don't know. I think so." Her stomach churned. Whoever the woman with Rocky was, a bad association accompanied her. But why? She could be someone August had a terrible falling-out with, but that didn't mean murder.

"Do you have a key to the marina?"

"I have a code. The gates to the ramps are electronic."

August took a deep breath. "I want to go down there. I need to see that woman."

Or, more precisely, I need her to see me.

Chapter Ten

Geoffrey punched his code into the electronic keypad to the section of the marina where the dog and its owner were last seen, and the gate's lock released with a shrill buzzing sound. After guiding August through, he circled her shoulders with his arm. The reassuring gesture relieved her fear. She pressed close as they walked side-by-side down the narrow ramp to the main section.

August had hoped she would find some familiarity when they entered the marina, but no technical names or jargon entered her mind as she glanced about at the rigging, lines, and sailing gear on the various boats.

"There it is," Geoffrey said, pointing. She caught a glimpse of the black dog loping down one of the long center piers, playfully chasing gulls into the sky.

The dog bolted from a slip and turned in the opposite direction. Would the woman at the end of the dock be the final key in unlocking her past? August realized that in a matter of minutes, she might be on the road back to her old life, no longer in need of Geoffrey's sanctuary.

No, that wasn't entirely true. He'd become important to her, even before her attraction had budded and blossomed. Even if she found an entire town full of family and friends somewhere else, Geoffrey would always remain fixed in her heart.

The red-haired woman stepped out from a slipway, lifting her arms toward the black Lab. "What 'ya got there, Poncho?" she said in doggie sweet-talk. The dog dropped a twisted piece of driftwood at her feet.

All at once August's fear and morbid hope disappeared. She had never seen this woman before.

As they'd approached the dock, she had been waiting for the sight of the woman's face to fill in the gaps between the whispers of familiarity brushing at her memory like the tendrils of a peacock feather. She'd been certain that if this was the red-haired woman from her past, all it would take was a first glimpse of her face.

But now that August saw this stranger, it seemed even those fog-like vapors were gone. Had she imagined the whole thing?

The woman straightened up and smiled when she saw them. "Hi, Geoffrey. Haven't seen you out here in a while. *Penny*'s looking nice."

"Rachel, hi." He glanced questioningly at August.

She shook her head.

"Er, Rachel, this is August."

"Hey there, August. What happened to your arm?"

"I fell," she answered simply. "I broke it in two places."

"Ouch. That must have been some fall." Rachel grabbed the dog by the collar when he lunged forward to introduce himself a little too enthusiastically. "Poncho, no! Sorry, he thinks people like to be trampled with muddy paws."

When the dog calmed, Rachel let him loose. Geoffrey knelt down and rubbed Poncho's head. "I don't remember you having a dog."

"I adopted him in March from the Humane Society. He's a handful, but the most loyal man in my life." She laughed at her own joke. "How have you been? I don't think I've seen you since the New Year's Eve yacht club celebration."

"We've been good. I'm staying at the summer house to help out with Jocelyn." He stood, and Poncho trotted back to Rachel. "I was going to give August a tour of *Penny Lane* when she saw you and mentioned you looked familiar."

"But I had only seen your hair, and your dog. I have a friend with a black Lab, but she doesn't live around here. I don't know why I would have thought you were her."

She was rambling. Did her story sound as hokey to Rachel as it did to her?

"Oh, where are you from?"

"Um." August swallowed. "Up north. Near Seattle."

The girl smiled warmly. "Well, it's nice to meet you, August. Are you two going to enter the Thanksgiving Regatta?"

Geoffrey stood up and took August under his arm. "That depends on whether or not we can get *Penny Lane* fitted out in time."

"I heard Derek is back in town. Tell him don't be a stranger."

As they started away, August felt a strange mixture of relief and disappointment.

"She dated Derek for a while," Geoffrey explained. "She's a little wild and crazy, but still a better influence than any of the other girls he'd dated."

"The bits and pieces were stronger before I saw her face. Once I realized she wasn't the person I thought I'd remembered, all traces were wiped away."

"But you do know a red-haired woman with a black Labrador?"

She nodded as he held open the gate. "I think so."

Penny Lane was two docks over in one of the first slips. The gleaming deck August spied through the binoculars was even more impressive up close. A narrow wire running through stainless steel bars served as her railing. Geoffrey unhooked the section at the portable steps and held August's good hand as she carefully stepped onto the deck.

"Does anything look familiar?"

She wished she could say yes. Somehow she felt it all should be, but the knowledge was just out of her reach.

"Yes and no. I know things are there, and it makes me angry that I can't remember them." Aggravation welled inside her like a building tornado that wouldn't blow itself out.

"Don't try too hard. Here, have a seat and relax." He guided her to the rear of the vessel and onto a plush padded seat spanning the breadth of the deck.

"You take it easy while I polish up the...this um..."

"Compass. Nice try, Geoffrey, but even ten-year-old Girl Scouts know what a compass is." She smiled. He was so devilishly charming. "You're sweet."

"Actually, I'm rotten."

"I'll never believe that."

"It's true."

She narrowed her gaze. "Explain."

"Come with me to the banquet. There. Now you know the truth about me. I'm selfish."

"You aren't even close." She laughed, but Geoffrey's

expression remained somber.

"This wouldn't be a date; I know you aren't my date." He sighed and glanced at the channel leading out of the harbor. "Forget I asked. It's a bad idea. A public event is probably the last thing you should do."

"You're right, it probably is." Her expression softened. "But you've done so much for me. It's the least I can do in return."

"That's not a good reason to say yes." He shook his head. Sunlight glinted on the gold strands in his hair. "I don't want you to go because you feel you owe me."

"I want to go because I want to see my favorite person in Newport pick up an award I'm sure he deserves. How's that for a reason?"

"Well, I guess that would be a pretty good one." He grinned. "You want to think about it while I lean against this...thing here..."

"The wheel?"

"Is that getting old?"

She nodded and laughed. "It feels good to actually get one. Try another."

"This is the..." He touched a rope secured to a cleat.

"I have no idea."

"Main sheet. Don't worry, that's a tough one. Here's an easier one." He pointed to a polished silver fixture.

"That's a cleat." August rose, her gaze caught by a small door set flush in a fiberglass compartment in the low cabin roof. She crossed the deck and flipped it open. Inside was a flare gun with a safety pin securing it like a fire extinguisher might have, and a small plastic case of extra flares.

"Not what I thought," she said absently.

"That should be marked, according to code. I'm still

ironing out the kinks."

She glanced away, tamping down her increasing agitation. "How about a tour of the inside?"

"Vright zees vay. Through the grand double doors and into the foyer." He unlocked a set of louvered doors and pushed back a hatch-cover, and then offered his hand. "Watch your step."

A beam of sunlight cut through the small windows on the right side of the cabin.

"It looks like Derek's been here," August said.

He glanced to the empty pint bottle of vodka lying on the small galley counter. A muscle in his jaw twitched. "I'd say you're right," he said, shifting his gaze to the rumpled makeshift bed. "He's dog meat."

"Now, wait a minute. This is good."

He raised his eyebrows skeptically. "If you can prove that, I'll spare him."

"I know this—that's usually a table, right? You unscrew the table's support pole, and then use the table top to fill in the space and put a pad over it to make the bed."

Geoffrey nodded. "How did you know that?"

"I wish I knew." She shrugged. "So, is he off the hook?"

"Hmmm. I'm not sure."

"What if we make him chip barnacles?"

He laughed. "Barnacles? On *Penny Lane?*"

"We can pick some off the rocks and relocate them, just for Derek."

Geoffrey's smile washed away her frustration. "Deal."

◆ ◆ ◆

This was a huge risk, but not finding out as much as

she could was a bigger risk. She parked her car in the parking garage located behind the hospital and walked to the main entry.

The facility bustled with a high level of energy for a Saturday afternoon. The main desk was huge, but with several nurse attendants on duty, she didn't have to wait. She chose the youngest looking one, hoping she'd be easier to deceive.

"Do you think I'd be able to see an OBGYN? I'm five months pregnant and last night I started having terrible pains in my abdomen. I thought it might be constipation..." She smiled sheepishly. "But I'm not constipated. I have insurance."

The nurse's icy expression thawed at the mention of insurance. "I'm sure we can get you in. You did the right thing coming in, even if it is just constipation. What's your name, hon?"

"Sonja Davis." She handed over the insurance card for Blue Cross.

"Second trimester," the nurse said as she typed. "I need to see your ID."

Her heart jumped, and she really did feel a cramp in her gut. She fumbled getting the driver's license out of the plastic pocket of the wallet.

She handed it to the nurse, who looked at it, and then up at her. Her eyes flicked back and forth, suspicious.

"I had red hair when that was taken," she said. "Can't color it now, though, because of the baby."

"That's good to hear. You'd be surprised how many still do. Shouldn't do it while you're nursing, either, okay?"

She nodded along, obedient and agreeable. *So far, so*

good.

The nurse set the ID and insurance card on the front of her keyboard and typed in the information. "You're from Washington. So you've never been here before?"

She breathed out her relief. "No, I'm down here visiting friends. I can't tell you how happy I was to find you have this big, beautiful hospital here. I was really worried I would have to drive all the way back to Seattle."

The nurse beamed as she handed her back the driver's license and insurance card. A well-placed compliment was usually all it took to persuade the simple-minded.

"You're in luck. We have an appointment available."

A stylish woman in a lab coat entered the nurse's station, wearing expensive high heels. She handed a clipboard to another nurse, speaking in soft tones. She looked up when another doctor entered the station.

"Dr. Jessup, I wonder if you have a moment to discuss my amnesia patient?"

Her attention went to red-hot. *Amnesia?* Was it possible this was the mysterious traffic accident victim Vinnie found?

"The young woman found out on the coastal highway?" The male doctor she was talking to checked his watch. "Sure, I have time before my next appointment."

The room around her had increased by ten degrees. Her mind worked with the fantastic possibilities as she dimly heard the printer grinding out a plastic ID band with her details. The nurse fixed it around her wrist.

"Take a seat. They'll call you in about ten minutes.

I've indicated this is urgent. Dr. Freeman will be seeing you." The nurse winked. "She's a woman."

She gave a huge smile. "That's a relief. Thank you *so* much."

Could it really have been this easy? She'd known Emily had been in this hospital, but to have the bitch just fall into her lap...and with amnesia, no less! *Fuckin' A.*

In the promised ten minutes, a nurse practitioner called her name. Swiftly and efficiently, her blood pressure and temperature were taken, and she was weighed. This chubby nurse seemed generally disinterested—in anything other than cake and cookies, it would appear—and hardly said two words. She showed her into an examination room and sat down at a computer console.

"Take off everything and put the smock on, opening in the front." She gestured to the folded garments on the examination table. "Your birthdate?"

Shit. She swallowed. *Think, think, think!* Valentine's Day. "February fourteenth." Close one. Thank goodness it was an easy birthday to remember.

"You're in for stomach pains...and you're in your second trimester?"

"Yes."

"Have you eaten any spicy foods in the last twenty-four hours?"

"No. That would be bad for the baby."

The nurse looked at her like she'd insulted her intelligence. "The doctor will be with you in a few minutes."

The instant the door of the exam room closed, she bolted for the computer. The screen was still visible; the nurse hadn't locked it.

She didn't know much about computers, and certainly not hospital programs, but there was a search bar for patient names at the top of a user-friendly looking screen.

She typed "Emily Atkinson."

NO PATIENT FOUND.

"Dammit. Come on." She tried again, but got the same response. Vinnie had been right; whatever record might have been in this system had been deleted.

There was another search bar, presumably to search the system by other factors. She typed in "traffic accident" and waited while it searched. The computer spit out more than twenty pages, judging by the resulting page links numbered at the bottom.

"Shit."

She couldn't possibly find Emily in all these. She typed "amnesia," in the search bar and clicked the search symbol again. A single page of results came up for a Dr. Lohman in the psychiatry department. She quickly scanned through patient summaries before she realized the first one, a listing whose abbreviated description showed the word "amnesia" and "August Unknown–Barthlow," was the one she was looking for.

She clicked the link for the first entry. No picture, but she hadn't expected one. She didn't know what "Barthlow" meant, either, but figured it was somebody's name. She'd check it out later on her smart phone.

She scanned what she could as seconds ticked by. She couldn't be caught, and she couldn't go through with this appointment. She could not afford to be remembered here.

If this was Emily, she had walked in front of a car on

the night of September ninth on the Oregon Coastal Highway. She had broken her arm, and needed eight stitches in her forehead. She didn't remember what had happened before the accident.

"Bloody beautiful."

The address was listed as 19 Crestview Drive. That was easy enough to remember. She typed "Sonja Davis" into the search bar, bringing up the original patient record again, in case anyone needed reminding who had been assigned to this room and mysteriously disappeared before the doctor arrived.

She grabbed her purse and casually exited the examination room, looking like any other patient who'd finished with their appointment.

◆　◆　◆

"Wow, Uncle G. You're smokin'." Jocelyn giggled.

Geoffrey stopped in the doorway and met August's eyes in the mirror. She smiled as she looked over his tuxedo, and his insides turned quivery.

"I love that tux on you," Leah said. "Jocelyn, let August borrow your beige hair ribbon, okay? It'll go nice with my shawl."

Leah had woven August's long hair into a single French braid and coiled the length of it into a bun at the nape of her neck.

A sliver of guilt needled its way in to his gut. Had August asked Leah to disguise her by hiding her hair?

"It's a little cool for this outfit this time of year, so this shawl will be perfect to drape over your cast. It's wool, but it's not too scratchy." Leah tied the cream colored shawl over August's shoulder as Jocelyn came bounding back into the room with the tiny ribbon bow.

"Let me put it on."

August sat on the edge of the bed and Jocelyn knelt behind her on the mattress. She gingerly slipped the bobby-pin into the center of the bun.

"Perfect," Leah said, surveying her work. "With the shawl, you can hardly tell you have a broken arm."

"Except for this ugly body sling," August said. She stood, and after glancing over her reflection, met Geoffrey's eyes again in the mirror.

She looked beautiful in the borrowed turquoise dress and strappy high-heeled sandals. Wispy bangs brushed over her forehead, and Geoffrey saw Leah had replaced the Sesame Street bandage at August's forehead with a smaller, flesh-colored one. A subtle touch of rose-toned makeup accentuated her natural coloring, and her lips were shiny with pink gloss.

Another wave of guilt surged through him. If anything happened to her tonight, he would never forgive himself.

He was being selfish. He'd watched his brothers parade around with beautiful women his whole life, and tonight was just another desperate effort to leap out of their shadows. Having her with him would make him feel a little less like an outcast in a room full of strangers.

Those were foolish thoughts. August was no more his girlfriend than Yaquina Head was his lighthouse.

The guilt morphed into something darker. Even if he and August both agreed this wasn't a date, the plain and simple truth was his feelings were becoming dangerous. Feelings he wasn't ready for.

"Are you sure you're up for this?" he asked, looking to justify his own excuse.

"Sure, bro. After I get her all dressed up, now you're

trying to back out?" Leah teased.

"I did her nails," Jocelyn volunteered.

"It sounds like you're trying to talk me out of it." August turned from the mirror and approached him. "Something wrong with the dress?"

"God no. August, you're gorgeous." Pale hints of pink eye shadow made her blue eyes more brilliant than a summer sky. The frosty-pink lip-gloss had turned her lips downright edible.

This is wrong. Somehow, I'm betraying Christina.

The hand August placed on his arm squeezed reassuringly. "I'm beginning to feel silly with all this paranoia. All that worrying was for nothing, right? I mean, who even knows if I have an enemy with red hair?"

He took her hand from his arm and wrapped it in his own. "You need to trust your gut. If this isn't right, tell me."

"It's right. Don't worry."

He wasn't convinced. Even if she felt safe, a nagging voice whispering in his ear told him taking August out was wrong. But was it the angelic side of his conscience, or the devilish?

Even though she clearly enjoyed his company, August truly wasn't his, just like Christina had never truly been his. Geoffrey felt himself being pulled north and south by his emotions, but heaven help him, he liked being around her too much.

"The award, one drink, and we'll skip out before dinner."

"I don't even get dinner?"

She smiled, and her eyes twinkled. Lord, he could watch that happen for the rest of his life.

"Geez, you're a stingy date."

Date. There, she'd said it. He didn't know how to respond. Heat crawled into his face as an uncomfortable second stretched into an uncomfortable minute.

"Can I come, too?" Jocelyn asked.

"No, honey, it's grown-up stuff," Leah told her. "Besides, I thought we were going to bake a blueberry pie?" She shooed them out of the room. "Get going, you two, before Geoffrey misses his award."

August took his arm as they walked down the hall. When Derek caught sight of them, he whistled.

"Whoa, don't you two look like the dapper duo. Nice penguin suit, dude. Tonight's your tree-hugging thing, isn't it?"

Geoffrey clenched his jaw. "Yeah. The tree-hugging thing."

"Hey, I'm all for it. Save the trees, you know. Too much logging, too much pavement."

"That's funny, considering you're most at home in New York City."

"Actually, Derek," Leah cut in, "two years ago a fire started by campers destroyed 165 acres of national forest. This family—those members who were present anyhow—was primarily responsible for organizing and funding the reseeding. Geoffrey headed up the project, so the Newport Chamber of Commerce and the Sierra Foundation are presenting him with the Mayor's Volunteer of the Year award."

"To me and my very large group of volunteers," he interrupted his sister before she embarrassed him to death. "The people who were actually shoveling and planting deserve the most recognition."

Another miserable wave of heat crawled over his

face. How he hated ceremonial foo-fa like this. He much preferred to wield his influence from the anonymity of his office, and keep it that way: anonymous.

"I think it's wonderful," August said, tightening the link of her arm around his. She eased closer, enveloping him in a wonderful essence of roses and citrus. "It's always so sad when nature gets destroyed, especially from careless human error. People need to take more responsibility for this planet."

"I would have helped out, if I'da been here," Derek mumbled. He looked genuinely pouty. Geoffrey joined the others in ignoring him.

"Let's go, shall we? The sooner we get there, the sooner we leave."

August laughed. "It sounds like you don't want to do this."

"What gave me away?" He guided her to the door.

"It'll be fun."

Already, with August at his side, it was starting to be.

◆   ◆   ◆

"This is one of your hotels?" August asked him.

"The first one." Geoffrey sounded as uneasy as she felt.

Nerves had started as tiny pin-pricks during the short ride to town. Anxiety morphed into worry as they got out of the car and started toward the Palisades' entry. She had the strangest sensation she was being watched.

But the worry turned to full-fledged terror when they entered the grand ballroom and found nearly a thousand people milling about. The buzz of conversation was deafening, and as soon as they saw

Geoffrey, the people closest surrounded him, offering handshakes and congratulatory pats on the back. It was obvious he was well-known and well-liked in Newport. Their voices rang in her ears and August was overwhelmed by the sudden crush. She sidled behind him, lost in a sea of tuxedo-clad men and elegantly dressed women.

"It's about time. I was wondering when you'd get here."

August hardly recognized Gran Millie. She'd shed her Mirthful Mermaid's t-shirt and apron for a glittering black gown. For the first time, instead of her tight ponytail, August saw a perfectly coiffed page-boy hairdo. She looked like a movie star. For all her sixty-seven years, she'd retained an air of elegant beauty.

"Watch it, people, she's got a broken arm. Come this way, darling. We're sitting up front at a reserved table."

Suddenly all attention turned toward August, and she heard a woman loudly ask, "Geoffrey, dear, who is your date?"

He kissed his grandmother on the cheek and took August under his arm. "This is a friend of the family. August, uh, Smith. August, this is Maxine Crawford, president of the ladies' auxiliary."

August shook her hand, and then allowed herself to be introduced to several other people whose names she'd never remember. She felt as if everyone in the room was staring at her, and even imagined she could hear their whispers.

Someone bumped her arm. Bright agony zinged down her forearm, followed by a surge of nausea. Suddenly everyone seemed threatening. Was one of the people in this room the person who had hurt her?

She was glad when Gran Millie pulled her away. "You look so pretty tonight, dear. I'm glad to see some color back in those cheeks."

"It's painted on." She swallowed. "I think I need to sit down."

Millie guided her to the nearest chair. "Is your arm hurting?"

"Someone bumped it. I'll be fine in a minute."

"Clumsy clods. You can dress 'em up but you can't take 'em out." Millie poured her a glass of ice water from the carafe on the table. "Did you take a pain pill tonight?"

She desperately looked around for Geoffrey. "I flushed them. We were afraid Derek would try to find them."

"Oh, for God's sake! Where is that grandson of mine?"

"I didn't like them. They make my head foggy." She forced a smile. "I'm better now. It's just a little overwhelming, all these people."

Gran Millie gave her a narrowed glance. "Are you sure coming tonight was a good idea?"

August nodded. "I have to stop living in fear of every person I see." She mustered a weak laugh. "The way I figure it, I need to give the person who did this to me a big surprise."

"We're talking about a would-be murderer." Millie frowned and chuckled at the same time, shaking her head. "You've got moxie, I'll give you that, kiddo."

Geoffrey slipped out of the crowd. "Hey, you two, I turned around and you were gone."

August breathed a sigh of relief. He was so handsome in his tux, she could drink him in for hours

With his short-trimmed, rusty-blond beard and wavy golden hair against the black tuxedo, he looked as though he'd stepped out of a James Bond movie.

"You're not keeping a close enough eye on her, what with a killer running around," his grandmother snapped. "And what's this I hear about you making her dump her pain pills?"

At that moment, the microphone shrieked. The announcer took the podium and asked everyone to take their seats.

"Thank you, everyone. We know you're all hungry and eager for this to begin, so we're going to serve you dinner as our keynote speaker, James McTierney, begins with some announcements. Then we'll move on to our very special awards."

Millie carried August's water glass as they made their way to their reserved table at the front. She took a seat facing the stage so that her back was to the rest of the room. One glance over her shoulder at the immense ballroom was enough to send her stomach jumping all over again.

"Here, take this with your food," Millie said, passing her a pill. "It's Tylenol with a low level of codeine."

August was thankful dinner was easy-to-eat: ravioli with green salad and sliced baguettes. The keynote speaker stuttered and stumbled over his speech, and a mischievous part of August was glad someone else was more nervous than she. Fortunately, the man was spared by the sounds of dozens of servers putting out hundreds of meals, and the wind-chime like music of the guests' forks and knives tinkling against their plates.

They were finishing a bland dessert of frozen-strawberry topped cheesecake as the poor man stammered over his conclusion.

Millie shook her fork at Geoffrey. "This tastes like paste. You need to speak to the operations manager about changing caterers for these events," she teased. She leaned over and whispered in August's ear. "You've got to try my triple chocolate layer cake; it's decadent.'

All her discomfort vanished as Geoffrey was introduced. He rose amid thundering applause, climbed the stairs and moved across the stage elegantly, a striking vision in black and white. He accepted his award with a charming smile. August held her breath, wondering what kind of speaker he would be.

"He is such a handsome man."

"He certainly is," Millie agreed.

August hadn't realized she'd spoken out loud. She shot a look at Millie, afraid she'd made a huge blunder.

"It's about time a decent woman recognized that. I can't tell you how many worthless gold-diggers have come sniffing around my grandsons."

Geoffrey began his speech humbly, as she knew he would.

"This is a great privilege I am honored to receive. I'm happy to say that as of September first, the burned acreage was completely re-seeded."

A second boom of applause shook the ballroom Geoffrey smiled proudly from the podium, waiting for the ruckus to die down.

Millie leaned closer. "All his life he's trailed in his brothers' footsteps without realizing what a great catch he is."

August smiled. She could see how that was possible. Even Derek, with his grunge-rocker good looks, made a pretty picture. She'd only seen photos of Geoffrey's other two brothers, but their handsome looks were extraordinary.

Justin, kneeling on a football field with his padded shoulders and flawless smile, was an all-star golden boy. David, regally posed with a beautiful date at a high school prom, fit the image of a confident ladies man. They made a picture-perfect family, but if anyone searching for a more meaningful relationship looked deeper, they would see that Geoffrey, with his earthy charm, gentle manner, and generous nature, was the premier catch in the family.

She believed Millie's complaint that superficial women had pursued them for the family's money. She pushed away an uneasy suspicion about herself—had she come from a wealthy family? If she learned that she hadn't, would she still be able to yearn for a future with Geoffrey with a clear conscience?

Am I yearning for a future with him?

She watched the gorgeous man at the podium, admiring his poise and debonair style.

Yes, she realized with a tremor in her belly. *I'm falling in love with him.*

Chapter Eleven

The introductory speaker resumed the podium and concluded the ceremony before Geoffrey had reached his seat.

"Wow. I'm glad that's over. Did I embarrass myself?"

Millie swatted at him with her napkin.

"Exactly the opposite," August assured him. "You were incredible."

The lights dimmed and soft music tinkled across the ballroom. Immediately the murmur of the crowd rose. While a few people made their way to the small dance floor in front of the stage, most of them milled about, socializing.

Geoffrey took a single bite of cheesecake, and then put his fork down and looked at his grandmother. "You're right. That's terrible."

"Isn't mine, that's for sure."

He glanced at August. "Ready to go?"

She did want to leave, but it would be selfish of her to go now. *This is Geoffrey's night. He deserves to enjoy it.* She was feeling comfortable enough; so far no attackers had sprung out of the crowd.

"The night is just beginning. Dance with me?" She rose to her feet and reached for his hand before he could protest.

"I don't dance very well," he warned her.

"Perfect. Neither do I."

They walked to the small dance floor and he took her gingerly around the waist. August slipped her hand around his neck and pulled him close, placing her broken arm between them.

"Doesn't it hurt?" he asked as they slowly started moving.

She shook her head. "Gran Millie gave me a painkiller."

He laughed. "That would explain the dreamy look in your eyes. She's always got something good in that big bag of tricks of hers."

"She's a wonderful woman, your grandmother. I wonder if I have a grandmother."

"We'll find out. Soon."

August wasn't so sure she wanted to anymore. She pulled on his shoulder and instinctively Geoffrey drew her closer. She was dancing on air, safe and adored in Geoffrey's strong embrace.

"Tomorrow we'll drive down the coast. Mike gave me the addresses of the four burger joints still standing that match your description."

She sighed. "All right."

"You don't have to worry. You'll have all your answers soon. I won't stop until you do."

"I know." She turned her head and rested her cheek on his shoulder, not wanting to talk about it anymore. She wanted this dance, and this wonderful night, to go on forever.

Would finding the answers mean the end to their time together? August almost didn't want to find them. The whole idea scared the daylights out of her. Maybe it was cowardly, but she didn't want to know anymore. She wanted to go forward, not back.

"August?"

"Hmmm?"

"The music has stopped."

She kept her arm around his neck and Geoffrey didn't let go. Before she could wonder if another slow song would play, bouncy modern rock began thumping through the speakers and people began dancing faster. Geoffrey stepped back and his arms slipped away from her waist.

They wove their way through the dwindling crowd and back to their table.

For the next few hours, Geoffrey and Millie visited with friends who stopped by their table. While most congratulated Geoffrey and talked about the wonderful accomplishments the volunteers had made, many of them chatted about other subjects, and August could see the Barthlow family had put down solid roots in Newport. The people were nice, and made a genuine effort to include her in their conversations, but after a while she got tired of answering the same questions about her arm, over and over again.

A waiter made a final pass at their table. "Are you finished, ma'am?" he asked of Gran Millie's dessert plate.

"Oh yeah," she said emphatically.

"I'm finished, too," August said.

Gran Millie collected her purse. "I know it's almost midnight, but if you're up for dessert you can actually eat, I've got a triple layer chocolate cake back at the Mermaid. It'll put this to shame, if I do say so myself.'

Geoffrey glanced at August. "How about it?"

"I'd love some." Like him, she'd taken a single bite of the cheesecake before putting down her fork.

They drove the four blocks to the Mirthful Mermaid in separate cars. As he drove, August picked up the plaque they'd awarded Geoffrey and ran her fingers over the inscription. *Geoffrey Barthlow*. Reading his name in bronze sent a warm, comfortable feeling rippling through her.

I *am* in love with this man, she thought. The idea both terrified her, and brought intense joy. *I don't know what lies in my past, but I'm certain I have never felt this way about anyone before.*

Admitting as much lifted a great weight from her shoulders. What a wonderful feeling to finally be sure about something.

He parked the car next to his grandmother's in a mostly empty parking lot. Gran Millie unlocked the door and led them inside the dark restaurant.

The Mirthful Mermaid had a different feel after hours. Quiet and dark, August breathed deeply of its aged, salty smell. She was grateful for something familiar. The restaurant was cozy, comfortable, and emitted the powerful essence of family.

After rummaging around in the kitchen, Millie emerged with three plates, each with a gigantic slice of chocolate cake. She sat beside August.

"Where's my grandson?"

"In the restroom, washing up," August said, taking a bite of the most delicious cake ever baked. "Mmmm. You weren't lying."

"That was nice, seeing you two dancing together tonight," Millie said in a reserved voice. "You two look good together."

"I like him," August said, certain his grandmother's statement was leading somewhere.

"Do ya, now?"

"A lot."

"I don't want to see him hurt again."

Again. She wished she knew what had happened, so she could do something to make it better. Or at least make sure it never happened again. The idea of sweet Geoffrey in pain made her heart ache.

"I don't want to hurt him. Believe me when I say that." It would kill her to be the person to do it.

Millie patted August's hand. "I know." She took a bite of cake and chewed, deep in thought for a long moment. "It's going to happen, though. You're going to find out you've got another life somewhere, and then you'll go back to it."

August set down her fork. "I'm not so sure of that."

The older woman's eyebrows rose, but she remained silent.

"Someone went pretty far to get their point across. I'm not wanted there."

"That doesn't mean your whole life was people who hated you."

"I'd like to think that if someone did do this to me on purpose, it was just one person. But if I did have a good life otherwise, wouldn't I be yearning for it? Honestly, Gran Millie, I don't feel it in here." She placed her hand over her heart. "One thing I know, I've never met anyone like Geoffrey. And I'm sure my family wasn't like yours. It will be terrible if I never remember, but staying here wouldn't be so bad at all."

"Do you say that because of what you think you didn't have before, or because of what you've found here?"

Before she could answer, Geoffrey emerged from the restroom and crossed the empty dining room. "What have you two lovely ladies been talking about?"

"Girl stuff." Gran Millie took a bite of cake and winked at August.

He glanced from one to the other. "Why does that make me nervous?"

◆ ◆ ◆

Geoffrey hadn't paid much attention to the dark-haired woman sitting alone at an unoccupied table in the back of the ballroom. But when a lone pair of headlights flashed on and the car began following them away from the Mirthful Mermaid, his wariness bristled.

He'd first noticed her when he took the podium. She'd caught his attention when she slipped into the ballroom and took a seat at an empty table in the back, looking like a puzzle piece that didn't fit. She'd glanced around the room like a party-crasher waiting to get caught. Dressed in faded jeans and an even older-looking denim jacket, she certainly hadn't come prepared for the banquet.

"You have a wonderful life," August said quietly. She'd been so silent, with her head leaned back against the seat, that he thought she might have fallen asleep.

"I do?" He glanced over. Her blue eyes were pale in the dim light seeping into the SUV's cabin.

"Take it from someone who doesn't know anything about her own. I can only hope to find myself with such a great life. You have a loving family, a good job, a beautiful home. You're well educated, respected by your community, lots of friends. These are good things. For all we know about me, I could have spent the last five years in jail."

He laughed. "I seriously doubt that."

"Why? It might very well be true."

"You would have more tattoos."

"I don't have any tattoos!"

"There you go."

She settled back into the seat, smiling. "It was nice tonight. It felt good. Dancing with you felt good."

Geoffrey swallowed back a mouthful of regret. It almost seemed wrong that dancing with her had been so nice, when the single memory he had of dancing with his late wife, at their wedding, had been unpleasant. Christina had been half sloshed at the time, and had snapped at him when he suggested she ease up on the champagne. If she couldn't celebrate at her own wedding, when could she?

Geoffrey glanced into the rearview mirror, but didn't mention the woman from the ballroom. The car maintained a steady distance out onto the lonely ocean highway. His unease mounted, and Geoffrey bit down on a pang of guilt. Had taking August with him been a mistake?

"I'm glad I came," August continued. "The cheesecake was gross, but your grandmother made up for it. I like her."

"She likes you, too. Believe me, you'd know if she didn't."

Gran Millie hadn't liked Christina. Even after she'd eventually warmed up to her, she had always remained slightly intolerant, and slow to forgive Christina's many mistakes.

"It was nice getting out tonight. I'm glad I went."

He turned onto Crestview Drive, watching as

moments later the headlights appeared behind him on their narrow street. The car matched his slowed speed, following around the turns and bends that led to the house. He angled into the driveway and parked in his normal spot under the oleander tree. The car following them slowed as it passed the house. In the dark, he couldn't see through its windows.

Of course, there was a sharp curve after their driveway. Anyone who lived in the neighborhood knew to slow down for it, or risk sliding into the tall dune on the outer bend. And he knew several of his neighbors, also volunteers on the project, had attended the awards tonight.

"It was almost like a date," he said, watching the side mirror to see if the car made another pass. After he'd said it, he realized what he'd intimated. "I mean—"

"It *was* like a date," August agreed.

Only the silvery light of the moon illuminated the SUV. He found her smiling, as if the idea pleased her. He wondered if she could see the heat filling his face.

"About this time on a date, I always start to wonder...not that I go on many dates."

"Wonder about what?" She gave him a teasing smile, as though she already knew.

"Whether or not I should give you a good-night kiss."

Still smiling, she bit her lower lip. She was bashful, too, he realized. How endearing. A warm feeling swirled in his stomach.

"Do you want to kiss me?" Her question came out in the barest whisper.

He glanced down at the keys in his hand. *Just say it, idiot. Yes, I do.*

He met her eyes. Before he could say anything, she leaned over and placed a gentle kiss on his lips.

It was a sweet, soft kiss, hardly more than a brush of lips really, but it ignited a spark inside him that immediately roared into flames.

She leaned away with a squeak from the leather seat, carefully adjusting her cast away from the center armrest.

Geoffrey leaned over and kissed her again, more deeply this time. She tilted her head to receive it, and parted her lips when he grew more intense. He breathed in lemons, flowers, and sunshine. She met his kiss with equal ardor, gently responding to the sweep of his tongue across hers.

She caught his lower lip between her teeth.

He groaned low in his chest. "God, August." He cupped her face, caressing her cheek with his thumb.

At his age it felt silly, magnificently silly, making out in the car like a couple of teenagers.

She breathed his name on a soft moan between kisses pecked to the corners of his mouth. He cupped her face, caressing her cheek with his thumb. When his lips found hers again, their kiss slowed and nearly stopped, so achingly tender it made his heart seize.

Geoffrey slid his hand across her thigh, leaving soft silk for even softer skin through the high slit in her dress.

August stiffened. "Geoffrey—"

He drew back. "I'm sorry. That was rude."

"No, it wasn't." She slid back into the cup of the leather seat. "It was my fault. I didn't realize I was getting so carried away."

He angled himself to face forward again and

gripped the steering wheel. "You don't have to worry. That won't happen again."

She twisted around, reaching over her cast to place her hand on his arm. "It was wonderful. You're wonderful." She smiled that pathetic, pitying smile that would soon be followed with a *but*.

"But until I know everything about me, I don't think we should take it any further."

He nodded. "You're right."

"I'm sorry."

He mustered his own well-practiced *that's okay* smile. "Don't be." He reached for the door handle.

"Wait a minute."

She slid closer and squeezed his arm. "I don't want to end tonight like this. Kiss me one more time."

The tension rushed out of him in a whoosh. He did, gladly, eagerly, but this time with the reverence of a man about to step onto the gallows. And likewise, she was tender, gentle and cherishing. This time it was she who reached over to brush her fingers along his jaw.

If it was just one kiss, it was a very long kiss. She showed no signs of stopping, and heaven help him, neither would he.

He didn't know what he'd done to discover this delicate angel, but it must have been something good. He felt like the luckiest man alive, yet at the same time, doomed to lose. He would be a fool not to recognize exactly how uncertain his time with her was.

She wasn't his.

After tonight, letting her go would be even harder than before, and only yesterday he'd thought it would be impossible.

This time, when she stilled their kiss, it was on a

sigh. "Geoffrey?"

He stopped, reluctant to open his eyes. "Yes?"

She smiled sheepishly. "I have to pee."

Chapter Twelve

Colin's breath plumed in the crisp air as he crunched across the gravel driveway. He emerged from the shadows of the house into the warm, orange light of the rising sun.

He used to love the dawn, when he and Emily would launch the *Maraschino* onto a cobalt ocean. The colors usually held their deepest contrast at this time of day: the sky a deep cornflower blue, the ocean's surface shining like polished silver, the boat's white hull gleaming in the new light. And all of it pale in comparison to the hue of Emily's eyes, the light in her smile.

He ached for those days with her, when before he hadn't realized how good they felt.

He looked up in surprise at an approaching figure. Sonja crossed the driveway at an angle. He cringed at the sight of her. He hadn't even heard her pull up.

"Colin. We need to talk."

He opened the door to his battered Jeep and tossed his duffel bag to the passenger side. "Not now. I need to get on the road."

"When are you coming back?"

He glanced over the marshes to the water. Pristine white seabirds circled a fishing boat returning early, trailing for fish scraps the fishermen tossed over as they cleaned their catch. Today, the morning held the promise of that renewed beauty he hadn't known in so long. He had his first lead on Emily.

But Sonja, and her needy persistence, threatened to destroy that.

"Where are you going?" she added to the unanswered question. Her eyes were red-rimmed and her face pale, as though she'd been up all night crying.

"Chelsie found a lead on a Jane Doe in a coma in a Seattle hospital. She has blond hair."

"It isn't Emily. Colin, dammit!" He turned away but she grabbed his arm. "Emily is dead. When are you going to accept that?"

He leaned towards her and shouted his answer. "When I see a body!"

Sonja pushed the door shut and stepped between him and the Jeep. "Emily is gone. I'm here. Colin, I'm five months along. You need to do right by this baby."

He blasted an angry sigh and scrubbed a hand over his face. God, how was he going to explain this to his father?

Her voice grew softer and this time when she placed her hand on his arm, she was gentler. "Can't you see that I love you?"

He shook his head and fought the urge to shrink out of her grasp. "You don't—you're just scared and you want to provide for your baby. I understand that, Sonja—"

"You love me, too, Colin. I know it. I could feel it when you touched me."

"No. Jesus, I was drunk that night. You said, 'Do you want to have some fun?' Christ, that's all it was. I wish I'd never done it."

Her hand formed a fist at the collar of his coat. "How can you say that? We made love. We made a baby!"

He pried her fingers away. "I love Emily. She's alive—I know it. I'm going to find her."

He slipped into the Jeep and pulled the door shut. She stayed where she was in the driveway as he pulled away, making him feel like an A-number one dirt-bag.

Jesus, how he wished he'd never messed around with Sonja. The girl was out of her mind, plain and simple. She knew he'd never leave Emily, yet she'd tried to lure him away anyhow. What an idiot he'd been. Why hadn't he valued Emily as she deserved? Was he being punished? In all those years she'd refused to set a wedding date, he'd still considered himself a free man, and he'd strayed.

More than once, he'd strayed.

But it had always been Emily he'd gone back to, always Emily he knew he'd spend his life with. She owned his heart. Why hadn't he let the head with the brain do his thinking for him? God. A baby on the way.

He refused to believe Emily was dead. There was a piece of his heart that was connected with her, that continued to glow with her life force. When Chelsie told him about the young woman in a coma in Seattle, he had known in an instant it was Emily. She was alive, but unable to contact him. It made perfect sense.

His energy increased as he drove north, munching on pretzels and an apple. His father would surely run him up one side of the mizzen and down the other when he found out about Sonja, but hopefully Colin could keep her quiet about the baby until he and Emily were married.

He intended to provide for it, to fill a place in the child's life. But Sonja had to find a husband of her own. It was an old-fashioned notion to expect him to marry her just because she was pregnant. If a girl was modern enough to sleep around before marriage, she should be modern enough for single parenthood.

His anxiety increased with each hour on the road. Gnawing hunger poked at his belly. He used the john at a gas station, but the munchies in the Jeep would have to do.

The only thing on his mind was reaching Seattle, and finding Emily.

◆ ◆ ◆

August awoke late feeling groggy, but she didn't think it was from the pill Gran Millie had given her last night. She'd been up late, thinking about that kiss over and over again.

She rose from the bed and padded to the mirror, smiling to herself as she wondered if Geoffrey had as much trouble sleeping, too.

He'd been a wonderful kisser, but she'd known he would be. There was something so enchanting about a humble man. His beard hadn't been prickly, after all. His skin, and the gentle brush of his eyelashes across her cheek, had been magically soft.

She brushed her teeth and dragged a comb through her hair before venturing into the main part of the house. A quick glance outside showed Leah's Lexus missing, and August remembered her saying she was taking Jocelyn shopping this morning.

"Geoffrey?" The house was eerily silent. "Derek?"

The patio door to the deck was open, just the screen closed, letting in the cool morning air. She expected to find Derek outside, but the deck was empty.

The morning was crystal clear, giving her a bright view of the gleaming tower in the distance. Two or three miles down the beach, a familiar shape in black shorts jogged toward the house at the water's edge where receding waves left the sand hard. *Geoffrey.* Even at this distance, she could make out his blond hair and muscular physique.

August went back in and stuck a mug of hot water into the microwave for tea. A little caffeine would clear her head. She started a teabag steeping in the hot water and opened the dishwasher. Unloading dishes and vacuuming were the only tasks she could manage with one hand, and she'd quickly learned where things went in the orderly kitchen.

A sound from the back of the house seized her attention. She went still, all the hairs on her body prickling.

"Derek?" His room was at the other end of the house, next to Geoffrey's.

She slotted the last knife into the butcher block holder, closed the dishwasher, and started down the hall in the direction the sound had come from.

Cold shivers of unease slid over her flesh. She cleared her throat. "Derek?"

Silence answered her. It was the first time she'd felt uncomfortable in this house. August turned around and went back to the kitchen.

She was imagining things, that was all. She needed the tea to wake up and clear her head. The pain pill Gran Millie had given her last night made her more fuzzy-headed than she realized.

She went back to the kitchen and toward the

steaming cup on the counter. Halfway there, she froze.

One of the knives was missing from the butcher block.

Her body grew hot and hissing rose in her ears.

She glanced around the kitchen, searching for the phone, but couldn't convince her feet to move. It was at the back of the long kitchen, by the doorway to the foyer.

A creak sounded from the hallway—the creak she had already come to recognize between Jocelyn's room and the entrance to the grand living room, directly on the other side of the foyer.

Someone was coming.

She turned and bolted through the living room to the patio door. Her fingers fumbled on the latch, but she couldn't stop her momentum. Her body hit the screen and she stumbled, knocking it off the track. She fell to her knees on the deck and nearly went flat on her face. With her good hand, she shoved herself upright and scrambled to her feet.

She leaped onto the stairs and crashed into Geoffrey.

"Whoa, what is it?" He grabbed her by the shoulders.

"Someone is in the house!"

He glanced past her. "Who? Did you see them?"

She turned around, nearly choking on her fear. Was someone coming with the kitchen knife, or a gun, to finish the job they started?

"I heard a noise when I was unloading the dishwasher. I thought it might be Derek, but he didn't answer."

He took her hand and stepped around her.

"Wait, Geoffrey—no."

"We have to call the police."

She pulled on his hand. "Can't we go to a neighbor's house?"

A female voice called out a hello from inside the house.

Geoffrey's features relaxed. "It's Leah."

But it hadn't been Leah. August jerked free and rushed up the stairs. Leah was in danger, didn't he realize that? There was someone else in the house!

His footsteps thumped behind her on the wooden steps.

Leah set a bag of groceries on the counter and smiled when she saw August. "Hi. What happened to the screen?"

August glanced around. The house appeared the same as it always did.

"Where is Derek?" Geoffrey asked his sister.

"I took him to Gran's. What's going on?"

Jocelyn came through the front door carrying a grocery bag and a little sac from a boutique. She handed the groceries to her mother and started the other way.

"Jocelyn." August stopped her. "Come here for a minute, please."

"What's up, August?"

She smiled, not wanting to upset the little girl. "What did you buy?"

"Mom got me these really cool beads to make a friendship bracelet for me and my best friend, Amy Knoeller. I'm going to make one for you, too." She sat down on the couch and opened her bag, but stopped. "What's going on? Why does everyone look so weird?"

August turned around and met Geoffrey's eyes.

"Someone *was* just here," she whispered.

"Leah, did you see anyone on your way in?"

His sister shook her head. Leah had shifted into full-fledged worry; August could read it in her body language.

"Call Mike."

Leah turned and grabbed the phone.

"Jocelyn, why don't we take a walk down to the beach?" August held out her hand. She could hear Leah asking for her brother-in-law in the background.

"What's going on?" Jocelyn pressed. "I'm not a baby, you know. Was there a burglar?"

Leah hung up the phone and they all headed out onto the deck together.

"August got scared, that's all," Geoffrey explained gently. He looked at the side of the house. August grabbed his arm when it seemed he was going to investigate.

"Then why is Mike coming?" Jocelyn's voice took on a new hint of fear.

"We just want to make sure. Come on, let's watch for him."

A section of the road could be seen from the far end of the deck. In less than ten minutes, Mike's black sedan angled around the bend, followed by a squad car.

Leah, August, and Jocelyn waited outside while Geoffrey explained the situation. After Mike and the two officers with him thoroughly checked the house, they went back inside and Jocelyn was allowed to go listen to music in her room.

"We didn't find anything. The glass door to your father's room was unlocked, but nothing to indicate someone had been here."

They grouped in the kitchen, all of them looking at August like she was crazy.

"There was someone here," she insisted. "I heard them in the hall. I thought it might be Derek, but he didn't answer."

"I took Derek with me this morning," Leah confirmed. "There was no one in the house."

"Are you sure you didn't just hear the house settling?"

"When I came back to the kitchen, I saw that a knife was missing out of the butcher block. I had just unloaded the dishwasher and I'm sure the block was full. Every knife was clean."

She could practically hear the swish of all five heads turning toward the butcher block.

"All the knives were there," she repeated. "Then I heard someone step on the creak in the hallway. That's when I ran to the glass door to the deck and fell through the screen."

Leah went over to the dishwasher and cracked the door. She pulled it all the way open, bent, and retrieved a knife from the bottom rack. "This one?"

A wave of heat rushed from head to toe. She wasn't crazy! "I put that in the block, I'm...I'm sure of it."

"You're certain you didn't leave that one behind? It's small; you might not have seen it in the silverware tray."

"I remember replacing all five knives in their rightful place. That's the paring knife. It goes in the bottom, rightmost slot." She glanced away, certain that if she let go the tears stinging the back of her eyes, she'd lose all credibility in the officers' eyes. "I'm not imagining this. I heard someone in the hall."

"There's something else," Geoffrey added. He sighed. "I didn't think it was important so I didn't want to worry you with it. Now I'm not so sure."

Her heart did a flip-flop. What did he know that he hadn't told her? She swallowed back the burning in her throat and waited while Geoffrey turned to his brother-in-law.

He briefly explained the eerie feelings August had every time she saw the marina, and her memory of a red-haired woman "Then last night at the banquet, I noticed a strange woman sitting at the back of the ballroom at an empty table. She didn't look like she belonged. She was dressed casually and didn't talk to anyone."

"Why didn't you tell me?" August didn't mean to shout, but at the same time she couldn't believe Geoffrey had kept this from her.

"Her hair was dark, almost black, and I didn't think anything of it at the time." The voice he returned sounded hurt. "I noticed a car had followed us out of town, but I didn't put two and two together."

"My God, Geoffrey, you endangered your family!" One tear slipped free, and August lost her hold on the others. She turned sideways and wiped at them with her good hand.

Geoffrey stepped closer and slipped his arm around her shoulders. "Listen, we still don't know it's anything to worry about. You may have left the knife behind, and this old house creaks all the time."

He wiped a tear from her cheek. When he gathered her into his arms, she melted against him. She could feel the others watching them in silence.

"I think you may be overreacting," Officer Mike

finally said. "After all, if someone were after you, why would they put the knife back into the dishwasher?"

August pulled out of Geoffrey's grip but wiped the tears from her face before turning back to face the group.

"I wish I had the answers. Believe me."

"I know you do, and nobody blames you," Mike said. "What can you tell me about the marina? Do you think it's possible you were on a boat that night?"

August shook her head. "I don't know. Geoffrey took me onto *Penny Lane*, but nothing looked familiar. Only the red-haired woman and her black Labrador were right at the edge of my memory."

"Did you talk to Dr. Lohman about it?"

August shook her head. She didn't want to admit she wasn't going back to the psychiatrist. Thinking about it now, though, maybe she should.

"August isn't comfortable with Dr. Lohman," Geoffrey said. He stepped up behind her and placed a hand on her shoulder. She felt a rush of gratitude for his support, and guilt churned in her stomach for snapping at him.

Mike's frown said he disapproved, but he didn't comment. "Well, the house is clear, and I locked that sliding door in your father's room. I'll send a patrol car past every few hours."

"Can you issue an alert to pull over any cars with out-of-state license plates?" Geoffrey asked. "Just to check license and registration for any red-haired women from out of town? The woman last night might have been wearing a disguise. At least we could get a name."

"Not officially, of course," Mike said. "But I'll see

what I can do. Leah, when are you heading back to Portland?"

Geoffrey's sister turned a sympathetic smile toward August. "I'm sorry, sweetie. In light of this, I think we should go today. Believe me, if Jocelyn were with her father, I'd stay here and help you kick some ass."

August grasped her hand. "Don't apologize. I don't want anyone hurt because of me. I couldn't live with myself."

The officers departed and Leah went to pack, leaving Geoffrey and August alone in the kitchen.

She leaned against the counter and stared at the butcher block. Was she going crazy? When she'd seen the empty slot, she'd been so sure she had replaced all five knives. Now, she couldn't even remember closing the dishwasher. She hadn't imagined it, had she?

"Maybe we should put off our trip," Geoffrey said.

"No. I definitely want to go. I need answers."

He put his hands on her shoulders. "All right."

He touched her chin with the tip of his finger and smiled down at her. His presence helped calm her nerves. Drawn against his chest, she felt safer in the protection of his muscular embrace. She could tell he wanted to kiss her, but she didn't invite it. With her nerves as tight as a guitar string, she was in no mood. The kisses last night had been a mistake, a misguided prelude to something that could never be. She felt wretched for allowing them, leading Geoffrey up just to drop him down. She hadn't intended to be cruel, but it had turned out that way anyhow.

"I'll go shower." He stepped back, as though sensing her need for space.

August sat at the kitchen table as those soft kisses

repeated in her thoughts. While her head knew they had been wrong, her heart had enjoyed them so much. They had been wonderful, beautiful, delightful. She wouldn't trade last night for anything.

But now she realized the risk Geoffrey and his family faced just for knowing her. She had nothing to offer him but danger. Nothing to promise him but uncertainty.

Would her answers lie somewhere between here and California? She was almost afraid of what she would find. She might be a bad person, someone Geoffrey would never otherwise associate with.

A small part of her didn't want to know, but the rest of her had to.

Chapter Thirteen

"You're awfully quiet." Geoffrey glanced over from the driver's seat. "I'm sorry I didn't mention the woman."

She put on her best smile. "Don't be. It's not your fault. You can't be suspicious of every unfamiliar person."

"I should have realized. She looked so out of place."

"You said it yourself. We don't even know if there is a woman from my past, red-haired or otherwise. Maybe I'm reliving that age-old feud between blondes and redheads."

He laughed. "There's such a thing?"

"Of course. Don't you know? Blondes have more fun, but redheads have more fire."

"I think I'll take fun over fire any day."

She sighed and glanced out the passenger window. "I'm afraid I'm not much fun today."

"Nonsense. We can have some fun while we drive. My family used to play a game called 'The Alphabet List' to pass the time on road trips."

He'd opted for the ocean highway instead of heading inland to the interstate freeway. Despite the terror of the morning, it had blossomed into a beautiful autumn day.

"Alright, how do you play?"

"Just call out a sign with a word starting with *A*, and so on. First person to get through the alphabet wins. Cannon City Animal Shelter."

"No fair. I wasn't prepared." She laughed, grateful for his efforts to lift her spirits.

"You can't use the same word, unless you see it written again."

"Asphalt. Watch out, Barthlow, I'm right on your tail."

"Bed and—"

"Breakfast!" She grabbed the next one, too. "County—"

"Courthouse, next right. You're good at this."

The ocean highway wove in and out of the rolling coastline, each time catching a glance of the sparkling sea disappearing into a misty sky. The effect was magical and August felt a melancholy tightening in her chest that she couldn't exactly identify.

"Detour ahead—"

"Expect Delays. *D* and *E*." She laughed, wishing it sounded more enthusiastic. "I think I've played this game before."

A moment passed where August could sense Geoffrey's unspoken tension. "Have you thought about what you'll do if you recognize one of these places?" He phrased the question carefully.

She could tell from his tone it had been lingering on his mind. "Not really. I'm more scared than anything."

"About what happened this morning?"

"Yes, about what happened this morning, and about what I might find today." August sighed. "About what I'm going to do tomorrow."

He glanced her way. "Tomorrow?"

Bad things had followed her out of her mysterious past. How good could her life have been if someone wanted her dead? She wished she could forget the past—write it off, and start new.

With Geoffrey.

But she couldn't, not while his life, and the lives of his family, were in danger. She didn't doubt for a minute that someone had been in the house—that someone had been after her. Gone as far as to take a knife from the butcher block to stalk her with, and then return it to the dishwasher to mess with her mind and make her look like a fool.

Whoever it was, they were smart and calculating, effectively destroying her credibility with her new friends *and* the police.

"I can't keep living at your house if someone is after me." The words burned in the back of her throat. Whoever this was who had tried to kill her was now threatening her future with Geoffrey. "What if Leah and Jocelyn had come home before you got back to the house? I don't want to even think—"

He reached over and gently grasped the fingers extending from her cast. "They didn't. Nothing happened. Hey look, Evergreen Fairways Golf and Country Club. *E-F-G.*"

He was trying to make light of the situation. She knew he was doing it to ease her fears, and she couldn't help but smile. That was her sweet Geoffrey. She felt another sad pull as she realized he wasn't *her* Geoffrey, and he probably never would be.

"No fair. You've been here before. Gas, food and lodging next exit. *F* and *G*. Ha!"

She sensed he didn't truly believe someone had

been in the house, but she was certain. That meant the threat, and her past life, was close to Newport. Obviously someone had seen her at the award ceremony, or at the Mirthful Mermaid.

The miles passed in silence except for the game, and they were both stuck on the letter *Q* by the time they reached the first burger joint in southern Oregon. August was deep in thought, wondering how she would move out of Geoffrey's house—how she would find work with a broken arm to *afford* to move out—when his GPS told him to turn into the driveway at a remodeled fast-food joint.

"It doesn't look like a 50s sock hop," he said, glancing at the paper showing the address. They got out and walked halfway around it. If she had ever seen the place before, she didn't recognize it now.

August looked at the roof. Under the remodeled gutter, there was a band of bright green paint and bracket marks where neon used to be attached. She turned around, looking at the quaint streets surrounding them. The small Oregon town was a jewel in an emerald green forest, but held not a sliver of familiarity.

"Why don't we take a short walk, stretch our legs?" He locked the SUV remotely. "Are you hungry?"

"Not for burgers," she said sourly, but in truth she was ravenous. After this morning's fright, her stomach had been too jittery to eat. Now, almost four hours later, it rumbled with emptiness, and she was beginning to feel run-down.

One block over, they found a pub restaurant similar to the Mirthful Mermaid, but with a motorcycle kind of feel. They sat in a corner of the darkly paneled room decorated with unique, roadside memorabilia, listening to honky-tonk music emanating from an old-fashioned jukebox.

Geoffrey ordered a barbequed beef sandwich and August ordered what turned out to be a gorgeous mountain of delicious pasta Alfredo with fresh, succulent vegetables.

"Did Dr. Carlson ever give you the information on that woman's shelter in Corvallis?"

About to take a bite, Geoffrey put down his sandwich and picked up his napkin, slowly wiping away a small dab of barbeque sauce from one finger. His expression turned dark.

"We told him it wouldn't be necessary. Look, August, you don't need to worry. You're safe at my house."

"But *you* aren't. And Leah isn't, and Jocelyn isn't. Even Derek isn't, despite his city street-smarts. I can't live with myself if someone breaks in again."

"We don't even know for sure someone did."

She glanced away, not wanting to start an argument.

"Okay, someone may have been there," he conceded. "Maybe it was even the red-haired woman. But we called the police so fast it made whoever it was run like hell. I doubt they'll be back."

"This is a *killer* we're talking about." At least Gran Millie understood that. August glanced down at her plate, but her appetite was lost. "Someone who has to finish the job before I can identify them."

"Jesus, August." Geoffrey's tone fell low with horror. "Don't talk that way."

"It could be true!" She lowered her voice when a

young man at a nearby table glanced over. "It makes perfect sense, when almost nothing else does."

"How would this person even know you've lost your memory? The only people who know are family, Dr. Lohman, and Mike. No one else at the police station even knows. Derek and Leah sure wouldn't tell anybody."

"Jocelyn?"

"Jocelyn is smart enough to tell her mom if any strangers tried to talk to her—about *anything*."

"What about Gran Millie? There are lots of people in and out of the Mirthful Mermaid."

Geoffrey reached across the table and grasped her good hand. She laced her fingers with his. "You're safer with me."

"But you're safer *without* me," she argued.

"I'm not putting you out because of that."

She hadn't wanted an argument, but that was exactly what she got. It was pointless, she realized, because her mind was set.

"I'll take you to Portland if you want. My loft has a doorman and a security system. No one can get in."

August speared a crisp snow pea and forced herself to eat it. "Maybe."

"Stop thinking of yourself as a burden."

"You have no reason to do this. You've already done too much as it is."

"I have a good reason."

And she was dying to know what that reason was. But just because she was curious wasn't a good enough reason to endanger his family. Whatever obligation he felt he owed, he would get over it.

And she had enough of her own problems. She'd

developed feelings for this man. Her first mistake.

She'd endangered his family, and his home. Her second mistake.

She had a life to return to, even if it was a lonely apartment, a dull job and an old cat.

"I'm running out of clean clothes anyway," he told her.

"You have a maid come once a week."

The waitress brought the check and collected Geoffrey's empty plate. "You want a box for that, hon?"

"No, thank you. I'm finished."

"Y'all come back real soon, ya hear?"

"Definitely," Geoffrey told her. "That was the best pulled pork I've ever had." He rose and helped August out of her chair. "Back on the road again?"

She nodded and took a deep breath. "Back on the road."

◆ ◆ ◆

It was four thirty in the afternoon when they reached the third burger joint. The second had been a run-down pit in a not-so-good part of town, and August was almost thankful when she didn't recognize a thing.

This one was run-down, too, but only because it was abandoned, a falling-down relic of yesteryear. Geoffrey stood by the SUV on the cracked asphalt parking lot while August walked around and faced the front.

She tried to imagine it freshly painted, with gleaming neon lights running from the empty outlets at the edges of the face.

A gas station attendant told them the town had once been bustling, but when the nickel mine petered out, the only industry left was fishing.

Had she lived here then? Was she from a fishing family? A mining family?

It was picking up again, though, the man at the station had explained in an enthusiastic voice. A shoe company that used only natural and environmentally friendly products had moved its factory here and created a thousand new jobs.

She turned around to find Geoffrey watching her expectantly. She shook her head. "Nothing."

"I'm sorry, August."

A convertible raced past on the main road with a group of smiling teenagers listening to too-loud music. Once, somewhere, that had been her.

"Don't be," she told him as they trudged back to the SUV. "It was a long shot."

"There's one more."

She slipped back inside the SUV and waited for Geoffrey to get in on the driver's side. "It's too late. We'll never make it back tonight. You must be exhausted from all this driving."

"Let me worry about that."

"It's a waste of time. Let's just go." She was beginning to feel sorry for herself, and in a wretched way, the pity felt comforting.

"The last one is only six miles away. We've come too far to turn away so close."

She sighed. "All right."

◆　◆　◆

When they swung open the hotel door to the room, both August and Geoffrey froze.

"He said this room had double beds," August snapped. She stalked across the room and picked up the phone. She winced as she jerked her arm in an instinctive effort to dial with her left hand. She bit back an oath and punched zero with a finger of the hand clutching the receiver. She was sick and tired of struggling through life with one arm.

"Yes, Mrs. Barthlow?" the operator answered automatically. August gritted her teeth with irritation but didn't correct the woman.

"May I speak to the man who checked us in?"

"He's on his dinner break. Is there a problem I can help you with?"

"He promised us a room with double beds, but this room has one king. My arm is broken. I can't share a bed."

"I'm sorry, Mrs. Barthlow, but it's the last room in the hotel. We're sold out for the Seafood Festival tomorrow. If you'd like, I can call our sister hotel in Grandview."

"Where is that?" August asked her.

"It's nine miles south of here on Highway 101."

She glanced at Geoffrey. He was tired; she could see it in his sloping shoulders and the weak smile he mustered.

"Never mind. This will have to do, thank you."

Geoffrey tossed his jacket on the chair beside the bed. "I can sleep on the floor."

"Good. That'll work."

He stared at her, and she laughed. "That was a joke. Of course you won't. I trust you to behave yourself."

He sank into the chair. "Good, because I'm bushed."

She took a deep breath, forcing herself to relax. She'd been acting cranky and rude. Geoffrey had done her a great favor today. She went over and sat on the edge of the bed near him.

"I haven't thanked you yet for bringing me here." She reached out and took his hand.

"Yes you have. But you're welcome again." He gave her fingers a squeeze. "Nothing came to you at all?"

"Nothing that I didn't force myself to see." She rose and walked around the bed to the mirror. She tried to imagine herself with other people, but nothing would come. "It's been two weeks. I'm beginning to think my memory will never come back."

He stood beside her and looped one arm around her shoulders. August leaned against him and let him wrap her in his warm strength.

"It will. Don't worry. But until it does, let's stop talking about that woman's shelter."

She met his eyes in the mirror. If something happened to any one of them because of her...A smattering of chills rolled over her arms.

"I think it may be the best solution."

"Listen." He turned her to face him. "Stop worrying so much. We're a resilient bunch, us Barthlows."

She smiled, but it was strained. She would never be able to make him understand how she felt.

"Besides, I have a much better idea, and I think you're just spunky enough to make it work."

"Me? Spunky? You must know something about me that I don't." She chuckled. "Okay, I'll consider anything. What's your idea?"

"We lure this person out in the open...using you as the bait."

"Me as the bait?" August rolled her eyes. "Sounds like a brilliant plan."

"If you find out who it is stalking you, it might jar your memory."

"I don't know."

"I can arrange something with Mike. You'd be perfectly safe."

"That's not what I'm afraid of."

She wasn't ready to let herself be shocked into remembering that way. She couldn't admit to him that during the drive here, she had been hoping she wouldn't remember. It was only when she didn't that had she become so irritated

He pulled her gently by the hand, and August leaned against him, her legs suddenly rubbery. At once, his warmth and the reassurance she drew from his touch made her strong again.

"Hey." He lifted her chin with a finger. "Do you think I would let anything happen to you?"

She felt herself easing toward him as he gazed down at her, one finger gently tracing under her chin. She wished he would kiss her again while at the same time, she knew she should put a steady distance between them.

His lips brushed hers and August leaned closer, lifting her mouth to his as if she had no control over her body. Their soft kiss turned serious, and all at once August's frustration drained away.

She would have liked the kiss to go on forever, but she remembered their situation.

One room, one bed.

She couldn't let this slide out of control. While under any other circumstance she would welcome Geoffrey as her boyfriend and lover, an exclusive significant other, she had to make sure her past was clear so she could freely make that choice for her future.

She drew away and a second later opened her eyes.

"We'd better keep things G-rated."

He stepped back and raised his hands. "You're right. That was my fault."

"Uh-uh." She grinned. "That was my fault."

"Sweetheart, you're great for my ego."

She turned around and faced the bed. "I guess we're stuck with this room. I'll take the left side so you don't bump my arm."

"Deal." Two red spots appeared in his cheeks. August found it adorable.

"Why don't you look at the room service menu? I'm going to take a shower."

"Ugh! When this cast comes off, I'm going to take the longest, hottest shower ever!" She peered into the small bathroom. "Thank goodness, a north pointing tub."

He looked at her questioningly.

"I can lean against the back with my cast on the outer edge. The bathtub at your house faces the other way, so I lean back on the faucet and drain lever to rest on the edge."

"Why didn't you say something?"

She shrugged. "It wasn't a big deal. I just sat up. Besides, what could you do?"

"Well, you'll be glad to know the tub in my loft is a 'north pointing' tub, too."

She turned back to the room, deliberately avoiding the subject. "I'll check out the menu."

She didn't want to tell him she wasn't going to be part of any "trap" for her attacker, and she wasn't going with him to Portland.

She intended to move out of Geoffrey's house as soon as they returned to Newport.

Chapter Fourteen

Colin pulled into his driveway and shut off the Jeep, dead tired but at the same time, buzzing with nerves and anguish. He stared across the dunes at the glistening night sea. Tears welled in his eyes, sending starbursts shimmering across the silvery path cast by the low moon.

After waiting three hours in Seattle for a uniformed officer to show up and then spend an eternity taking his credentials, he was finally shown into the room where the unknown woman he prayed was Emily lay in a coma.

It wasn't her. Even though the woman's face was swollen and pale and she had bandages across her nose and tubes coming out of her mouth, he knew right away. It wasn't his Emily.

God, could his fiancée really be dead?

He banged his fist against the steering wheel. *No.* He refused to believe it. He wasn't giving up on her. Dammit, he could feel her inside himself. He would know if she were dead. A piece of him would be dead, too.

The door to the kitchen opened, spilling a slice of yellow light onto the driveway. The silhouette of his father's burly frame filled the doorway.

"Come inside, Colin. I need to talk to you."

His heart sank. Even with the Jeep's window rolled up, he could hear the tone in his father's voice: level and low, but very resolute. That tone always meant bad news to come, or he was in trouble for something.

Christ, he hadn't learned about Sonja, had he?

It would be just like her to go running to his father if she didn't get what she wanted from him.

Graham left the kitchen door standing open. Colin slipped out of the Jeep and slammed the door behind him. His feet crunched across the driveway, the only sound in an otherwise deathly still night. He couldn't even hear the never-ending crash of waves over the cottony hum of the highway still thrumming in his ears.

He closed the kitchen door, but didn't join his father at the table. Graham sat motionless, holding a steaming cup of coffee between two hands.

Colin saw it on the table beside the mug: Emily's engagement ring. His heart lurched in his chest.

"I found it today." His father picked it up and held it out to him.

Colin rushed across the tiny kitchen and grabbed it. "Where?"

"In one of the electronics compartments on the *Maraschino*."

He stared at the delicate ring pinched in his fingers.

"She was wearing it that night," Graham said, as if he needed to be reminded.

A sharp sliver of ice plunged into his gut as he met his father's suspicious gaze.

"You want to tell me what's going on, Colin?"

He shook his head, unable to form words.

"Why would she take it off? There's something you're not telling me."

"Like what?" Colin demanded. Sudden rage flared inside him like a wildfire. "Are you saying she dumped me so I threw her overboard? Jesus Christ, Dad. How could you even insinuate—"

"Calm down. I'm not saying that at all."

Graham stood and placed a hand on his shoulder. Colin shrugged it off. His father frowned.

"I'm asking you what would make her so upset she would take off her engagement ring."

Colin turned and paced across the tiny kitchen. He ran a hand through his hair. "Maybe she didn't want to catch it on something when she was working."

Or maybe somehow she found out about Sonja. Christ, when I get my hands on that bitch—

"Colin, come clean with me now. If there was something that made her so upset—"

"What? That she jumped? Emily wasn't like that."

Holy hell, this was getting worse by the minute. Sonja had probably already been here and told Graham everything. His father was probably baiting him into a confession, like he was a toddler caught in a lie. Shit, that pissed him off.

But when he looked into his father's eyes, the compassion and the sadness he saw made him crumble inside. He'd loved Emily like his own daughter, certainly more than her own father ever had. When they'd gotten engaged, his father had been almost as happy as he was.

Colin sat at the table and pressed his fingers to his eyebrows. The fatigue from six hours on the road could be rubbed away; this situation could not.

He heard his father pull out the chair and sit beside him. Other than a drawn sigh, Graham said nothing as he waited.

"Sonja's pregnant."

The weight suddenly came off Colin's shoulders like a dozen fat seagulls taking flight from an overstressed telephone wire.

He looked up at his father. Graham stared at a speck on the table, his expression gray with raw grief. He suddenly looked every one of his fifty-eight years.

"It's mine," Colin added, and then felt like an idiot. No kidding, it was his. He clutched his head in his hands as a long moment of miserable silence ticked by.

"How far along is she?"

"Almost five months." He lifted his head and looked at his father. "We weren't having an affair. I never would have done that to Emily. We were just...fooling around. I was drunk that night—at Spring Fling. Jesus, I didn't even want to do it."

Except for another drawn sigh, his father didn't condemn him, and Colin felt a hot rush of gratitude. He wished he'd told his father as soon as he'd learned himself. He'd always been there for him, supporting him no matter what, and now Colin felt like an undeserving brat.

"Did Emily know?"

"I don't know. But even if she did, she wouldn't have jumped."

"I know that." His father patted him on the shoulder, and this time Colin relished in the familial touch. "But she very well might have taken off her ring, and thought about a hundred ways to get your balls in a vise."

"Yeah, that sounds more like Emily." He almost chuckled as he thought of his fiancée with her gander up. She never did put up with his BS.

"Was Sonja below with you when Emily went overboard?"

Colin's attention snapped clear and bright, as though he'd been doused with icy water. "What are you saying?"

"Is it possible the two girls were fighting on deck?"

His stomach twisted. It was too horrible to consider. "No. No! Sonja would never do that. She and Emily were best friends!"

"It could have been a terrible accident. We don't know until we talk to her."

"Oh, God." Colin shot out of his chair. He turned and paced across the floor as the horrific images played in his mind like a living nightmare. "Fuck. Please. Oh, shit."

Graham rose and caught him by the shoulders. "Colin, get hold of yourself."

"Jesus, Dad." He shook his head, unable to fathom the intensity of what his father said. "Sonja couldn't have—"

"I don't want to believe it either."

Colin covered his face with his hands and let go the first tears since that night on the boat. His father pulled him into a hug and let him cry like a baby, and for a moment Colin wished he *was* a baby again. No problems, no responsibility. No heartache. *If only such a thing were possible.*

"I think it's time we called the police," Graham finally said.

Colin nodded. He dropped into the kitchen chair, numb and raw, almost detached from his physical self.

"Do you know what this means?" He looked up at his father, his last crumb of hope wiped away. "My fiancée died because I cheated on her."

◆ ◆ ◆

Room service knocked on the door just as Geoffrey heard the tub start to drain. A few minutes later, August emerged from the bathroom wearing her knit shirt and a towel wrapped around her legs.

She sat at the small table and wound the length of her hair behind her back with her good hand. "Mmmm, smells wonderful."

Geoffrey removed the silver dome and placed a plate in front of her. "German waffles with whipped cream, maple syrup, hash browns, hot chocolate, and sliced honeydew melon."

"Yum, breakfast for dinner. I love it." She picked up a fat waffle. "Excuse me while I eat with my fingers."

Geoffrey laughed. "No problem." It was just one more of her endearing traits that was so uniquely, adorably August. Only she could eat with her fingers and still look perfectly mannered. He poured a generous helping of syrup onto a saucer and slid it over to her.

"Anything interesting on the news?" She leaned over to see the screen.

"A storm, due to hit by Tuesday. No missing persons' reports."

She tipped her head to one side and offered him a lopsided grin. "Wishful thinking." She dipped the corner of the waffle in the syrup, bit off a hunk, and chewed thoughtfully. "I really appreciate your bringing me up here. Sorry it was a bust."

"I wish for your sake it wasn't." He wasn't sure if he was lying or not.

She swallowed a mouthful of potatoes. "Maybe it's better this way. I was really scared, and almost hoping I didn't recognize anything." She glanced at him sheepishly. "I think this is my mind's way of telling me I'm not ready to remember yet."

He wondered if she'd become as content in Newport as he had with her there. He was torn between his loyalty to her and his selfish desire to have her all to himself.

"Nothing at all looked familiar?"

She leaned back in her chair and sipped her hot chocolate. "Not a thing."

The news broadcast flipped back to the storm warning, showing cartoon animations representing the sleet and frigid winds coming from the arctic region.

After finishing the honeydew melon he'd served her, August rose and went over to the bed to get a better view of the television. She slipped under the covers and tossed the bath towel onto the chair.

Geoffrey swallowed and pretended interest in his nearly empty plate.

What had he been thinking, agreeing to this room? He never imagined he and August would spend so intimate a night together under circumstances like this. It should be passionate, spontaneous, and desired by both sides. Instead of looking forward to a new level of closeness with her, the whole situation left him feeling miserable.

He stood and turned around. "Maybe I *should* set up camp on the floor."

"Don't be ridiculous. There's plenty of room. You won't bump me." She downed the last of her hot chocolate. "I will use this extra pillow, though. This fiberglass cast may seem light at first, but try sleeping with it."

"It's yours."

"Top me off?" She held up her cup. Realizing he stood in the middle of the room like a gawky teenager, Geoffrey pried his feet from the floor and took it.

August placed the pillow at her hip to rest the weight of her cast. She settled in and used her good hand to pull her hair out from under her neck.

"We've talked so much about me. I want to hear more about Geoffrey."

The knot of tension in his shoulders tightened another notch. He poured the last of the hot chocolate into her cup.

"There isn't much to tell." He took his time rolling the dining cart into the hall.

She pressed the mute button on the remote control, silencing the droning newscaster's voice. "Tell me about Berkeley. Maybe hearing about college will remind me if I went."

He suddenly wished he had calls to make, papers to read, or anything to occupy him while she fell asleep. What should he do? Climb into bed as if he belonged? Or sit in the chair a polite distance away?

After standing in the middle of the room like a dolt for another long minute, he flipped off the light and shuffled to the far side of the bed by the glow of the television. He sat on the edge.

"Some people call it 'Berzerkely.' There were a lot of unique characters there, including this guy who walked around naked."

She laughed. "No way."

Geoffrey nodded. "He considered it his constitutional right."

She glanced at the television. "You want me to turn it off?"

Oh great, he'd hesitated for so long she thought he was afraid to be seen in his boxers. In truth he was, but not for physical reasons. Years of dedicated exercise and a healthy diet had left him lean and muscular. He knew he looked okay, especially in front of someone who had never compared him with Justin or David. He just couldn't shake the feeling he was pushing her too far. Well, she'd seen him in his running shorts after he'd removed his t-shirt. This was almost the same thing.

Then why does it feel so different?

"Um, leave it on until the news ends," he said. "You never know, we might see something."

He shrugged off his jeans and slipped under the blanket. Only then did he wonder if he'd just made a huge mistake. Had she wanted him to leave the jeans on? Was he exposing himself to her like a horny frat boy?

She shifted onto her side to face him. "A naked guy, huh. I think that would gross me out."

Uh oh.

"Wouldn't it be kind of...drafty? And I can only imagine what the bottoms of his feet looked like."

"I didn't have the wild time a lot of people did at Berkeley," he said, pretending nonchalance. In truth, his heart was racing. "In fact, I spent a lot of my time in San Francisco at bookstores and poetry bars."

"Now *that* I can believe."

He leaned up on one elbow. "Why?"

Her smile softened, but didn't dim. "You're sensitive."

Sensitive. That wasn't the highest compliment. He rolled onto his back, hoping the bluish light from the television hid his growing embarrassment.

"Were you on any sports teams?"

Sports were his brothers' thing. "Track. I like the way running clears my head."

August giggled. "Let me guess. The mile. Two mile?"

"The mile. How did you know?"

"You don't strike me as a sprinter. You're a long-haul kind of guy."

How did she see these things in him? Was it that she was really good at reading people, or she was the first person to take the time to look more closely?

"What else?" he asked her.

"Hmmm." She narrowed her gaze. "Debate team."

"Only for one year. It was too intense for me."

"And...you volunteered at the soup kitchens."

"At Thanksgiving and Christmas. August, you're amazing."

She shook her head. "No. You're amazing, Geoffrey Barthlow. If it weren't those things specifically, it would be something similar. That's the kind of person you are. I'm surprised you don't own a dog that was once a stray."

He laughed, wondering if it would be passé to tell her about Scruffy, the family's terrier mutt who had come sniffing around the beach house one year. The poor thing had obviously been abandoned by one of the high-season residents. They'd taken him in and kept him fat and happy until he died a ripe old dog.

"You give me too much credit. I have a confession to make: I hope your past life was boring."

After he'd said it, he realized how callous it sounded, but August surprised him by laughing. He deserved her anger for such a selfish and inappropriate statement.

"That was rude of me. I'm sure the opposite was true."

She was still giggling. "You know, I'm hoping it was boring, too."

"There's something to be said for a quiet life."

He almost wished he had never met Christina, that he'd never endured the pain that every day chiseled away at his heart, that he'd never been thrust into this wretched situation with his brother. Almost as if reading his mind, she asked the question he knew she'd been wondering about.

"You said you met Christina at Berkeley." When he hesitated, she gave him his out. "You don't have to tell me about her if you don't want to."

Geoffrey sighed. "I should have told you about Christina right away." He figured he owed her as much, since she had fallen into the middle of his feud with Derek.

He wondered how to begin. No matter which words he chose, the subject always churned his guts. He'd never actually talked about her with anyone outside the family, even though Leah had nagged him damn near to death that seeing a therapist would help.

"I met her in the tutoring center. She was at risk of losing her scholarship because of her grades."

That wasn't as hard as he'd thought it would be. Surprisingly, once he got started, the rest flowed out of him. "Christina was from Oakland and received her scholarship as part of an outreach program for students from low-income families. She got her BA and I got my master's in the same year, and we were married two weeks after graduation. I was her ticket out of Oakland, and she couldn't wait to leave."

"So she moved up to Portland with you."

He nodded. On the silenced television screen, images of fire trucks in front of a blazing building reflected the turbulent memories that accompanied thoughts of Christina.

"She was beautiful, and I loved her with all my heart. I think in her own way, she loved me, too."

August had rolled onto her side to face him. She balanced her cast on her hip and leaned on her good arm. "I'm sure she did."

"But even the simplest things about marriage with her were hard. She had a lot of problems. She'd used drugs as a teenager and she was constantly fighting with depression. Prescription meds helped her short term, but after a time, they made her sick and sapped her energy, so she stopped taking them. It was a cycle with us."

"Did she use drugs during your marriage?"

He swallowed. Would it have been the lesser evil if she had? He would never know. "By then she was drinking, which was worse because alcohol is a depressant."

August nodded. He met her eyes. Hers were wide and sad, as if she didn't want to know but couldn't stop listening, like someone who happens upon a car wreck but can't force themselves to look away.

"Once she disappeared for two and a half weeks. We went as far as to issue a missing person's report, and visit the morgue when a woman matching her description was brought in. It was the hardest thing I've ever had to do." He took a deep breath and let it out slowly. "That's how I understand what the people in your life are going through."

He looked back in time to see her glance away, her long lashes hiding glossy tears.

"But I'm alive. And someday I'm going to find those people."

"Someday soon," he promised, and meant it. "I'm going to help you."

She brushed his shoulder with the backs of her fingers, a barely there, feather-light caress.

"Christina came home on her own, very obviously strung out. I never knew where she was or what happened to her, but I can only assume she'd hit rock bottom because in the next three months she tried harder to be my wife and fit in with our family than she ever had."

The memories were almost too much to bear. Even those last, pleasant days didn't bring any peace because now after the fact, he recognized how phony they had been. Their entire marriage had been a precarious dance on a high-wire, with his family as the audience below, holding their breath at the edges of their seats.

"Then Derek came home. He and I have always had our differences, and when he was in New York, I was glad he was as far away as he could be. He'd made buckets of money on the runways and he was a lead model for Ralph Lauren, but he blew it all—his career and his savings—on drugs. Putting him and Christina together was like mixing nitro and glycerin."

He glanced over at August. She stared off into the darkness with a far-away look in her eye. "What if I'm like that?" she asked softly. "What if I have this really terrible past, where I did horrible things?"

"You're not that kind of person," he said quickly. He was sure of it. Sweet, kind August could never be even half as cruel and self-destructive as Christina and Derek both were.

"You don't know that. What if my family are thieves, or con artists? I'm not exactly ugly—"

Geoffrey laughed but August remained rigidly serious.

"I could have used my looks to take advantage of trusting people. Maybe I'm subconsciously doing it to you."

Wariness bristled along the edges of his thoughts. "I'd like to think that even if that's who you were, you've changed."

She looked back at him and smiled. "You're too good to me." Her expression grew somber. "I'm sorry. I didn't mean to interrupt. Please go on. You said Derek came home."

Geoffrey took a deep breath, trying to formulate the least humiliating way to explain what happened. There was none.

"They had an affair," he said bluntly.

"No."

August frowned in that pitying way people did to show sympathy. Usually it left him feeling ashamed, but from August it was the kind of encouragement he needed, especially now that Derek was back in his life.

"I had no idea he could sink so low. I trusted you that there was something big between you two, but I had no idea it was so awful. That is the worst thing a brother can do." She softened her tone. "You've been very tolerant of him, considering."

"Supposedly, it wasn't really an affair. They only...were together twice."

"Sheesh! Even if it was once, it was an affair. And

even if it was only once, it's still unforgivable."

She was the first person to agree with him on that. Everyone else had coddled poor Derek, the baby of the family, with his drug problem and his broken finances, led astray by the big city. It made Geoffrey want to punch his hand through a wall.

"I keep a lot of my anger to myself. It wouldn't do my family any good to start a war with him. Besides, where Derek is concerned, my father just won't listen. He loves to carry him out of trouble. I wish he'd realize he's only making Derek worse."

"It's called 'enabling.'" She glanced off and frowned, as if she wasn't sure how she knew that.

As tired as he was when he'd climbed out of the SUV, now he was wide awake and alert, aware of every nuance of their intimacy.

"Was Derek driving the car?"

It took him a moment to realize what she'd meant.

"No, Derek wasn't even in Oregon. Leah had caught him and Christina together and made him catch the first available flight back to New York."

"Good for her. She's tough. I like her." August pursed her lips. "But I have to admit, I have less respect now for Derek."

He choked out a forlorn laugh. "In all truth, I can't really blame Derek. Christina was always looking for bigger and better things, and she was seduced by his lifestyle. The parties, the celebrities, the prestige that came with being a model. He put stars in her eyes. He had her convinced she could be a model, too, and truly, she could have been. Not only was she beautiful, she had incredible bone structure and she photographed well. But that lifestyle would have destroyed her."

"Like it did Derek."

"They're both a lot alike: weak in the face of temptation."

"Obviously." She chewed her lip. "But as bad as things are between you, I don't want you to blame him for what happened that morning he scared me. He really hadn't done anything wrong; it was all me. I don't want to make things worse between you."

She shifted, bending her arm again to touch his shoulder with the backs of her fingers. Her warmth, and the unwavering strength she'd displayed these past few weeks, seeped into him and made him feel stronger, too.

"Healing is good for the soul," she said. "That's probably what everyone has been telling you."

"Yeah, in one way or another." He sighed. "I know. I also know now it was Christina who instigated what happened between them. I was never enough for her. I should have known that from the start."

August shook her head. "You are such a special man. I wish she could have seen that."

His emotions surged. He loved that she took the time to look, but it had been so much more than his failed relationship with Christina that had made him crawl off and cower in the corners of his life. August hadn't yet met his overachieving older brothers, whose shadows he'd always trailed in.

"We were living at the beach house that last summer, and I had gone to the office in Portland for a day that had turned into three. Leah told Christina, in no uncertain terms, that when I got back she had to tell me everything. She was so upset she started drinking. When I got home, she blurted everything, and told me she was leaving me. She was going to New York, so

Derek could introduce her into the business."

"Oh, Geoffrey, I'm so sorry."

"It was bound to happen sooner or later, for one reason or another. She couldn't live the simple life I provided for her."

"She didn't know how good she had it." August sighed. "What I wouldn't give to find I have a simple life even half as wonderful."

"I wouldn't have tried to stop her if she hadn't been drunk. I would have let her go."

August laid her head down on the pillow and shifted her body closer to his. She looked down past her feet to the silent television as butterflies fluttered across a digitally created meadow in a fabric softener commercial. She swiped at her eye as though trying to hide the fact she was teary.

"You deserve so much better." Her trembling voice betrayed her.

He swallowed and finished with the hardest part. "When I tried to stop her, she grabbed the keys to both cars and ran out the front door. She threw my keys into the ice plant and drove off in her car. As soon as I found mine, I went after her. I was nearly to town when I came upon the accident. Her car was on its roof and Christina had crawled out. She didn't look hurt, standing there in the road. When I got to her, she collapsed into my arms."

She lifted her hand and when he shifted, they brushed together. He turned his hand to take hers and August laced her fingers within his.

"A witness had already called an ambulance. I thought she would be okay, but when I arrived behind them at the hospital, they told me she died on the way."

"I'm so sorry...for her. That she didn't realize how good she had it with you. That she ever took drugs the first time. What a tragic waste."

"I should have seen it coming. I should have tried harder to help her. She needed therapy. I shouldn't have thought I could help her just by keeping her away from the city. If only I had done more for her, she might still be alive."

"You don't know that."

"And unfortunately I never will. Don't you see why I'm helping you? I couldn't live with myself if another woman died because I didn't offer my help. I need to do this, or I'll never find any peace."

Chapter Fifteen

August stared out the window at rolling country as his words echoed in her mind. "*I need to do this, or I'll never find any peace.*"

She knew he hadn't meant it as it sounded, that she wasn't some charity case to appease his guilt. But she understood where he was coming from, and it made it harder to stay true to her decision.

She had to leave the beach house. Even if Leah and Jocelyn were gone, she couldn't be responsible for endangering the Barthlow family in any way. But Geoffrey wouldn't see it that way. He would see it as her leaving him, just like Christina had.

The idea she might hurt him made her stomach clench. If only she could find a way to make him understand.

He glanced at her, but didn't comment on her quiet mood. She felt wretched.

They reached the Oregon border faster on the interstate, and when they pulled off at the exit for Newport, she asked him if they could stop at the Mirthful Mermaid for some clam chowder.

It was nearly three thirty when they arrived at the restaurant, and only two groups sat in the huge dining room.

"Well, hello there, you two." Gran Millie greeted

them from the bar. "Any luck?"

August shook her head. "It was a lovely drive, but nothing came to me."

"Well, don't push it. The brain is a complicated engine that doesn't like to be over-revved."

August smiled. Gran Millie always had a direct and simple way of putting things that made terrific sense. "I thought your clam chowder would help. Can we take that table by the window?"

Gran Millie shooed them away with a wave of her towel. "Go on, I'll be right over."

"All right, August," Geoffrey said as he helped her into a chair. "What's up? You seem...focused."

"I've been thinking about your idea of a trap, of sorts."

He sat across from her and eyed her warily. This wasn't going to be easy, but she was determined to make him see it her way.

"And?"

"I think it's worth looking into."

Gran Millie ambled over, carrying a tray with two huge bowls of Boston clam chowder and iced tea for them both.

"Thanks, Gran Millie."

"Be back in a snap with some soda crackers."

Geoffrey waited until his grandmother was out of earshot. "But?"

She sipped an almost too-hot spoonful carefully, biding her time. "Can you read me that easily?"

He frowned. "Yes."

She took a deep breath, trying to find the gentlest words. "I like the idea...just not from the house."

"From where, then?" He hadn't touched his spoon.

"I want to talk to your grandmother about that."

He looked down, and then away. He could sense where this was going, and he wasn't happy about it. A wave of guilt heated her blood. She had to be careful, make sure he understood she wasn't leaving *him*, only the house.

"I don't want to put your family in any more danger."

"Leah and Jocelyn have gone back to Portland. Derek is the only one there."

"And you."

"I can take care of myself."

She reached across the table and placed her hand on top of his. "It's because of you, Geoffrey. I'd die if anything happened to you."

He shook his head, shrugging her protests away. "I understand where you're coming from, and I love you for it, but you're worried over nothing."

"It isn't *nothing*." She sighed and straightened her napkin, trying to find the words to make him understand without hurting him at the same time. "There's more to it than that. I need to occupy my day with more than just trying to remember the past. I think I've been trying so hard to reclaim my memory that's precisely why I haven't."

"I told you, we can head to my loft in Portland. We'll leave some sort of clue for whoever this is—"

"Your grandmother still needs lunch help. I want you to ask her about letting me stay in the room above the bar."

He caught his breath. Stared at her. Something inside her crumbled.

"You haven't even seen it. It's a closet. Besides, what

can you do with only one hand?"

"I'm not exactly helpless. Look at my hands; I still have calluses. I worked hard, whatever I did before."

He shook his head. "I'm not saying you didn't—"

"It's this, or the women's shelter in Corvallis."

The ultimatum rolled bitterly off her tongue, and after she'd dropped it, she wished she could take it back. After his revelation about Christina last night, she knew it sounded like she was leaving him, too. But even though their relationship had advanced from more than simple friendship, he shouldn't feel that they were "breaking up." Neither should she.

And yet she did. He leaned back in his chair and gave her a long look. "It sounds like you've made up your mind."

"I need to work. I need to feel useful. I can't remain your guest until I remember. What if it takes six months? A year?"

"You can remain my guest as long as it takes." He clenched his jaw.

She softened her tone, trying to smooth over the mood that had effectively turned sour. "I know you feel responsible and you need to do this for your conscience—"

"That's not what this is about." Geoffrey leaned forward and reclaimed her hand. He gave her a resolute squeeze. "I care for you very deeply, August. I would be happy if you never left."

A warm rush of pleasure made her tingle, and she couldn't help but smile. His expression softened and he managed to smile back.

"Then do this for me," she said in a softly pleading voice. "Understand that this is what I need right now.

Give me a reference with your grandmother."

Gran Millie approached the table cautiously. "This looks serious."

"Would you sit with us for a moment?" August asked. "We have something to ask you."

"I think it's a bad idea. You're not safer here."

"All right, you two. What's going on?" Gran Millie dragged a chair around from the next table and sat on it backward.

With a grimace and an exasperated sigh, Geoffrey leaned against the backrest of his chair. "August wants to move into the apartment above the bar. She wants to work here."

Gran Millie's brows shot up. "She does, does she? I never knew anyone who'd trade a suite at the beach house for the room over the bar."

"Tell her everything, Geoffrey."

Gran Millie crossed her arms over the back of the chair. "Spill it, grandson."

He relayed what August told him about working and occupying her day, and with the feeling she was being followed by an unknown red-haired woman.

Gran Millie glanced sidelong at August. "Mike told me he went out there yesterday."

"August thought someone was in the house," Geoffrey told her.

"Someone *was* in the house," she insisted. "I can't stand the fact an intruder broke in because of me."

"Did Mike find any evidence?"

"Just an unlocked patio door," Geoffrey answered.

August swiveled toward Gran Millie. "I don't want to put you in an uncomfortable position. The truth is I would feel safer here than I would at the woman's shelter in Corvallis. We know it's a young woman following me—"

"We don't know anything for certain," Geoffrey argued.

"What it comes down to is I need a job. I need to keep busy and get my mind off the fact I can't remember anything, and then maybe I will."

"Well, August, I think having a cute little thing like you around could only be good for business, even if you do have only one hand." She glanced at Geoffrey. "But I don't want to come between you and my grandson."

Geoffrey clenched his jaw, but remained silent.

"It's up to you, Geoffrey." Gran Millie smiled as she lifted her brows at him. "It looks like you've got two choices, and one of 'em's all the way in Corvallis."

He rolled his eyes and grumbled. "Fine. If August wants to move in here, I guess that's better than going all the way to Corvallis."

◆ ◆ ◆

The room was definitely small. One window looked out over the street, so high an intruder would have to use a twenty-foot ladder just to peek over the bottom sill. Inside, a small box underneath held an emergency rope ladder in case of fire. To exit quickly, she only had to flip open the swinging pane and toss the ladder out the window. It would be difficult climbing with only one hand, but the ladder was reassuring anyhow. She could escape quickly if her life depended on it.

The room was at the end of a long hall, past two storage rooms and Gran Millie's office. Crates of extra supplies lined one side of the hall. At the opposite end, Gran Millie's full-sized apartment spanned the other half of the second floor.

The door was strong and had a slide bolt, dead bolt, and a locking knob. The tiny room was a combination bedroom-bathroom, with an antique claw foot bathtub and a pedestal sink under a small mirror. The day bed sat against the far wall.

"I'll get the sheets," Gran Millie said. With a glance at Geoffrey, she scurried off.

"I told you it was small."

"It's cozy," she said, hopping onto the bed. Squeaky bedsprings shrieked. Someone had put the bed there precisely for the view of the ocean. From this angle, she couldn't see the highway separating them from the marina and jetty, just the tips of some of the taller masts, and miles and miles of blue.

"Can I change your mind?"

She shook her head, smiling. August wished this wasn't so hard on him. It was hard on her, too, and she hovered on the verge of changing her mind already. But her reasons were the wrong ones. A romantic relationship was impossible until she remembered her past.

And then...she forced her fears away. One day at a time. Wasn't that what Alcoholics Anonymous taught?

"Will you at least come back to the house to pick what you want to bring?"

She hopped off the bed, crossed the room and gave him a quick peck on the lips. "Absolutely."

◆ ◆ ◆

Geoffrey awoke to a painfully quiet house. Since Derek's shift washing dishes at the Mirthful Mermaid was from two until eleven, he would be asleep until noon.

Geoffrey threw his arm up over his brow. He had

learned Derek was working there only after August had decided to move out. The idea sat like sour milk. It wasn't that he didn't trust her, but he definitely didn't trust Derek.

He stared back at his reflection after brushing his teeth. August was smart and strong. Even if Derek were to "put the moves on her," as he so charmingly put it, August would put him in his place. Still, Geoffrey didn't like it. He'd developed strong feelings for her, and he missed her. He would even say he loved her, if he were to speak his feelings aloud.

His skeptical reflection stared back at him. He wasn't quite ready to admit as much to himself, out loud.

It would be pushy to go down to the restaurant. August needed to work, she needed to occupy her time and her mind, and she needed to be independent.

She needed her space.

Sooner or later, all women said that to him.

He did his best to occupy his time as well, but found the ten a.m. conference call with Portland and New York had been cancelled. His email box was surprisingly empty. He phoned his secretary and sent a message to his linen vendor. Finally, when his stomach rumbled with hunger, he headed to the kitchen.

Derek sat at the table, bleary eyed and haggard. "Dude." He rubbed at his eyes. "What time is it?"

Geoffrey glanced at the digital clock on the range. "Twelve thirty."

Derek moaned something incomprehensible, followed by "coffee."

"Dude." Geoffrey tipped his chin toward the counter. "There's the brewer."

He pulled a loaf of wheat bread, mustard, mayonnaise, and a package of sliced ham out of the refrigerator in one armful.

"Hey—are you going to visit August?"

Geoffrey sliced a tomato and slapped together a quick sandwich using up the last of the ham. "Why?"

"I could use a ride, that's why."

All week Derek had been grumbling about riding their dad's bicycle if he wanted to go to town. Although his father was generally too lenient with Derek, three wrecked cars in two years had put an end to Derek's driving the family vehicles.

Geoffrey frowned. "It's mostly downhill."

"But the way back isn't." Derek grinned. "You could go visit her again, say, around ten thirty tonight?"

"Jesus, Derek." Geoffrey narrowed his gaze at his brother.

"Come on. I'll buy you a beer. August'll be happy to see you."

And he would be happy to see her, too. "Go get dressed. I'll drop you by."

"And pick me up, too?"

Geoffrey started off toward his office. "We'll put your bike on the back of the car."

When Geoffrey found him ready to go, Derek was on his cell phone with a friend from New York.

He hopped into the front seat and put his foot up on the dash. Geoffrey bit back the urge to say something, but opted for being ignored instead. He listened while Derek complained about his dishwashing job to someone named Roland, and asked about his agent.

"Yeah, I told her I'll be available again at the first of the month. No, man, I can't do that, but I'll do the

Fiorenzi show. I don't care how bad the clothes are. I need the money."

Geoffrey swallowed a twinge of guilt. Was it wrong for him to be glad his brother would be leaving soon?

At nearly one thirty, the lunch crowd at the Mirthful Mermaid was still in full swing, and busier than Geoffrey had ever seen it.

August was behind the bar, working by herself. Her face brightened when she saw Geoffrey.

"Hey there, handsome."

"Hi, August," Derek said.

She slid a narrowed glance at Derek. "I was speaking to Geoffrey. But hey to you, too."

Amusement bubbled inside him. He slipped onto a barstool. "The place is packed. Are you holding up okay?"

She popped open two bottles of beer with the opener mounted under the bar. "I'm fine. This isn't exactly a mixed-drink crowd."

"I'll have Sex on the Beach," Derek said, and then laughed at his own wit.

Gran Millie appeared behind the bar with a clean tray of beer glasses. "Aren't you supposed to be in the kitchen?"

"It's not two yet," Derek said in a whiney voice.

"We're more than busy today and Hector could use the extra help. Git."

August hid the most adorable smile as Derek muttered under his breath and sidled away.

"You've got him under control, Gran Millie," she whispered.

"I don't take any gruff from my grandson. He's dished out far more than his fair share."

"What about this grandson—does he get a beer on the house?"

"Well, now of course he does. He's my favorite one."

"She says that to all of us," Geoffrey said.

August popped a bottle and slid it over.

"Hey August, how 'bout another Guinness?" someone called from the far end.

"Coming right up, Frank."

Geoffrey watched as she nimbly held a glass tilted under the tap with her left hand and ran the lever with her right.

When August moved away to serve another customer, Geoffrey found himself under his grandmother's inquisitive gaze.

"I'm grateful you gave her the chance," he volunteered before she could say something contradictory.

"She took to it like a fish to water." Gran looked over at August chatting with the two older men. "She's worked as a waitress before."

"That doesn't matter to me. I don't care if she cleaned toilets for a living; she's the only person who's ever looked at me like I was more than the football captain's brother."

"Easy, Geoffrey. First of all, that isn't true. It's all in your mind and you know it. All I meant is she's quite capable of hard work. And since she's done the job before, it might help bring memories back to her."

He withered. "You think I'm smothering her?"

Gran Millie shook her head and leaned her elbows on the bar. "I think you blame yourself for too much."

Christina. Even though they were talking about August, she meant Christina just as much. Geoffrey's chest tightened.

"You've done all right by her after the accident and that's real fine of you, but you shouldn't blame yourself for her problems with her memory." She grinned and poked him in the forearm. "The broken arm, that's your fault. But the amnesia..." She pointed at her temple. "That comes from whatever happened to her before."

He glanced down the bar. August smiled brightly at another patron who asked for a refill. He said something that made her laugh. A dimple formed in her cheek, and it seemed she gave off her own brand of sunshine. The man grinned back at her like a lovesick fool.

How anyone could hurt that angelic girl was beyond him.

Suddenly Geoffrey knew; he wanted to protect her forever.

"I love her." He realized too late he'd said it out loud.

He gulped and looked back at his grandmother, but she didn't appear surprised at all.

"I know you do."

Chapter Sixteen

Nearly a week had passed since the incident with the police, and Sonja still wasn't speaking to him.

Graham had called the authorities the night he returned from Seattle. Colin had been exhausted from the drive that night and heartbroken at the discovery it hadn't been Emily in the hospital, and his nerves had only become more frazzled during the three-hour meeting with the cops.

They had asked the same infuriating questions again and again. It was as if they suspected it was he and his father who killed Emily and tossed her overboard, and the two of them were trying to frame an innocent young woman left pregnant by her evil, coldhearted lover.

At first, even he hadn't believed Sonja would do such a thing, or even be capable of it. But now, with a few days to mull it over, he'd begun to wonder if it were possible.

Had she fought with Emily on deck—over him, for God's sake—and knocked Emily overboard?

He remembered it clearly now; his father had discovered Emily missing and Sonja, soaking wet and still in her gear, had told them Emily went up on deck to pull in the sheet on the storm sail as Graham had asked her.

Still, their suspicions alone hadn't been enough to convince the police, and Sonja had been released. Before noon the next day, the truth about her pregnancy was no longer a secret.

A few of his closest friends had been supportive, but most people he knew thought him a rat. Several had called up to cuss him out. The answering machine was full of nasty messages.

It would have been easier to accept if something had come of Sonja's questioning. She admitted to being on deck and confessing her pregnancy to Emily, but maintained she had nothing to do with her disappearance. The police had no evidence, and very little cause, to hold her.

It had been another painful blow to learn Emily had died knowing he'd cheated.

A crisp wind filled the sails but the weather was otherwise clear as they sailed toward Freeport. Today's trip was just Colin and his father, Chelsie, Joseph, and Will, chartering old Mr. Hudson and his obscenely young girlfriend for a day trip. The old man pretended he liked the privacy afforded on the boat, but it was obvious he liked to flaunt his money in front of his hot young lay, and flaunt his hot young lay in front of everyone else. Colin thought the old guy was crazy as a loon, but if he wanted to rent them for the day, it was fine by him.

He needed to work to keep his brain from turning to sludge. He tramped through each day with little enthusiasm, not caring if *he* were to fall overboard and drown. Every hour dragged painfully into the next. He had nothing to hope for, nothing to look forward to. He was lost of all desire, existing as little more than a sailing zombie.

Since the storm that had taken Emily, the weather had mockingly remained clear as a bell, but he knew the fog would start soon. Misty mornings where the ocean was so still and the air so milky you couldn't discern where horizon met sky, and a sailor had better know his instruments or he'd meet a tragic end on the rocks, or get lost a hundred miles off course. The type of weather Emily was better sailing in than him. She'd aced her tests, while he'd barely passed. So much about his life wouldn't be the same without her, down to the business he hoped to inherit.

They docked at an unusually busy Gold Coast marina in Freeport. The mild weather this late in the season brought out the 'yachties' or, fair-weather-freaks, as they used to call them in jest. As Emily used to call them in jest.

His father clapped him on the back, pasting on that forced smile he wore so often now. "Come up to the bar for a beer? I'm buying."

"Come on, Colin. Mr. Hudson's going to be a while," Joseph said. "Game's probably on the big screen."

Chelsie, Joseph, and Will waited with his father, expectant looks on their faces. They had stood behind him through all this, but he couldn't force himself to look wholehearted.

"You guys go on ahead. I'll be up as soon as I splice this line."

"All right," Chelsie said, brushing her hand over his forearm as she passed. "Don't be long."

He took his time with the line, planning to skip the beer altogether. He wasn't in the mood for the meaningless conversation they always tried to coax out of him. But when he finished the line with a dry mouth and sheen of sweat on his forehead, the idea of an ice-cold beer from the tap sounded a lot better than a lukewarm soda from the chest.

He walked up the dock, sidling around a group of tourists preparing to board a small catamaran for an afternoon trip. A young girl sat on the foredeck of the squatting vessel, holding her arms out while one of the crew fitted her into a lifejacket.

Colin froze, blinking his eyes to make sure he wasn't imagining what he saw.

"Hey!" He jumped over a small boy sitting on the slip and ran around to the cat's dock step. "Where did you get that lifejacket?" He made it onto the cat's deck before the crewmember, a preppy young girl probably not even twenty, looked up.

"Where did you get this lifejacket?" he demanded again. The child regarded him with wide eyes, and even the crewmember looked a little frightened.

"Answer me! This is important!"

"What's going on here?" A man emerged from the cabin. "Can I help you?"

Colin whirled around. "That lifejacket came from the *Maraschino*." He thrust his arm out, pointing down the ramp toward his boat. The man glanced over him, and then to the little girl.

The front of Emily's lifejacket still had some of the embroidered stitching spelling out "*Maraschino*" on the left shoulder, and "Emily" on the right. What had once been a top-of-the-line custom-fitted lifejacket was now faded and scrappy. Where the stitching was missing, the neoprene beneath was a shade darker, revealing the letters that had once been there.

The man's gaze flicked back to Colin. "Hey, no problem, man. You can have it. Lisa, get her another one out of the bin."

Colin stalked toward him fast enough to make the man take a step back. "Listen to me. A girl went overboard wearing that lifejacket." He enunciated his last words slowly. "I need to know where you found it."

"Colin, what are you doing?"

He turned around to find his father, Joseph, and Chelsie staring up at him from the dock.

"That's Emily's lifejacket." He pointed to the little girl.

Chelsie's eyes grew wide. "Oh my God."

"Look, I found it on the beach. If I'd seen your boat there I would have given it back."

Colin turned back, his heart pounding painfully fast in his chest. "*Where* on the beach?"

"In Newport—it was caught on the rocks at the jetty near that hundred-year-old place, the Mirthful Mermaid."

Chapter Seventeen

Geoffrey couldn't concentrate. He paced his office, rushing to the computer when it beeped to alert him to a new email, but ignoring the message when the subject promised another boring topic.

He opened the wall safe to look for a document, and the sight of the black velvet box containing his late mother's wedding ring sent his mind reeling.

His father had given it to him the year she died. Geoffrey hadn't given it to Christina when he'd proposed. Her fingers hadn't been as slender as his mother's, and Christina was a big rock kind of girl. Her ring had been a flashy, pear shaped diamond surrounded by a cluster of small rounds mounted in a wide band.

His mother's ring was smaller and very tasteful, the band narrow and the main stone's mounting in a cluster of smaller diamonds so the half-carat center stone looked like a rose.

He put it back in its box, closed the safe and resumed pacing.

August would say no. Surely she was the kind of girl who would marry someone more...someone like David.

She hadn't expressed her desire for a more exciting, flashy life, but neither had Christina, at first. August was vivacious, energetic, and dazzling. She was destined for bigger things than small-town life. Even Portland seemed too drab and drizzly for her. No, August was more of a sunshine girl, pretty enough to get noticed in Hollywood.

Still, he'd faced rejection before. What was the worst that could happen?

August might be insulted, and the rest of their time together would be spent in awkward discomfort, that's what.

Besides, the last thing he could bear to hear from her lips would be the "I only like you as a friend," spiel. From her, it would be like an ice pick to the heart. He'd never loved any of the women he'd asked out before. Besides Christina, he'd not wanted to marry any of them.

But spending the rest of his life alone was the ending he was headed toward now. Considering such a bleak future, what did he have to lose?

◆ ◆ ◆

Fat, turbulent clouds sat low on the ocean, capturing the setting sun's rays magnificently. Darkness fell fast in the fall, August remembered. But from where?

A few glimpses of that stunning sunset were all she had on her half-hour break, as the evening rush was almost as busy as the lunch. And then the incredible sunset was gone, nothing left but purple edges distantly visible through the darkness.

These past few days working at the Mirthful Mermaid had left her bone weary, but it felt good. For the first time in almost three weeks, her entire day hadn't been spent frustrated by her inability to remember. Things came to her naturally, like how to tip a mug to keep the beer from foaming, how to fill the dishwashing tray, and even how to work the old ACME cash register. Somewhere, she'd done these things before. If she could remember this, why couldn't she remember her own name?

"It's ten to eleven," Gran Millie said. She slipped a loose lock of hair behind August's ear. "Why don't you call it quits? We're nearly empty."

August glanced at the dining room. A group at a table in the center was paying their bill, and the only patron at the bar was a flirty old fellow she suspected was sweet on Gran Millie.

"I'm waiting for Geoffrey to come back. Derek says he's going to pick him up again."

Derek emerged from the kitchen with a clean tray of glasses. He slipped them under the counter and retrieved the tray August had filled with dirty mugs.

"I thought you were biking home," Gran Millie said.

He looked up. "Aw, Gran, it isn't safe riding out on the highway at night. I heard some girl got hit out there and broke her arm." He grinned. "Besides, I kind of put it in G's head to come back and visit August, so I'm betting I won't have to."

"That's the third night this week he's picked you up." His grandmother rolled her eyes. "You're incorrigible." She swatted at him with her towel as Derek headed back to the kitchen.

She turned back to August, grinning. "I'll take that wager. We'll see my other grandson, then."

August laughed. "Hope so."

Gran Millie took her under one arm. August's face bloomed with heat. She sensed something important coming.

"My grandson has it bad for you."

Her heart gave a little jump. "Well, you know what, Gran Millie? I've got it pretty bad for him, too."

"Hmmm?" She peered at August. "I sense a 'but' coming."

"I hope there isn't one." The excitement that had just filled her heart turned to anxiety. She had tried not to let herself fall in love with him, but in the end she'd had no control over it. In a way, she was glad. It was a beautiful feeling, loving Geoffrey.

Gran Millie moved away and started transferring the clean glasses from the dishwashing tray onto the shelf below the bar. "I want you to know that I'm very fond of you, and whatever happens, I'm glad you brought Geoffrey happiness. He's been so miserable for the last year..."

"I'm glad, too." Was that a tear the older woman was trying to hide from her? "Why don't you let me unload those glasses, Gran Millie?"

"Naw, I've got it." She turned her head away and gave a quick dab at her eye. "You can take out that bag of garbage, though. The cans are right out the side door at the end of the alley."

She knew where they were, having done it before. August grabbed the small plastic bundle by the twisted neck and headed to the side door. It opened before she reached it as Jose, the busboy, came in from a cigarette break.

He held the door open for her. "Want me to get that?"

She smiled. "I got it. Mmmm, fresh sea air."

The cans were near the mouth of the alley. A single lamp high up at the corner of the building lit the narrow passageway in dingy light.

Cold wind slipped through her clothes like ominous, roving fingers. Suddenly, August wished she had given the bag to Jose. It was only eleven, but it seemed this part of town rolled up its sidewalks early. Other than the Mirthful Mermaid, the row of buildings possessed shops that closed at eight during the week.

She walked slowly toward the end of the alley in growing uneasiness. Not a single car passed on the road. August set the bag down, removed the lid, and then hefted the bag inside.

She was holding the lid again when a sound behind her made her start. She whirled around in time to see an orange tabby cat go over the fence separating them from the next building.

August let out a fast breath. She was jumpy, that was all. She fitted the lid back on the can tightly, so raccoons couldn't get in.

A glint of light from the street caught her attention. She looked up. The breath froze in her throat as a dark silhouette moved toward her.

A woman...holding a knife.

Chapter Eighteen

August backed away, transfixed by the long blade. She tripped over something and spun around awkwardly. Losing her balance, she spiraled toward the ground.

Her good hand landed on something solid—a stack of wooden crates—and just as quickly she regained her balance. She shoved forward and sent the crates toppling behind her.

"Shit!" a voice behind her hissed. Her pursuer crashed into the crates. She heard one scrape against the pavement, followed by another crash.

"Help!" August screamed. She reached the door. It was locked! It had been open just a few minutes ago—

She pulled on the knob, but it wouldn't budge. The figure was moving over the pile, holding the knife out in front of her body. August pounded on the door.

"Help me! Somebody open the door!"

Her attacker kept coming. August pounded harder. Her throat burned from screaming, but in her terror, she couldn't even hear her own voice.

The door burst open, nearly knocking her over.

"Christ, August—"

She flew into Derek's arms, turning to glance behind her as the door slammed shut. "There's someone in the alley with a knife!"

◆ ◆ ◆

The first thing Geoffrey saw was August, in Derek's arms. He choked on his own tongue.

His brother sidled around her and reached for the restaurant's side door.

She grabbed for his arm, fumbled, and ended up with only a handful of his damp apron. "Don't go out there!"

"What is it—what's going on?" Gran Millie crossed the empty dining room.

August turned around and saw him. She rushed over and threw herself into his arms. "Geoffrey! I'm so glad you're here."

He placed his hands on her shoulders, not sure what to make of the situation.

Derek stood in the doorway, peering into the alley. He came back in and let the door shut behind him. "There's no one there."

August wrenched free. "I am not imagining this!"

Gran Millie turned and ran back to the bar. "I'm calling Mike."

"The empty produce crates fell over," Derek said. "Are you sure that's not what scared you?"

Geoffrey gently turned her around. "What did you see?"

August was pale and shaking. Her voice trembled as she spoke.

"Someone was out there! She cursed at me."

"She?"

"It was a woman's voice...at least I think so." She pressed her hand to her forehead. "I knocked over the crates and she ran into them. My God, she would have gotten me if I hadn't knocked them over—"

Geoffrey pulled her close. "Shhh. It's all right, you're okay."

She melted against him and pressed her face to his chest. "I saw a knife. There was someone out there with a knife!"

He looked toward the bar at the sound of his grandmother hanging up the phone.

"Mike's on his way."

Had he been out of his mind to consider laying a trap for this stalker? Geoffrey leaned back and held August at arm's length. "Now will you come back up to the house?"

She sniffled and looked at him for a long second before shaking her head. "I don't feel safer there. She knows about the house, too."

He guided her to a table and after easing her into a chair, pulled another close and sat beside her.

"Then where? Tell me what you want me to do, and I'll do it."

She smiled even as she started crying all over again. "You're so wonderful." She reached up and touched his cheek. "Looks like the trap plan backfired."

He took her hand and grasped it in both of his. "This has gone too far. We need to start treating this situation as dangerous."

Flashing blue and red lights filled the empty restaurant as the sheriff pulled up at the front of the windows.

August blew out a long breath. "You're right. We'll ask Mike what he thinks we should do. I'll do whatever he suggests."

Gran Millie unlocked the front door to let Mike in. They all converged in the center of the room and August recounted the incident. Geoffrey's heart kicked into high gear as he heard her terrifying story.

He'd almost lost her tonight. It made him sick to his stomach. Had he really thought twice about proposing? He knew now, his life would never be the same without her.

Mike checked the immediate area and sent an all-points bulletin to Newport's sixteen other units to look out for a red-haired woman on foot, or driving a car with out-of-state plates.

"There isn't much more we can do," he said. Geoffrey noted the uneasiness in his eyes when his brother-in-law's gaze fell on him. "I can't say one place is safer than the other to spend the night, but whatever you choose, August shouldn't be alone. Just let me know what you decide and I'll have a patrol make a few passes throughout the night."

Still holding his hand, she gave his fingers a squeeze. "Will you stay with me tonight?"

"Here?" Geoffrey asked.

Derek snorted. "As if you'd have to ask him twice."

August whirled around. "Do you *try* to get on his last nerve, or does it just come naturally?"

His sneer faded away. "Sorry. I get itchy when I'm nervous."

Her shoulders sagged. "No, I'm sorry. That was uncalled for."

"He knows I don't mean it personally." Derek raised his hand and offered his brother a high-five, which Geoffrey reluctantly accepted. "Don't you, bro?"

"Sure."

Mike flipped his notepad open. "August, do you have any idea who this red-headed woman is?"

She shook her head. "I wish I did." Her voice trembled as she fought tears everyone could see coming. "I'm not even sure she has red hair. I couldn't see anything but a dark silhouette tonight, and Geoffrey says the woman he saw at the banquet had black hair."

"That could have been anyone," he said before Mike could question him. "I have no reason to think she didn't belong, other than her casual clothes."

When August shot him a look, he reached for her hand.

"I'm sorry, but there really was nothing to indicate that woman was there because of you."

Her shoulders dropped. "I know what I saw tonight. And I know someone was in the house."

"How tall would you say this person is? Was she thin, or heavyset? Is there anything about this person that jars a memory?"

"Taller than me, that was all I could tell." August shook her head at his list of questions. "I keep wracking my brain, but things only slip farther away when I try too hard."

Mike sighed heavily. "When we first met, you told me you wanted to remember your past before I made inquiries. I think now the situation warrants a full investigation." Mike wore his rigid policeman's face. "With your permission, of course," he added in a slightly gentler tone.

She nodded. "Do I have to sign papers or something?"

"Not at all." Mike smiled, and Geoffrey was immensely grateful for his brother-in-law's courtesy. "My assistant is back from vacation tomorrow. I'll put her on it first thing."

She took a deep breath and let it out slowly, rubbing her arm above her cast as if she had a chill.

"I think this will be for the best," Geoffrey said. "If we find out who you are, we can investigate your closest relations. We'll find this mystery woman before she can get any closer." Saying it made him feel better, even though the idea of finding her old life, and watching her return to it, filled him with a strange, dark envy.

"Yeah, you'll be all right, August," Derek said, trying to be agreeable for once. "Come back to the house tonight and we'll stay up all night and keep watch. Play a game of Parcheesi, or something."

Though his brother sounded like an idiot, Geoffrey was even grateful to Derek for his attempt to cheer her up.

"We have to work tomorrow." When she looked up at Geoffrey, her eyes were wide and watery, betraying the fear she tried to keep hidden. "What if she's up at the house now? She could be breaking in at this very moment."

"I'll go with you," Mike volunteered. "I'll do a check of the house before anyone goes inside."

"And of course we'll set the alarm," Geoffrey promised. "If anyone tries to break in, the siren will wake up the whole neighborhood."

"And alert us." Mike put on his hat. "Millie, I'd like you to be especially careful, too. Lock up, set the alarm, and don't go out again."

"What for?" Gran Millie fairly shrieked. "It isn't me this nutcase is after. No crazy woman with a knife is going to make me a prisoner in my own home."

Mike grinned. "You'll be here alone tonight, and you're frail, helpless, and senile."

"Watch it, buddy." She frowned and slowly swiveled to August, keeping her narrowed eye on the sheriff as long as possible. "What do you say, kiddo? You going home with these two capable protectors?"

"All right. I'll go to the house." The tension slid out of her shoulders. "I feel safer already, knowing there are two strong men keeping watch over me."

Mike started toward the door. "All right then. Geoffrey, you'll follow me."

"This is cool!" Derek sang happily. "I get a ride home."

◆ ◆ ◆

By the time they arrived at the beach house, August regretted her decision. She told herself it was only for one night, or two, until Sheriff Mike found out who she was. He'd assured her no one from her past would learn about her until she'd been given all the information, and she would be allowed to make her own decision on how to proceed.

But what if they didn't find anything? How long could she go on living with Geoffrey? What if she was hundreds of miles from home? What if she'd been on the run for years? What if she didn't have any family or friends?

There was nothing wrong with accepting his charity, but still August wanted independence. She'd tasted it this week, working at the Mirthful Mermaid. These were the first days that hadn't been filled with desperate, frustrating attempts to reach into the mud clogging her memory. Maybe it was because she'd taken her mind off it altogether, but the bartender's job at the Mirthful Mermaid was fast-paced and fun. Millie's regulars were a rowdy bunch, and they weren't stingy

Ava Bradley

tippers, either.

Mike gave the all-clear, and they filed into the kitchen.

"Anyone up for microwave popcorn?" Derek asked.

"Not me. I ate leftover meatballs at the Mermaid," August said wearily. She wanted a hot bath, and then to disappear under the covers. "Besides, the kernels get stuck in my teeth, and flossing with one hand is hard enough as it is."

"I've got to get back on duty," Mike said. "Geoffrey, August—I'll be in touch tomorrow morning."

They closed the door behind him. With every light blazing in the house, August felt somewhat safer.

"How 'bout you, bro?"

"I want to talk to August for a minute."

"Geez, what a bunch of party poopers. Well, I'm going to nuke some up."

August's uneasiness grew as she followed Geoffrey down the hall to his room. It was upstairs from the room she'd been using, and at the opposite end of the house.

Was he going to suggest they share a room tonight? The hotel had been one thing, but she wasn't sure how she felt about sleeping in the same room in his house, stalker or not.

Once inside the masculinely decorated room, he took her hand and urged her to sit on the edge of the bed.

"I know you had a terrifying experience tonight and this probably isn't the best time..."

He took a deep breath. She could tell he was trying to put something difficult into words. Her heart kicked up its speed with a mixture of excitement and worry.

"But I realize how close I came to losing you tonight, and it scared the hell out of me."

Her sweet, humble Geoffrey. A tinge of pink had crept into his cheeks. His eyes were soft velvet under a row of thick lashes that swept down as he glanced to the floor for a long minute.

"I knew almost since the beginning that I loved you—"

"Shhh." She put a finger to his lips. "Geoffrey, I love you, too."

It felt wonderful saying so. She smiled even as new tears burned.

"To hear you say that is the greatest thing I could have hoped for. I would say that I can't live without you, but I know I could lose you to your past. I'm okay with that. Because more than anything, I want you to have the life you deserve. I know you didn't just fall out of the sky. You're going to find your family, your friends—"

"Let's not worry about what we don't know."

"I need to." He took her good hand and grasped her fingers. "What I can't bear to lose you to is a senseless tragedy like the one that took Christina. After she died, I wished I had done more to help her." His eyes misted over but he continued to smile warmly and tenderly. "I realize now I have the perfect opportunity to do something, and I can't pass it up."

He produced a small velvet box. August caught her breath.

Geoffrey slipped to his knee on the floor. "I love you, August. I would be honored if you would be my wife."

He flipped open the lid. Inside was the most beautiful diamond ring she'd ever seen. Shimmery starbursts exploded around it as her eyes blurred with tears. She stared, thunderstruck, unable to find words.

Geoffrey removed the ring and placed it on her finger. Her limbs turned warm and ticklish.

She splayed the fingers on her broken arm, watching the stunning diamond sparkle as it caught the light. It fit perfectly, as though custom made for her.

"It was my mother's. My father gave it to me when she died."

"It's lovely." She sniffled. "But you don't even know me. *I* don't even know me."

He shook his head. "I know you, August. I know the person you are inside. If I find out you're heiress to the Pet Rock fortune or a bank robber on the run, I'll love you just the same."

She choked out a single burst of laughter. "Oh Geoffrey."

"I don't expect an answer now," he said quickly. "In fact, I don't want one. I just want you to know that I love you. No matter what you find in your past, no matter how good, bad, or ugly—you have a home here with me if you want it."

She slid her arm around his neck and kissed him. He wiped her tears away with his thumb.

"If I knew for certain there was nothing in my past to keep me from you, my answer would be 'yes' right now."

He smiled. "That's good enough for me."

She kissed him again, tiny pecks all over his face as she tried to squeeze back what were now happy tears.

"Hey, yo's, last chance on the popcorn—" Derek stopped in the doorway. "Whoa, looks like I interrupted something important."

Geoffrey rocked back on his heels and stood. "I've

asked August to marry me."

◆   ◆   ◆

It wasn't the loud snoring that kept her awake. Nor was it her fear of the mysterious woman haunting her memories. She'd hardly given her stalker another thought.

Geoffrey wanted to marry her!

Her heart sang with joy, and excitement raced through her blood like a high-speed pinball. He wanted to marry her, even if she had a less than desirable past.

The enormous dog at the foot of the bed grunted in her sleep and rolled over, nearly crushing August's foot. Geoffrey had used his cell phone on the ride home to call someone named Howard and inquire about Eunice, but she had no idea Eunice was a two-hundred-pound Mastiff. The gigantic dog was sweet as could be, but had a commanding bark, and August had no doubt the muscular animal could bring down the largest of men.

Geoffrey's sweet gesture nearly made her cry again, but she fell into a fit of giggles when the dog rolled, groaned, and let loose a loud flatulence.

The potted juniper outside the window rustled in the wind and the dog jerked upright.

"Good girl, Eunice. At least I know you can hear intruders over your own snoring."

The dog gazed at her and licked her giant chops. She relaxed, her panting breaths shaking the entire bed.

"You and I are going to become good friends," she promised the dog.

But in the back of her mind, August could not shake the uneasy feeling that with this great happiness would also come great sadness.

As hard as she tried, the uncomfortable feeling was

there, just out of reach: something would keep her from staying in Newport.

◆ ◆ ◆

Geoffrey's phone rang as he was driving August back to the Mirthful Mermaid for her shift. He saw the number and knew it was Mike calling about August.

"Let me call you back in ten minutes." He didn't identify his brother-in-law. The last thing he wanted was to make August anxious before her shift. She seemed so happy, gazing at the ring on her finger.

He pulled into a parking space at the Mirthful Mermaid and snapped the phone shut. "I think we should tell her together."

Gran Millie eyed them suspiciously as they came through the door. "All right you two, what's going on? You look funny."

The ring must have glinted because she looked down at August's hand and gasped. "Let me see that. Oh, my goodness. You're just a bucket of surprises, aren't you, grandson?"

"I asked August to marry me...when we get our lives all sorted out."

"And she said yes, of course. I'm so happy you gave her Susan's ring. It fits you, dear." Gran Millie looked up with shining eyes. Her voice grew soft and whispery. "I couldn't be happier. Let me be the first to welcome you to the family."

She pulled August into a hug, and then turned to Geoffrey. "I'm happy for you, too, grandson. Nice to see you out of your funk." She stepped back and dabbed at her eyes. "Don't think this means you can deliver her late to work."

"Does she still get a lunch break?" Geoffrey asked

his grandmother.

"Between two thirty and five, and I'm gonna make sure she takes it today," Millie answered for her.

August turned to him. "If you can get away, we could walk out to the end of the jetty."

"I'll try. I've got a conference call at two, but I'll come down after. Don't go anywhere until I get here."

"Don't worry." She leaned over to kiss him. A burst of joy jumped in his chest. "I'll go up to my little room and bolt the door. Derek will be here by then, anyway. His shift starts at two."

If only he could be on the receiving end of those sweet kisses for the rest of his life. He tamped down the tension coiling in his belly, anxious to return Mike's call. Before he could slip away, Gran Millie yanked him into a bear hug.

"Come here, grandson." She squeezed the breath out of him. "Congratulations."

"Thanks."

"I'm so happy, I could just cry."

"You are crying."

"Oh, go on." She shooed him away.

He went back to the car, but sat in the front seat without turning on the engine.

The heavy tone in his brother-in-law's voice had put Geoffrey on edge, and when he answered Geoffrey's returned call, it was no different. Geoffrey was learning to hate Mike's policeman's voice.

"I've got something you should see," was all he would say.

"Is it bad?"

"I think it would be best if you saw for yourself."

Geoffrey drove to the police station with the dread

in his stomach growing more acidic by the minute.

He sat in front of Mike's desk and waited while his brother-in-law concluded a phone call, and then got up and closed the door before taking his seat again.

"I know you have become very fond of August," he started.

"Don't," Geoffrey said sharply. He took a deep, calming breath. "Don't talk to me like you're a doctor trying to find a gentle way to tell me I have three weeks to live. Just give it to me straight."

Mike glanced down. He opened a manila folder and handed over a single sheet of paper to Geoffrey. "It took Wendy all of ten minutes to find her this morning."

It was a missing person's report for Emily Atkinson of Astoria, Washington. Geoffrey's heart froze in his chest. In the center was a photo of August.

◆ ◆ ◆

"Colin, don't do this to yourself."

He kept his back to his father as he stuffed a change of clothes into a duffel bag. This time, he wasn't coming home in the same day. He might have to camp out in Newport for a few days until...Hell, he wasn't coming back until he'd found her.

"It's a lead, Dad. My first *real* lead." He should have left last night. He would have been in southern Oregon by now.

"Colin, it's been three weeks. If she's alive, why hasn't she come home?"

"I'm going to check the hospitals. She could be like that woman in Seattle."

"Don't you think the authorities would have answered the missing person's report?"

They hadn't called about the woman in the Seattle

hospital. Colin shook his head, but didn't respond. It was useless arguing about it.

"It's obvious she came out of her lifejacket." Graham grabbed him by the elbow and spun him around.

Colin jerked his arm free.

"No," he barked a degree too harshly. "It was too small for her. You said so yourself; you had been trying to get her to buy a new one. She couldn't have come out of it. Besides, that guy said it was unbuckled. She took it off, or someone took it off her."

"Colin, you're setting yourself up for heartbreak again. I hate to see you doing this to yourself."

Colin grabbed his bag and zipped it shut with a shrill *whirr*. He turned around and snatched his car keys from the dresser.

"Then don't watch."

Chapter Nineteen

He read the report in silence. By the time he finished, his blood roared in his ears.

"We shouldn't treat this as a surprise." Mike cleared his throat. "We knew there was someone, somewhere, missing her."

Geoffrey nodded. It would have been stupid to assume otherwise. It had been stupid to *hope* otherwise.

"She's engaged," Mike said.

He swallowed. There was no response to that.

"When I conducted my first search, this missing person's file had been closed. She'd been listed as deceased, her drowning ruled an accident."

Geoffrey's stomach flip-flopped.

"After she found this, Wendy did an inquiry with the sheriff's office up there. Without revealing anything, of course."

He nodded. "Thank you."

"Everyone still believes she's dead. The fiancé is the only one who wouldn't let it drop. He's been searching high and low."

Of course he was. It was no less than Geoffrey would do, if the situation were reversed.

"They had a funeral."

He leaned his elbow on the armrest and pressed his fingertips to his forehead. *Good God.*

"Our hunch she was on a boat that night is correct. From what Wendy could find, her family used to own the fishing and charter fleet her fiancé's family bought out when her old man retired after a back injury. The two of them—Emily and her fiancé—work with his father."

Geoffrey grappled for something to say, anything, other than sitting there like a fool.

"She holds a captain's rating."

August was engaged. His August. *Emily Atkinson*.

"She didn't recognize anything on *Penny Lane*" Nothing except the table. The same kind of table most RVs and campers had.

"Whatever happened that night, it was enough to completely wipe her memory of sailing," Mike surmised.

"Jesus." Geoffrey's mind whirled with a million thoughts, but none of them solid, each one more confusing than the last.

"It's not so bad. She's engaged, not married."

He lifted his gaze to meet his brother-in-law's. He almost felt guilty. He would be sick if the situation were reversed, if someone else had found August—*Emily*—when she was engaged to him.

"Last night, I gave her a ring."

Mike rocked his wooden drafter's chair backward with a loud creak from the spring. "Then the lady has a choice to make."

Geoffrey's head ached. He took a deep breath and straightened his shoulders. Now was not the time to worry about that. "Do we know anything about her family, her circle of friends? This guy she's supposed to marry—"

"Colin Ridgley." Mike shook his head. "You're asking

if any of her friends have red hair."

Geoffrey nodded. He was about to lose his last remaining sliver of composure.

"The Coast Guard and the local PD conducted a full investigation. Foul play was ruled out."

"That doesn't mean squat to me. If that were true, then why is someone trying to kill her?"

"You don't even know for sure someone was in the house that day. And she might have misunderstood what she saw in the alley. When a person has the heebie-jeebies already, the mind can play tricks. And we both know she's suffered a pretty severe head injury."

"You think she's schizo because she took a knock to the head?" Geoffrey shot back. "She's lost her memory so what else is going wrong in her mind?"

Mike shook his head and leaned forward to place his elbows on his desk. "No, not at all. I just think she's sensitive to things. She's frightened, alone. And even though she has you, she's alone because she's lost her entire life."

"So she's conjuring a stalker?"

Mike shrugged. "She may have seen Stinky Stan. You know he sleeps in the alleys around the Mirthful Mermaid because your grandmother feeds him. Maybe he thought August—er, Emily—was Millie."

"No," Geoffrey said, shaking his head. "I believe her."

Mike sighed. A long minute ticked by. "I have a friend in the Coast Guard stationed up in Seattle. I could call him, if you want. Get him to do some checking under the guise of a continued investigation. He owes me a favor."

"You did some work for him?" Geoffrey's voice shook with the thundering of his heart. This was the worst he could have imagined, second only to her being married.

"I covered for him with his wife while we were in Vegas." Mike grinned. "So it's a *big* favor."

Geoffrey couldn't be convinced to laugh with his brother-in-law.

"I don't see how that will help. The woman with red hair is here."

"Well, you never know what might turn up. I'll give him a call."

He looked down at the paper in his hand. August's—no, *Emily*'s—beautiful portrait stared back. There was a light in her eyes that revealed the deeper beauty and happiness she possessed before this tragedy hit. When she remembered everything, would that light return?

And the biggest question of all—would she stay?

◆ ◆ ◆

Colin intended to check the hospital in Agate and the two others in nearby Newport right away, but the first thing he wanted was to see the jetty where Emily's lifejacket had been found.

When he'd stopped for gas, the station attendant had known the Mirthful Mermaid right away. "Down yonder at the edge of town. Try some of Millie's clam chowder; it's the best you'll find this side of Boston."

He found the place easily enough. The two-story building gleamed like polished lead in the afternoon sun, its wood bleached over the years without so much as an attempt at painting. The only color was a giant blue-green emblem of a mermaid sitting on a sea rock inside a circle, imprinted on the front of the building as though stamped there with an old-fashioned branding iron. A similar carved wooden sign hung over the door.

Had he not been so anxious, he would have appreciated the place a lot more. Its resistance to modern strip-mall urbanization impressed him. Next to the restaurant was a hardware store literally named *Mom & Pop's*. On the other side, a small real estate agent's office and next to that, *Ocean Outfitter*, a boating supplies place.

He parked the Jeep at the far end of the shared lot and flipped open his cell phone. A quick call to his dad to let him know he'd arrived safely would put the old man at ease.

He'd been too harsh on his father before he left. He knew Graham only had his best interests at heart, but it bothered Colin that he was so eager to give up on Emily.

He punched the number and brought the phone to his ear as he glanced out the window at the marina on the far side of the narrow two-lane road leading out of town. The only thing to keep him from thinking he was looking at a scenic postcard photo was the gentle movement of masts swaying to and fro in front of Yaquina Bay Bridge, and swirling sea birds caught on a thermal.

"Hello, Colin?" His father had answered from the kitchen where the phone displayed his caller ID.

"Hey, Dad. I'm in Newport."

Up the road a bit at the far end of the parking lot, a man and woman paused while a car drove by, and then stepped into the crosswalk leading to the marina.

Colin's entire world stopped turning. He couldn't draw a breath. Graham said something, but Colin didn't hear him.

He would recognize that flowing, platinum blond

hair anywhere, the way natural waves rippled in its lengths, the curl that formed around her shoulders. Her slight build, the cute bounce to her walk.

"Colin, are you there?"

"I'll call you back."

He snapped the phone shut and jumped out of the Jeep. He ran to the crosswalk and dodged in front of a car. The driver blared the horn and swerved around him. Colin scooted out of the way and held up his hands. "Sorry!"

When he looked back, Emily was gone.

◆ ◆ ◆

Geoffrey had been strangely quiet when he returned for her break at three. "How about that walk you promised earlier?" was all he said before taking her by the hand and leading her to the jogging path that wound around the marina and up to the vista point.

The lunch shift had been another busy one and her feet were aching, but she loved the fresh air.

"It's going to be a pretty sunset tonight," she said as they walked toward the low-hanging sun. Fluffy clouds at the edge of the horizon would glow with rapidly changing colors when the sun passed behind them. Hopefully, she could get a short break to enjoy it.

Had she always lived in a coastal town where such beauty was a regular occurrence? She must have, because she looked forward to it with a thrill of eagerness she couldn't explain.

Geoffrey didn't comment. "Are you staying at the house again tonight?" he asked, bringing up her mysterious stalker instead.

Should she, now that he'd proposed? She wondered where they would live if they did get married. The idea of leaving Newport for Portland where he worked saddened her.

"I suppose I should, if Eunice is still going to be there. I wouldn't want you footing her kibble bill if she's not going to make herself useful."

Geoffrey didn't chuckle at the joke, and his mood remained oddly stiff. It wasn't so much the way he spoke or his choice of words, but August could feel something different in him.

"Is everything all right?" She reached across with her right hand, and then turned in front of him to walk on his left side so she could hold his hand.

"Fine," he answered simply, but there was still a strain in his voice.

They walked down the path that wound around the marina's parking lot and headed toward the gates to the piers.

"Let's go to *Penny Lane's* slip," he said.

In the distance, she heard a man shouting. The voice sounded strangely familiar. August stopped.

"Emily?"

She looked up at Geoffrey. His eyes were soft, almost sad.

"Emily!"

He glanced over his shoulder, and she followed his gaze.

A young man wearing a linen coat and blue jeans ran toward them. Flashes of familiarity raced through her. His curly golden hair in the sun. The smattering of freckles across his nose. His stocky build, the length of his gait as he moved with intent.

He slowed, almost came to a stop. His eyes held a mixture of awe and disbelief. "Emily," he repeated again, this time in little more than a whisper.

Geoffrey pulled his hand free of hers.

"My God!" The young man ran the last few steps and threw his arms around her. He lifted her off her feet and spun her around. "I knew it. I knew you were alive!"

All at once his touch, his scent, and his voice were clear, as if she'd never forgotten.

He set her back on her feet and circled her tighter, sobbing into her hair. She slipped her good arm around his back.

"God, I knew it. I never gave up hope." He held her tenderly, gripping a handful of her hair, trailing a rainfall of kisses across her cheek to her lips. She kissed him back knowingly, remembering this touch before she could even recall his name.

When she drew back, his eyes were glossy with tears.

"Where have you been?"

She could only stare back as a flurry of memories whipped through her mind.

"Emily, don't you know me?"

She drew in a sharp breath. "Colin."

Chapter Twenty

"August, you know this man?" she heard Geoffrey ask.

"Her name is Emily, and who the hell are you?"

"Colin," Emily stammered. "This is Geoffrey Barthlow. He's been...helping me."

"Why haven't you called? Jesus, Emily, everyone thought you were dead."

She still couldn't sort out her thoughts. She recognized him, but didn't yet remember him. No, she did remember him, just not as completely as she knew she should.

"I..." She placed her hand to her forehead as her gaze slipped to the ground.

"She didn't remember. She was hit on the head."

Colin glanced fleetingly at Geoffrey. He gently smoothed back her bangs to reveal the angry pink scar that remained near her hairline. His expression shattered at the sight of it. "Oh fuck. Are you all right?"

"It looks worse than it is," she said vaguely.

When Dr. Carlson removed the stitches, it had looked downright monstrous, but he'd assured her the scar, and the tiny pink dots where the stitches had pierced her skin, would go away soon. She'd been putting vitamin E on it so it would fade.

"What happened to your arm?" He stood back and

gazed at her as though horrified by what he found.

"I fell." She could sense Colin's distrust of Geoffrey, and remembered his jealous streak well enough. There was no use making him angry with Geoffrey for something that hadn't been his fault.

"My God, I can hardly believe it. I've been looking everywhere for you."

"I'm sorry," was all she could think to say.

He gripped her by the shoulders, clearly growing frantic. "What does he mean you don't remember? Don't you know me?"

Geoffrey stepped forward and placed a hand on his arm. "Don't push her. She's not ready to remember."

"Back off." Colin jerked away. "She's my fiancée."

Both men looked to her hand.

"What the hell is this?" He grabbed the finger with Geoffrey's ring. She bit back a gasp as a sharp bolt zinged her elbow.

"If you're engaged, where's her ring?" Geoffrey asked.

Colin shot him with a glare. "Look, can you give us a minute?"

"I don't know you." Geoffrey remained rooted. "But I know she almost died, on *your* boat."

"She went overboard in a storm. It was an accident."

"Just because foul play was ruled out doesn't mean someone didn't push her," Geoffrey argued.

Suddenly all August's jumbled, whirling thoughts came to an abrupt halt. She faced Geoffrey. "You knew?"

"I learned this morning. Mike found the missing person's report on you. I was going to tell you now."

"I don't believe him," Colin shot.

Geoffrey glared back. "I don't care what you

believe."

Colin turned on him. "You can go now. She doesn't need you anymore." He poked Geoffrey in the shoulder in a definite challenge.

In a lightning fast reaction, Geoffrey grabbed his hand, twisted his arm behind his back and shoved him away.

Geoffrey was larger and more muscular, but Colin was strong, and used to heavy work. The last thing she wanted was to see a fight break out between them.

"Stop it!" she shouted. "Stop, now!"

Colin whirled around, but both men froze at the same instant, a distance apart.

She pressed her fingers to her forehead, rubbing away a rapidly growing ache. "I can't take this right now."

They both started shouting at the same instant.

"Stop!"

Emily took a deep breath. Her heart pounded in her throat.

"You! Go that way." She pointed behind Colin, and then turned to Geoffrey. "And you, go that way."

Colin's brows shot up. "Hell no! I'm not letting you out of my sight again."

"Where are you going?" Geoffrey asked.

"I'm going back to the Mirthful Mermaid to finish my shift. Alone!"

They both erupted in argument so fast and so loud, she couldn't distinguish any of it. She sliced through the air with her good hand.

"No buts! I need to sort this out. Do you hear me?"

Both men settled on their heels.

"And I won't tolerate any fighting." She held her

breath for a long moment, and was satisfied when they both kept quiet.

By the time she reached the Mirthful Mermaid, all the confusion seemed to have lifted like a fog that had suddenly blown off.

My name is Emily Atkinson. I am twenty-six years old.

She lived in a quiet suburb of Astoria, Oregon, renting the little house her parents hadn't been able to sell when they retired. The seventy-six foot ketch, her pride and joy, now belonged to Colin's father, Graham, and Northwest Expeditions, their fishing and charter company where she worked. Her heart surged with a happy ache. Graham! Dear, sweet Graham, how she missed him.

Gran Millie looked up when she walked through the door. She smiled. "Did you forget something, child?"

"No, I've remembered something." She strode across the nearly empty restaurant and extended her hand. "I'd like to introduce myself. I'm Emily Atkinson."

◆ ◆ ◆

So he'd found the little bitch. She watched from the car and couldn't help but snicker when Colin and Emily's new guy started swinging.

It was just like Emily to have two men fighting over her. Back in eighth grade, Colin got into a fistfight with Brent Nelson because Emily had asked him to the Sadie Hawkins dance.

I'd asked Brent first. A bitter taste accompanied the memory. But Brent had dropped her like a lump of dog shit when pretty, blue-eyed blond-haired Emily asked him. They'd been kids then, and as adults, incidents like that had been forgiven, chalked up to immaturity and childish antics. But never forgotten.

Brent had been my first crush, and the first time Emily had snatched it away. But not the last.

Emily looked confused. She muttered to herself as she left them both and strode back to the restaurant. She never even looked up, passing right in front of the parked car.

Wouldn't that be another pisser, to look up and see me sitting here?

She must not have remembered everything. Surely the police would be pulling up by now if she had.

"It's not too late for you, Emily."

Just because Colin had found her didn't mean it was too late to finish what should have been the end three weeks ago.

◆ ◆ ◆

"There now, this will make everything better." Gran Millie poured two cups of her magic tea blend and sat down at the table with Emily. "I suppose this is a real doosey for you."

"It's like my head is a blender set on high." She groaned, and then couldn't help but laugh. Her spirits were soaring.

She remembered! And it felt wonderful.

"There's all this information in there whirling around, but I can't quite pin it all down. I have to grab for things one at a time, or I won't get anything."

"Don't you worry about any of it. It'll come to you when it's good and ready." Gran Millie picked up her cup, and then urged Emily on with a wave of her hand.

She took a sip of her tea.

"Emily. I like that name, it's pretty."

"It feels a little...foreign." She smiled as she thought back to Geoffrey's teasing when they'd first met, when he'd wondered if her name was Prunella or Grizelda.

"I suppose a lot's going to feel strange to you over the next few days."

"It's all coming back fast. I remember my parents, and I remember Colin and his father, Graham."

"That's Colin, out there?" Gran Millie tipped her head. Emily twisted around in her seat. Colin sat on one of the short pylons connected with old ship chains that created the artistic fence around the parking lot, his hands stuffed into the pockets of his coat.

"I bought him that coat for his birthday last year," Emily said softly. "It's March twelfth. He's a Pisces." He looked so desperate, her heart lurched for him.

Far across the parking lot, Geoffrey paced in front of the SUV, using his cell phone. Both men glanced secretively at each other, careful not to let the other see it.

"What are you gonna do?"

Emily turned back to Gran Millie, but only shook her head. "I don't know."

The older woman smiled. "Well, you're a lucky woman, with two men panting at your heels."

"It was more like fighting than panting." Emily sipped her tea. "And I don't feel very lucky."

Of the confusion churning inside her, this was the most turbulent. What would she do?

She loved Geoffrey with the sharp, vivid intensity of new passion, but Colin...Colin was ingrained on her soul. She could feel it already, and she hadn't even remembered everything.

"I think the first thing we should do is talk about this woman who's been following you. Did he spark any memories of her?"

Emily shook her head.

"Maybe your young man will know who she is."

Your young man. A few hours ago, she would have put Geoffrey in that role. Now Colin had been returned to it, but she wasn't sure that was right, either.

"Well, we shouldn't leave them out there." Gran Millie rose from her chair and put her hands on her hips as she looked through the Mirthful Mermaid's front windows. "We need to talk this thing through."

She knew Gran Millie was right, but the idea made her heart flutter.

She turned back to Emily. "Shall I bring them in?"

Emily swallowed and nodded. Ready or not, they had to talk.

Gran Millie went to the front door and leaned out. She gestured to Colin, who leaped to his feet and started over, and then to Geoffrey. He snapped his phone shut and followed.

"Come on in, boys, and have a seat." She held the door open until they'd both come through. "My girl here is a little upset. So we're all going to try our best not to make it worse, aren't we?"

"Yes, ma'am," Colin said.

"Of course, Gran."

Colin sat down beside her and took her hand. He leaned forward, balancing his elbows on his knees, and brought her fingers to his lips. "I still can't believe it. I'm so glad you're all right." His eyes still had a glossy quality.

She smiled as she turned his hand in hers and gripped it. She then released him and stood, pacing a few steps away.

Geoffrey sat in the chair his grandmother had

vacated, watching them with sad eyes. She knew what was on his mind, and it broke her heart to imagine the pain he was feeling.

She took a deep breath and started in as even a tone as she could manage over the tremors wracking every muscle and nerve.

"I know that you both have a lot of questions for me, but right now I don't have the answers. I need some time to get my thoughts straight. I don't know what I'm going to do."

Colin jerked upright in his chair. "You're going to come home! People want to know what's happened to you; your family needs to know. For God's sake, Emily, your parents had a *funeral*. They buried an empty casket."

She had not been prepared to hear that. Emily sagged into a chair before her rubbery knees gave out.

Gran Millie returned to the table with two more teacups. "Let's all keep a cool head, now."

Colin let out a grumbling sigh. "How do you expect me to feel? I thought I'd lost my fiancée."

"Colin, last night somebody with a knife attacked me in the alley right outside that door." She pointed to the back hallway. "It was a woman. And someone broke into Geoffrey's house when I was there alone."

He stared at her with shocked disbelief written on his face. She shoved to her feet and stood before them. Both men looked so forlorn, a lance of misery sleeted through her chest.

"Do you have any idea who it might have been?" Geoffrey asked him.

Colin's brows drew together. "How would I know who it was?"

"Do any of our friends have red hair?" she asked him.

He glanced away, silent over whatever was going through his mind.

"I just remembered something."

Colin's gaze snapped back. "What?"

"That look. What are you not telling me?" When he remained silent, she pressed. "What happened the night I went overboard?"

He shoved out of his chair and paced away. "I don't know." He stopped and faced the group of them. Emily could feel everyone waiting on bated breath, most of all herself.

"I wish I did. My father and I suspected you and Sonja had an argument. The two of you had been...at odds lately. We told the police and they brought her in for questioning, but they didn't have anything to hold her on."

"Do you think this woman pushed Aug-Emily overboard?" Gran Millie asked.

Geoffrey leaned forward and set his elbows on his knees. He clasped his hands together and pressed them to his mouth as if trying to hold back an inappropriate comment.

"Pushed? No," Colin finally answered. He shook his head. "But was there a terrible accident? Only the two of you know for sure."

"Colin, I don't remember what happened that night on the boat. But I keep having these strange, transparent memories of a woman with red hair that scare me so badly I get sick to my stomach."

"Does this 'Sonja' have red hair?" Geoffrey asked. He'd been mostly silent until now.

Colin's shoulders sagged. "Yeah, she has red hair." He returned to his chair and sat heavily. "She's been your best friend since grade school. I can't believe she'd do something to hurt you. I sure as hell don't believe she's trying to kill you now."

"How can you be certain of that?" Geoffrey asked. "It seems to me you're the least informed person here."

Colin clenched his jaw but didn't respond. After a scalding glare Geoffrey's way, he rose from his chair again. "I need to make a phone call."

"Now hold on a minute." Geoffrey jumped to his feet. "Who are you calling?"

Colin swiveled around to face him. The tension between them was so sharp, Emily could almost smell its bitterness.

"My father."

Geoffrey glanced at Emily. She stepped forward. "Who else was on board that night?"

A horrified look slipped over Colin's features. "You can't possibly believe my father had anything to do with what happened!"

Emily approached him and reached for his hand. Colin took it and squeezed. His expression softened as he gazed down at her.

This, she remembered: his sweet smiles, his kind eyes, and the way he gazed at her as if she were a princess. She had loved this man with an intensity that had ruled her entire life. Bits and pieces came back stronger now, memories of the excitement and exuberance that had been life with Colin.

"Listen to me, Colin. I don't remember what happened that night, but I have these really bad feelings about it. Until I remember exactly what happened, I don't want anyone to know I'm alive."

"It would appear the person who wants to hurt you already knows," Gran Millie tossed in.

"I won't say anything," Colin promised. "If I told him I'd found you, he'd think I was crazy anyway. He'd probably assume I grabbed some poor woman who looks like you."

He flipped open his phone, dialed, and paced a few steps away.

"I don't like the way this feels," Geoffrey said.

"Nor do I," his grandmother agreed.

"Dad—" Colin glanced back at Emily as he spoke. "Sorry about that. No, there was a bad connection. Yeah, I got here okay. Listen, where's Sonja?"

Emily returned to her seat beside Geoffrey. Colin turned away, as if watching it upset him.

Heaven help me, what am I going to do? She loved two men, each in such a completely different way it couldn't be compared.

"When was the last time you saw her?" Colin turned back to them. "Are you sure? What time? All right, thanks...I don't know. I'll call you back soon. Yes, I'm fine—I swear. Dad...I love you."

He flipped the phone shut. "Sonja was in Astoria last night. My father saw her having dinner with her mother at Trudy's Café at about eight thirty."

"It's almost a three-hour drive from Astoria," Gran Millie said. "She would've had to drive like a bat out of hell to be here by eleven."

"Do I know anyone else with red hair?"

"And a black Labrador," Geoffrey added.

Colin's gaze flicked over him. "When we were in high school, Sonja had a black Lab named Rocky."

Emily was even more confused. "This doesn't make any sense. Who was in the alley?"

Geoffrey swiveled toward her and took her hand. "Are you sure you saw a woman?"

She didn't answer. She wasn't sure of anything, anymore.

He looked over his shoulder. "Gran, when did you last see Stinky Stan?"

"Who?" Emily asked shrilly.

"He's a transient who hangs around here," Millie told her. "I give him leftovers from the kitchen, so sometimes he sleeps in the alley. He's never bothered anyone, so I let him be."

Geoffrey faced her. "Are you sure it wasn't a man you saw in the alley? Mike was thinking—"

She shot to her feet. "He thinks I'm crazy. He didn't believe me that there was someone in the house, and now he thinks I saw a bum in the alley."

"You've suffered a very traumatic experience. If you did fight with this Sonja girl that night, it's possible your mind is conjuring a threat to compensate."

"Now you sound like Dr. Lohman."

"I believe you saw something," Geoffrey said quickly. "But even you said you only saw a shape."

"I heard a woman curse."

"Maybe he was headed up the alley, and you startled him when you knocked the boxes over," Gran Millie offered. "He does have sort of a high-pitched, raspy voice."

Colin stepped close and slipped his arms around her. "It doesn't matter. You're safe now. It's all over. I'm not going to let anything happen to you."

Chapter Twenty-One

Emily didn't know how to put into words what she needed to say. No matter how gentle she was, she knew Geoffrey would be hurt.

A long moment's silence passed as they all waited for her. Like entrants in a contest waiting to see who won, it seemed they all held their breath in anticipation.

"I need to see my parents," she finally said. "Colin, where is my car?"

Geoffrey glanced away. A sharp strike beat in her chest.

Colin smiled, obviously feeling like he was the winner. "At their house in Palos Verdes, with what's left of your stuff."

Emily realized the magnitude of what her family and friends must have gone through over the last month. "What about the house in Seaport?"

"It's empty. Your parents put it back on the market."

She should have expected as much. It was still technically their house; she had only been renting it. But the idea of her things being sold, or donated, broke her heart. That was her life, and as foreign as it still felt, now it was nothing more than garage-sale remnants. She swallowed, forcing the thought away. Why did she suddenly feel depressed, as if a great event had just come to an end?

Because I've realized that my life isn't here, but it isn't there anymore, either.

She took a deep breath. Wherever she chose it to be, her life needed to be rebuilt. She could survive. She wouldn't let this thing beat her.

She glanced back at Geoffrey. He stood quietly beside his grandmother, eyes downcast.

"Gran Millie, I know I only started here, but I'd like to keep my job."

Millie's expression brightened. "Of course. Customers adore you."

"What about your job at Northwest?" Colin interjected.

She turned back to face him. His expression had turned almost as forlorn as Geoffrey's. "I can hardly sail with a broken arm. Besides, I don't remember sailing."

His eyes grew wide. "Nothing? Jesus, Emily. You hold a captain's rating."

She shook her head. "Not a thing."

"But you live in Astoria."

She couldn't do this, not now. She took a breath, gathering her resolve. "I need to speak to Geoffrey alone. Could you wait outside at the car?"

"Yeah. Sure." He threw an uneasy glance at Geoffrey and Gran Millie, and then turned and headed out.

Sensing their need to be alone, Millie gave her a hug and a quick kiss on the forehead. "I'm here when you need me, honey pie." She then hurried away, subtly wiping the corner of her eye.

Emily took Geoffrey's hand. His was limp; he didn't squeeze her fingers as he always did.

"Geoffrey—"

He forced a smile. "It's okay, you don't have to

explain."

"Yes, I do."

This wasn't fair! Was she being punished? Whoever said "it was better to have loved and lost than never to have loved at all" had never had to choose between two men.

Her heart swelled with love and it took every ounce of strength she had to prepare to walk out the door.

"You said you didn't want an answer until I remembered my past."

He glanced at her hand where his mother's ring still adorned her finger.

"I still don't have an answer for you." The first sting of tears burned. She blinked them away. "But I meant what I said. I love you, Geoffrey. Nothing will ever change that."

Now his fingers did squeeze. "I know."

"I have to see my parents, or I wouldn't leave at all."

He only nodded.

"I'll be back in a couple of days."

He slipped his hand around her neck and pulled her close. Emily met his lips eagerly, drinking in his kiss like a lifesaving elixir. His tender touch renewed her strength and filled her with hope.

He kept his eyes closed for a few seconds, as if savoring a last taste of her.

"Be careful. I believe you about the woman in the alley." He mustered a thin smile. "As much as I hate to say this..." His gaze flicked past her to the window. "Don't go anywhere alone."

She held his hand as they moved apart. "Don't worry. I'm not taking any chances." Finally, with arms outstretched, she had to release him.

A seizure of pain filled her chest as she walked toward the door. She wanted to turn around, to take a last look at this man she had come to love so dearly, but she knew it would be her undoing. Instead, she concentrated on what she knew she had to do next.

◆ ◆ ◆

With a heart turned to solid stone, Geoffrey watched her leave the building.

Leave him.

That man, Colin Ridgley—*her fiancé*—stood outside looking through the window. When Emily stepped through the door, he pulled her under his arm.

That quickly, she was gone.

Gran Millie reached up and put a hand on his shoulder.

"You okay there, sport?"

"No." He shook his head. "I'm destined to lose."

She rubbed a circle on his back, like she used to do when he was little. "Don't say that. No use anticipating the worst."

He turned and faced his grandmother.

She smiled wanly. "I've got a feeling about her. She's special, that one."

As if he didn't know that better than Gran did.

His grandmother gave his hand a pat. "She'll be back."

Inside, he wasn't so sure. But it wasn't himself he was worried about; it was Emily.

"I just let the woman I love walk out of here with the person who very well may have pushed her overboard."

Chapter Twenty-Two

Colin took her under his arm and buried his nose in her hair as they walked to his Jeep. "I still almost can't believe it." He breathed deep and sighed a hot breath against her neck. "I never gave up on you."

She laughed. There was something wonderful about being near him, remembering him. They had a lifetime of memories together she was eager to reclaim as *her* memories. Memories someone had tried to take away from her.

He was like a book she'd read a long time ago. Opening the cover again would refresh her memory of the story within.

Still, she couldn't escape the uneasy feeling things were not as perfect as they should be. "Let me drive. You're distracted."

"Sure. That way I can stare at you the whole way back."

He handed her the keys and jogged around to the passenger side. In the back of her mind she knew if it were Geoffrey, he would have opened the door for her. They were two very different men, she realized. It only made her situation harder.

She started the Jeep and pulled onto the narrow highway. As her memory started slipping back, like a trickle of water slowly filling a bucket, she suddenly remembered Newport. Not what she knew of it now, but having visited it once before. They'd sailed into Copper Marina on the other side of the inlet. Still, though she remembered coming in on the boat, she didn't remember anything about operating it.

"My father is going to drop ten years when he sees you."

She couldn't wait to see him, too. Since the seventh grade, when her family's financial problems began and her father started drinking, Graham had been like her surrogate parent.

"You never told me who was on board that day." She could feel him watching her as she drove. She hoped she didn't sound too suspicious.

"You don't really think someone has been trying to kill you, do you?" When she didn't answer, he went on. "Well, Sonja, as you know. Tim, Sean, Will, Joseph, Chelsie, Jessica, me, my father...the passengers from the charter that day, but they were seasick as hell, puking their guts up below."

She tried to picture their friends. The only one who would come to mind was Graham.

"And Sonja has red hair?"

"You don't remember them at all?" He slid his hand over her thigh as he slipped closer on his seat. "Don't worry. It will all come back to you when you see them."

"I meant what I said, Colin. You can't tell anyone else about me until *I* say it's okay. I'm visiting my parents, then I'm coming back to Newport."

"Maybe after you see them, you won't want to."

It was pointless going round and round with him about it. A peculiar ache started in her stomach and grew stronger as they left town and merged onto the main highway north.

"Be straight with me." She used her firm voice. "Did we break up?"

He leaned away. "No. No way."

"Then why did I take off my ring?"

Colin pushed back into his seat. He glanced out his own window, avoiding her gaze. Another familiar trait of his.

"I don't know. I honestly don't. You didn't take it off in front of me." After a moment's silence, he added, "Are you asking because of that guy?"

"Geoffrey."

"Whatever." From the corner of her eye, she could see him gritting his teeth, as though saying Geoffrey's name tasted bad. "I saw him kiss you."

The need to defend herself sat sourly. "He and I have become very close." After she'd said it, she wished she hadn't. He had no right to intrude.

Something had happened between them that Colin wasn't telling her; she could feel it.

"How close?" Colin demanded. "Did you sleep with him?"

She scowled at him before quickly turning her eyes back to the road. "No."

"What really happened to your arm?"

She supposed that question was fair. "The night of the storm, I walked in front of a car."

"His car."

"Yes, *his* car," she snapped. "He took me to the hospital and paid my medical bills."

"And you've been with him this entire time?" This time when Colin spoke, there was so much hurt in his voice she couldn't hold onto her irritation, even though she had the inescapable feeling she was angry with him for something she didn't yet remember.

"He's been very generous. You should be grateful."

"Of course he was," Colin drawled. "He wanted a piece of ass."

"Colin!"

"Emily, look at yourself in the mirror sometime. You're gorgeous. What man wouldn't want to take you home? He was probably trying to keep you from remembering."

"He would never do that." Her anger mounted. He was out of bounds with accusations like that. She tried to imagine how he felt, and remembered he'd always had a jealous streak. Still, he was pushing her buttons the wrong way.

"You heard him," Colin continued. "He found the missing person's report this morning, but he didn't say anything."

She pulled the Jeep to a stop behind a line of traffic at the last stoplight before Highway 1's speed limit increased.

"Colin, listen. He was a perfect gentleman the whole time and he only acted in my best interests. It was either stay with him, or in a women's shelter."

He shifted closer again. "I suppose that was better than staying at a shelter." He forced his voice to remain low, but he still wore a scowl. "Remind me to send him a thank-you note, or something," he finished in a sarcastic tone.

Emily glanced sideways. "How did you find me?"

Maybe knowing how he found her would help her discover how her attacker had found her, too.

"I saw your lifejacket on a boat in Freeport

yesterday. They told me they found it on the jetty across from that restaurant."

Yesterday. Whoever had been following her, they'd found her long before that.

"Was anyone helping you look for me?"

"Chelsie, Sean, Tim, and Joe. They all were, for a while. Then everyone started to think I was crazy and I should accept that you were gone. Everyone went to your funeral except me."

She glanced at him, somewhat surprised. "You didn't go to my funeral?"

He shook his head. "I knew you weren't dead. I could feel you, alive." He put his hand over his heart. "In here."

Heat bloomed in her middle and a whole new rush of tears stung her eyes. "You never gave up on me."

"I told you that. I love you. I could never give up on you."

Her throat choked up and she could only manage a whisper. "I love you too, Colin."

Chapter Twenty-Three

Colin flipped open his phone. He glanced at her as he spoke to his father. "Can you meet me at the Atkinson's new house in about a half hour?"

She heard Graham's voice buzzing through the earpiece. She couldn't wait to see him, and her parents, and the looks on their faces when they saw her.

"Just meet me there. Dad, relax. You gotta trust me. Do you remember how to find it?"

She merged left, preparing to take the exit toward Palos Verdes. So far, she remembered where she was going.

"I'll be there in about thirty minutes. All right, see you." He flipped the phone shut. He slid closer on the seat and nuzzled her. "I would rather go to a hotel. I need to touch you."

She wanted to touch him, too. To close her eyes, let herself be drawn into his embrace, try to forget all this had happened. She was sure, broken arm aside, she would almost be able to imagine the last three weeks had never happened.

But she couldn't do that. She didn't want to forget Geoffrey. An unbearable ache had been twisting in her gut since leaving Newport. Since leaving him.

Her life with Colin had been set. She had her job, her engagement, her future. Now she had Geoffrey to consider too. Life with him and his wonderful family had been joyous and right.

But now she recognized a new feeling, or rather a memory, that she'd wanted to break free of the old life, where everything had been decided for her. Of course, not in such a drastic way, but deep inside Emily knew she'd been yearning to make her own choices.

Was that why she'd refused to set a date for the wedding for so long? So many parts of her past were still ungraspable, and now it was even more frustrating that she could see shapes and shadows but not be able to make them out clearly.

"I need some time," she said simply. "A lot's happened, and I still don't remember everything."

"I don't understand it, but I'll give you all the time you need."

"Thank you." She smiled at him. "Okay, don't tell me. Right up here at...Thorndike?"

The sky had gone from dusky purple to rich sapphire sprinkled with diamond chips. They pulled down the long gravel road through the pine trees leading to her parents' tiny woodland home. The windows glowed with golden light.

Her red Prelude with its dented door and cracked windshield sat in the driveway. Familiarity swelled through her with pleasing warmth. Cherry Pit, she jokingly called the car. Her parents' Oldsmobile sedan was parked in front of the garage door.

She stopped the Jeep beside Graham's pickup at the back of the circular drive and turned it off.

The front door opened and Graham came out, followed by her parents. When they saw her slip out of the front seat, her mother cried out and covered her mouth.

Graham froze, and then ran toward her. "I don't believe it!" He stopped only for an instant to hold her at arm's length, and then hauled her into a hug. He stepped back again, staring at her as though he still couldn't believe his eyes.

"Hi, Graham."

Her mother ran up and threw her arms around Emily. "My baby!" She rocked back and forth, sobbing.

"Mom." Her mother's familiar scent and the scratchy apron she never took off brought memories flooding back.

She heard her father's slow steps and the crunch of his cane spearing the gravel. She turned from her mother and approached him, giving a tentative hug. Emily realized the bad memories were as vivid as the good. She leaned back and smiled.

All at once, all three fired questions and exclamations.

"Now, now, everyone, let her come inside," Colin said. He never strayed more than a few feet from her side. "We've been on the road for three hours."

They sat her down in the front room. Her mother blotted her eyes with a tissue and passed the box around.

"Did I tell you?" Colin asked his father. "I knew she wasn't dead."

Graham swiped at his eye with a thumb. "You certainly did. I'm sorry I doubted you. I'm sorry, Emily."

"Where were you?" her mother asked. "Why didn't you call?"

She remembered her mother's name was Agnes. She glanced at her father. She felt as if she'd dived into cold water as she realized she could not remember her father's first name.

"Uh, it's difficult to explain."

"You couldn't call your own family?" her father said in his trademark grumbling voice. *That* she remembered.

The furniture in the house was familiar, but otherwise the place was foreign. She'd never lived here. When their cottage in Astoria didn't sell, they'd allowed her to rent it and bought this quiet house far from the ocean with the money from selling their boats.

"When I washed ashore that night, I was disoriented," she explained. "I had hypothermia. I was hit by a car on a dark road."

"That wonderful guy who was taking care of you is the reason you couldn't remember in the first place." Colin's voice held barely-contained anger. He sat next to her in a matching Queen Anne chair, his face scrunched into a grimace.

"What guy?" Graham asked.

"A family in Newport put me up." She shot Colin a look. "All I remember is walking along the ocean highway. My head hurt then. I was already injured. It must have happened when I went overboard. Whatever made me forget, it happened on board." She'd almost said the boat's name, but at the last minute it wouldn't come. This wasn't as easy as she'd hoped it would be.

Across the tiny living room, her mother mewled like a kitten. "Your head?"

"I had eight stitches." Emily pulled back her bangs. "But my arm was broken when I was hit by the car."

Graham swallowed. "There was blood on the cabin roof."

Her father glared at Graham. "What blood? You didn't say anything about any blood. Just how much did you cover up, Ridgley?"

"It wasn't Graham's fault, that much I know for certain," Emily said quickly. She should have known the accident would have caused bad blood between them.

Graham gave a terse nod, but his shoulders still looked bunched.

"I don't remember what happened that night," she continued, anticipating his next question. She swept her glance from him, over her father, to Agnes. "I didn't remember much for a long time. Fleeting memories here and there. The family who took care of me after I got out of the hospital drove me down south to see if I remembered anything, but it didn't help."

Colin leaned forward, his elbows on his knees, and drove his fingers through his short-cropped hair.

She didn't elaborate further. None of them needed to know about her time with Geoffrey. She suddenly felt protective over it, worried they would all be as possessive and jealous as Colin. Her time with Geoffrey, and the new memories they'd created, were precious.

"You didn't remember your own parents?" her father barked. "Hogwash."

"Now, now," her mother soothed.

"It's hard to explain how murky everything felt after the accident. I'm really sorry for any pain I caused."

"It's not your fault, Emily," Graham interjected. "Nobody blames you for what happened that night, or since. We're just glad you're back."

Her father snorted. "You're right at that; we knew whose fault it was. You're damned lucky, Ridgley." He shook his finger at Graham, and Emily cringed inwardly.

"Listen, everyone, let's not lose sight of what's important." Colin took her hand. "It's a good thing I found you. Otherwise we might never have known what happened to you."

She shook her head. "No, I would have remembered, sooner or later. The doctors who treated me said I would remember when I was ready."

She had to tell them about her fears to encourage them to keep her presence a secret for a while, but did so without confessing the attacks. Until she remembered what happened, no one else could know she was alive.

Her father wanted to call the police, and Graham agreed with him. But with Colin's help, she managed to convince them they had no more proof today than they did the day Graham and Colin spoke to them about Sonja. She still had a queasy feeling in her stomach when she thought about the red-haired girl, but Emily was dead-set against implicating Sonja any further if she wasn't sure.

For the next hour, she did her best to answer the barrage of questions fired at her. When she yawned, her mother jumped from her seat. "You must be hungry."

"Famished," she said, knowing it was what Agnes needed to hear. She loved cooking for her family.

"I'll make you a sandwich. Your favorite?" She hesitated.

"Turkey and tomato on French bread?" Emily confirmed, and Agnes beamed.

"Coming right up!"

"Well," Graham cleared his throat. "I suppose you two want to be alone."

Colin had inched progressively closer. He reached

over and took her hand. "I do want to talk to you," he whispered.

They walked to the door with Graham. Emily found herself captured in his big, gentle hug.

"I'm so glad you're all right," he said in a hoarse voice. "Part of me died that night, Em." Tears welled and spilled, but he smiled past them. Love burst in Emily's heart. Strong and sturdy Graham wasn't afraid to let anyone see him cry. "Now I feel alive again."

He dragged her into another hug.

"The minute I saw Colin, I remembered you, too," she whispered just for him. "And how very much you mean to me."

He chuckled, pretending the tears weren't streaking his cheeks, and turned to his truck without another word. He started the engine, looked at her again while grinning like a little boy, and then drove away.

"He missed you."

"I missed him."

Colin took her good hand, swinging it gently back and forth as they crunched slowly across the gravel to the edge of light spilling from the house. She could feel his longing, his pain of believing her dead.

"I've been living a nightmare for the past three weeks." He stopped and turned to her. She felt herself draw nearer. *Her Colin*. She had been missing something vital inside herself without him, too.

"Now it's over and you're back. It's the second chance we both deserve. It's a miracle."

She smiled, not sure if she was ready to chalk it up to a miracle.

"I don't know why you took this off that night..." He produced a small velvet box from his pocket. "But I'm asking you to put it back on."

He flipped open the box. Her ring gleamed in the wan light. She remembered it perfectly: the neat, quarter carat Marquis set prettily in its white-gold band.

"Colin—"

"I know you said you needed time, and I'll give you as much as you need. But just take off that ring, please."

She shook her head. "I can't do that."

His hand dropped a few inches. "Why?"

"Because..."

"Do you love him?"

Her stomach quavered with nervous tension. She drew a shuddering breath. "Yes. I do."

He snapped the velvet box shut and turned around, bringing both hands to his head. "I don't believe this."

"Colin, I haven't decided what I'm going to do."

"You mean you haven't chosen between us."

He turned back. She saw him take a deep breath and smother his anger. He stepped close again and placed his hands on her shoulders.

"It's all right. I know you've been through a lot, and it's confused you. Once you're back in your old life, you'll get used to us again."

His eyes were as she'd never seen them before. So filled with misery, so lost and hopeless. She understood the pain he'd been feeling the past three weeks, because now she was feeling it, too.

"I'm so sorry." She fought against the stinging in her throat. "I didn't do this on purpose."

He took her hand and placed the velvet box in her palm. "I know." A long moment passed before he lifted his gaze to meet hers. "I can't believe I found you again, only to lose you."

"You aren't losing me." She stepped forward and kissed him. He gripped her shoulders and dragged her hard against him. In his kiss, she felt his desperation, his tragic need. She wished she could make his pain go away.

She didn't want either man to hurt, but she could only choose one.

Chapter Twenty-Four

Agnes flitted about the house in a state of perpetual happiness, eagerly catering to Emily's every need. She didn't have the heart to tell her mother she only wanted some quiet time to think.

Colin had finally been convinced to return home with Graham, even though she believed him when he said he wouldn't be able to sleep again until she was beside him.

She missed him and Geoffrey terribly. The sadness had only gotten worse. Now it was a constant sharp stab at the apex of her ribs. In order to make one happy, she had to break the other's heart. How could she possibly choose between them? Colin had been a part of her life for so long that being without him would be like losing a finger, but Geoffrey was a unique and special man who brought light alive inside her.

"Son of a bitch." Her father dropped the invoice he'd just opened onto the kitchen table. "I wonder if we can dig up that coffin and return it."

"Bernard!" Agnes shrieked.

In an instant, her father's name sparked with familiarity. How could she have forgotten that? And worse, why hadn't she remembered it herself?

Her relationship with him had been a turbulent part of her life, with as many bad memories as good. Was she blocking out the less pleasant things from her life? Would she ever let herself remember that night on the boat?

The unease at the things missing from her memory came with a dark fear she could almost see. She racked her mind for a glimpse of the night she went overboard, but still nothing would come.

She gazed at the photographs on the mantel, but didn't have the heart to ask her mother to name the young people in the group shot taken aboard the *Maraschino*. She didn't want Agnes to know how much was missing from her memory. If it hadn't been for the photo of the boat's christening, she wouldn't have remembered its name, either.

The girl with red hair was obviously Sonja, but looking at her now was like looking at a complete stranger. She might as well have been the girl Emily and Geoffrey met on the dock that day.

Her father sank into a chair and popped open a beer, even though it was only ten thirty in the morning. "Hell, I'm still paying off that casket. I don't want to tell you how much that set me back." He shook a finger at her. "But twelve thousand dollars is a lot of money."

"Bernard. That isn't nice. Our baby has been brought back to us, and we should be rejoicing, not bickering." She wrapped her arms around Emily and kissed her cheek. "How's your arm, dear? Would you like something for it?"

"I'm fine," she lied. Her tension had grown tighter since waking up this morning and finding her father in his usual sour mood, griping at her mother in his usual fashion. It brought a dull pain that throbbed simultaneously in her head and arm.

Emily went to the guest room and picked up the phone. She dialed her bank and was surprised that she not only remembered the toll-free number, but her account number and her passwords, and the key strokes to move from one account to the other. She also remembered the balance in her savings account precisely.

She'd been saving the money for almost eight years, since graduating from high school and starting full time at Northwest Expeditions when her father still owned it and the *Maraschino*. The money had been for her honeymoon with Colin. They were going to sail Graham's thirty-five-foot gaff cutter, *Tigger Too*, down the coast and through the Panama Canal, across the northern coast of South America and up the chain of Caribbean islands.

Emily glanced down at Geoffrey's ring on her finger. Sudden longing for him made the spike in her gut dig deeper.

She now remembered the day she'd ridden in the back of the convertible.

It had been the day after senior prom. Colin had been her date, and they had been voted Prom King and Queen. She'd followed him up on the stage to be crowned, and right there in front of the whole school, Colin had knelt before her, presented his ring, and proposed.

It had been like a fairytale. They'd stayed up all night, she and Colin, Sonja and Joe, and Jessica and Tim. Though the others' faces were still hidden by shadows, she remembered the night perfectly. They ended up at the beach at Juniper Point, and each couple went their separate ways. She and Colin had made love on the beach to the sound of crashing waves.

The sun had risen at their backs as they sat on the beach, painting the offshore clouds with an amazing kaleidoscope of colors. When the others found them again, hunger drove them in to town for breakfast at Trudy's Café, still wearing their prom clothes. The six of them piled into Joe's Maverick convertible, she in the back seat beside Colin, with her arm on the side of the car, watching the diamond dazzle in the morning sun.

It had been the most magical time of her life, and Geoffrey had tried to help her find it.

Dear, sweet Geoffrey. The agony of missing him suddenly turned excruciating.

She went back to the kitchen and found her mother making her famous homemade chicken soup.

"I'm going back to Newport," she announced.

Her father didn't look up from the television. His favorite team was losing, and his mood had darkened.

"So soon?" Agnes pouted, but was clearly hesitant to start with her usual regimen of guilt-associated ultimatums. Only her father seemed more like himself, though even he was treating her as if she were made of glass.

This isn't how things used to be, Emily realized dimly. *They're only treating me carefully because they thought I'd died.*

Geoffrey had treated her like a queen from the start.

The cell phone she'd found stashed in Cherry Pit's glove compartment the night before was nearly done charging.

She retrieved her checkbook from her purse and sat down at the kitchen table to write out checks for some of the bills her parents had collected. She didn't have many, but would need to continue her car insurance and cell phone service.

Without telling them what she was doing, she wrote out a check for twelve thousand dollars to pay her father back for the casket. It nearly tapped out her savings, but she felt she owed him that much, and at least this way she wouldn't have to put up with his complaining.

"I have to," she told Agnes. She slipped the larger check in the middle of the stack and rose to kiss her mother on the cheek. "It's important."

◆ ◆ ◆

The drive back from Portland had been hellacious. A turned-over big-rig held up traffic for an hour and a half. When Geoffrey finally arrived home, it was to a dark house, all the outside lights turned off. Somebody had messed with the switch and the motion sensor light over the entry was deactivated. He bumped his shin painfully on the potted jade near the front door.

Inside, a messy kitchen greeted him. Derek ignored him from the living room, bathed in flashing, multicolored lights as he watched music videos from a floor pillow in the middle of the room with the set's headphones.

Thank God for small miracles.

Geoffrey idly flipped through the mail as he loosened his tie. All junk. With Christmas two months away, the catalogs were piling up. His foul mood soured.

The doorbell rang. Derek didn't move.

"Sure, I'll get it. Wouldn't want you to strain yourself," Geoffrey muttered. His mood had steadily plummeted since August—*Emily* had left.

He frowned as he saw the red Honda through the

window by the door. Who would be visiting at this hour? He pulled the door open.

"Emily."

"Hi."

She stepped through the threshold and he moved back to allow her in. "I needed to see you."

The first hints of alarm raced through him. Was she coming to return his ring?

She must have read the dumbfounded look on his face. "I still don't know what I'm going to do," she said quickly. Her eyes held a tint of worry she tried to hide behind a timid smile.

She stepped close and placed her hand on his chest. "But I know I want to be with you now."

"Of course." Just having her near had made the day's tension drain away.

"Can I stay here tonight?" She looked up, her eyes wide and innocent. "With you?"

"Sure." Like dawn rising after a cold night, he warmed from head to toe as he grasped her meaning. "Oh—um, yeah."

She leaned in, rose onto her tiptoes, and kissed him.

Instinctively, his arms went around her back. His heart kicked in his chest, leaping with joy but at the same time, seizing with pain. He would eagerly accept whatever she offered. A touch, a kiss. A minute or a lifetime. Or only a single night.

When her kiss slipped away and she settled on her heels, he grabbed her hand where it rested on his chest. She still wore his engagement ring on the other.

"I haven't decided what I'm going to do," she said again. "I can't make you any promises."

He didn't need promises; he needed this moment,

right now. If that was all she could give him, it would have to be enough.

That was a lie. A single night would be more painful than nothing at all, but he would never turn her away.

He scooped her up and carried her down the hall to his bedroom. Geoffrey laid her down across his bed and stood back to look at her. "Emily, are you sure?"

She reached for him. "Absolutely."

He perched on the edge of the bed, and she sat up and slipped her arm around his shoulders.

"Kiss me," she said. "Love me."

God, didn't she know he did? His lips found hers, and he drank in her scent, her taste, and the feel of her against him. How could he ever live without this?

Don't think about that. Just concentrate on the here and now.

She smiled. "You taste sweet."

"Chai tea latte on the way home from Portland."

She grasped his tie and slid her fingers through the buttons of his shirt. Geoffrey leaned away only to pry open the knot and shrug out of his shirt. He rose and kicked the door shut, locked it, but didn't bother to turn on the light. The rising moon shining through the window sheers illuminated the room just enough.

No, it wasn't enough. He wanted to see her. He used a fireplace match to light the decorative candle arrangement on the mantel. As the room filled with soft golden light, he made a mental note to tell Leah last year's Christmas gift wasn't frilly, after all.

Emily released the Velcro and removed her sling. "Can you help me with this?" She swung her knees over the side and sat up to remove her clingy knitted tee. She pulled it over her head to reveal a black lace bra, and eased her right arm free. "Stretch it over my cast."

For a moment he could only stand there, gazing at her. God, she was so beautiful. Her skin was like creamy milk, the lush curves of her body smooth and toned. Her breasts were generous, her stomach flat with lean lines.

He wrenched his feet from the floor where they seemed to have taken root, and knelt before her.

While she supported her arm at the elbow, Geoffrey gently stretched the sleeve and pulled it over her cast. She kicked her sneakers off and leaned back on the bed. With her good hand, she pulled her hair from beneath her neck. It fanned out across his pillow in shining gold ribbons.

She was the most gorgeous vision he'd ever seen, pure and real, lying there in nothing but that lacey bra and a pair of frayed Levi's jeans faded nearly white.

She sat up again, and started working the button on his pants.

"God, August," he said when she finally released them and pushed them over his hips. Too late, he realized his mistake. "Sorry."

"It's okay. Call me that if you like."

He moaned when she pulled on his boxers, tugging them over an embarrassingly high tent in the front. She took his hand, urging him down with her as she leaned back. In one fluid movement, he kicked off his loafers and the tangle of clothing swirling at his ankles.

And then skin came against skin in a glorious explosion of sensation, their bodies burning hot in comparison to the cool silk of the coverlet beneath them.

He held himself above her on one elbow as he brushed across her cheekbone with his thumb.

"Touch me," she told him.

He did: gladly, determinedly, desperately. She was more beautiful than he'd imagined, with hair like beams of moonlight, and skin as soft as rose petals. He would have liked to thrust himself inside her and close his eyes to lose himself forever, but a tiny nagging voice reminded him this might be the one and only time they would be together.

Make this last, fool, that voice told him. He was equally content to kiss a path across every inch of her, over the mounds and into the hollows, committing her to memory. He explored every bump and ridge as he made his way down her neck, across her throat, over her collarbone and between her breasts.

Would she regret this later? A selfish part of him didn't care, but he glanced into her eyes anyway, just to be sure. Hers held a dreamy pleasure, and he knew she had no second thoughts.

"Emily," he whispered.

"Love me," she said.

He did.

The rest of the world disappeared and it was only them, joined in the most primal and intimate way possible, moving with each other in simple, beautiful harmony.

◆ ◆ ◆

He awoke in the middle of the night to find her leaned up on her good arm, her cast balanced on the opposite hip as she stared down at him.

"Hi," she whispered. The nearly burnt candle tossed amber light over the curves of her body.

After the first time they'd made love, he'd risen, walked around the bed to look at her beautiful nakedness from all angles, and then pulled the blankets down so they could nest under the covers. The heat of their two bodies had become too much, and sometime later they'd kicked them off.

She'd straddled him, and he'd held her hand with one of his and balanced her cast with the other. He'd never imagined how erotic it could be to watch her love him this way. She'd gently lowered herself onto him, controlling every movement and sensation. He'd been content to lie back and let her take him on a slow, languid journey toward incomprehensible pleasure.

"Hi," he said back. When her stomach rumbled, he realized he hadn't eaten, either. "Hungry?"

"Hmmm, a little."

"Did you eat dinner?"

She shook her head. "I drove straight here without stopping."

"Gran's coffee cake is in the refrigerator."

She smiled, her eyes twinkling in the wan light. "Don't tempt me."

He wanted to tempt her, and so much more. He rose and padded to the dresser to retrieve a pair of silk pajamas. He slipped into the lower half, and then helped her into the top. After easing the wide sleeve carefully over her cast, he pulled the top over her head, and then hauled her close and kissed her deeply.

"Do you need your sling?"

She shook her head. "I'll be okay without it for a while."

He held her for a long moment, looking into her eyes. She stared up at him with that same, dreamy look. Was she thinking about a future here? Lord, if he only knew what he could say or do to help her choose to stay.

Before he could stop his thoughts, he wondered how she'd convinced that rambunctious young man to let her out of his sight.

"Does...Colin know you're here?" *Idiot, you always know the right thing to say.*

Her expression sobered ever so slightly. "He doesn't need to know." She grasped his hand, lacing her fingers within his. "What goes on between you and me doesn't concern him."

He didn't ask how long she would stay. He didn't want to know the answer. *Just enjoy what you have.*

They walked hand in hand through the dark house to the kitchen. The living room was still glowing blue. Peering in, they saw Derek sprawled across a floor pillow, snoring. A circle of saliva stained the fabric.

"Shhh." Geoffrey pulled her toward the foyer to go around the other way.

Emily stopped him and pointed. "Look."

An empty pint-sized bottle stuck out from under the edge of the pillow. Geoffrey shook his head, determined to ignore it.

But when he looked back at Emily, she was smiling wickedly. She crooked a finger at him to follow. Once in the kitchen, she retrieved a pen from the oversized coffee mug by the phone. "There's more than one way to teach someone a lesson." She removed its cap and pantomimed a curly mustache below her nose.

He grinned and took the pen. Her eyebrows crept up as Emily retrieved a permanent marker from the mug and offered it to him instead.

"You've got a mischievous streak."

"Do you like it?"

"I do." He pulled her close and kissed her. "But I

won't do anything that might keep him from taking that modeling job back in New York."

Emily shrugged and slotted the permanent marker back into the coffee mug.

They tiptoed back into the living room and ever so slowly, Geoffrey drew a Dick Dastardly mustache under Derek's nose.

"There. Now he's Derek Dastardly."

Emily covered her mouth to keep from laughing.

Derek was clearly out for the count, so they didn't bother being quiet as they went back to the kitchen. Geoffrey poured them each a glass of orange juice and served a single, giant slice of coffee cake onto a plate. Between bites, he fed Emily small mouthfuls, enjoying the way she delicately closed her lips over the fork each time.

He remembered how pale and sad she'd looked when he first saw her in the hospital, and how even then she'd been remarkably beautiful. Now, with her health and happiness restored, she positively glowed with vitality, exactly like he knew she would that first day.

She remembered her past, yet she's here with me. Geoffrey knew only of the determined young man who wanted her as his wife; yet he, and whatever else waited for her in her past, was not enough to convince her away.

She's here with me, he thought in awe. *Me, the football captain's brother.* It was amazing, miraculous and wonderful.

But would she stay?

◆　◆　◆

Morning sickness forced her out of bed before the

sun was up. A hot shower always made it better. Since she was dressed by six a.m., she decided to make another pass at the beach house.

Emily's car still sat next to Barthlow's gargantuan SUV. A sheen of dew pebbled the windshield. Now that the little bitch remembered who she was and where she lived, there could only be one reason she was here.

"And I'll bet it wasn't to stay in the guest room."

Emily was probably playing them both. *Tramp*. A bitch doesn't change her stripes.

Colin deserved better. Hell, Geoffrey deserved better, but she didn't give a shit about him.

Yesterday afternoon, she'd been relieved and excited to follow Emily back to Newport. Her choice to return to Geoffrey meant Colin might be free after all.

But after a wretched night spent puking up her dinner in the cheap hotel downtown, her mood was foul. She understood it didn't matter who Emily chose. Gone didn't mean forgotten. If the slut hadn't already remembered what happened on the boat, she would soon.

No, it was time to finish what was started the night of the storm.

Emily had to die.

◆ ◆ ◆

Emily quietly pulled the front door closed and breathed in the cold, moist air. The morning was blanketed in fog and the air held the coming chill of winter. On the other side of the house, the ocean crashed against the beach in its never-ending surge and pull.

It was wonderful here, but it was wonderful in Astoria, too. Colin had been her whole life, and there was sweet comfort in the familiar. Geoffrey was a magnificent new discovery, and there was brilliance in new love.

She hadn't slept at all, but the drowsy fatigue from a night of making love felt wonderful. After sharing the coffee cake, they'd returned to bed and made love a fourth time so slowly and tenderly it hadn't been so much an act, but a passage of time spent as one. Geoffrey was a fantastic, tender, and generous lover, whereas Colin could be called...energetic.

Last night had been beautiful, and she wouldn't take it back for the world, but it had not been fair to Geoffrey. What would happen to him if she chose Colin?

Emily now knew she could find her way in a new world, but did she want to? There was something deeply reassuring about familiarity, especially since she'd come so precariously close to losing it. But there was also something magical in new discoveries, and embarking on the unknown.

How could she ever choose between them? She loved them both so powerfully, and couldn't imagine being without either of them.

She started her car, ran the wipers once across the windshield, and pulled onto the narrow street leading to the highway. Once up on the crest above the house, she looked out over the water. In some places, she could see the frothy waves creeping over the sand, but on others, the ocean was completely obscured by the fog.

Colin hated sailing in weather like this, but it had always excited her. The day she'd passed her United States Coast Guard rating for stellar seamanship, the weather had been thick with fog like this. She now remembered that day, and how she'd handled the boat with confidence as the Coast Guard agent watched.

She thought back to the town she and Geoffrey had driven through and how she'd wondered if she came from a fishing family, or a mining family. In the early years when she helped out her dad, she had enjoyed herself, and later it had become her job, but she had never actually chosen seamanship for her future. It had gone unsaid, but been expected, that she would step into the family business.

Maybe she didn't need to make a choice now. Maybe this was time she deserved to claim for herself. She'd nearly died—she had the right to be a little selfish. She'd always flirted with the fantasy of attending culinary school. Maybe now was the time.

But she couldn't do that to Colin or Geoffrey. She was deeply embedded in both their lives, and they deserved an answer.

She pulled Cherry Pit into a front parking spot at the Mirthful Mermaid, and then realized it wasn't even eight a.m. The only other car there was the van driven by the owner of the hardware store next door.

She heard spraying water in the alley. Jose was hosing down the garbage cans.

"Good morning, Jose. Is Millie up yet?"

Jose looked up and smiled. "Oh, hello, Miss August. She gone to Woodland for farmers market. You want to go inside? The door is open here." He gestured to the side door.

Although a cup of hot coffee was almost too good to pass up, so was the first foggy morning of fall. "I think I'll go sit on the pier for a while. If Millie comes back, tell her I'll be back in about an hour."

She trotted across the deserted highway to the

marina. Cloaked in the haze, the foghorn rolled its deep call, and the harbor buoy's bell rang on the gently rolling waves.

She walked slowly down the path to pier fifteen and entered Geoffrey's code in the electronic keypad. Before she could finish, the gate eased open under the pressure of her fingers. There was something wrong with the lock.

Emily sat on the end of the pier beside *Penny Lane*'s slip. The fog had completely swallowed Yaquina Bay Bridge. Somewhere in the misty haze, screeching gulls followed the steadily louder hum of a returning boat. She smiled to herself. The gulls, and the early return, meant they'd had a good catch.

She stared into the fog and let the gentle swells of the glossy water soothe her mind.

Deciding between Colin and Geoffrey would be impossible. Not because she couldn't choose, but because she couldn't bring herself to hurt either of them by choosing the other.

She wished she'd never gone overboard, never found herself in Newport, never even gone out that day on the charter. Her life would be so much easier if none of this had ever happened.

As soon as she had the thought, her stomach clenched with regret. She couldn't bear to wish she'd never met Geoffrey. He was a wonderful man, and her life was richer for having known him. She loved him, pure and simple. Nothing could ever take that away.

Quick, light footsteps sounded on the pier behind her. For a fleeting moment, she thought it was Gran Millie.

A svelte silhouette emerged through the mist,

slowly taking on color. The figure was familiar, and Emily shivered under a blast of icy fear.

She stood and faced the raven-haired woman. Thick, oily terror slid into the pit of her stomach.

"Chelsie."

"Remember me, do you?" One hand was pushed under the lapel of her denim jacket, hiding something.

Emily sidled to the left, every molecule in her body screaming at her to run.

"Not so fast." Chelsie thrust her hand forward. Her fist wrapped around the thick black handle of a hunting knife, its silver blade gleaming in the wan light. "You've been a hard woman to get a moment alone with, Emily."

Chapter Twenty-Five

The sound of a car door slamming brought him from the edge of sleep. When the engine started and it pulled away, he understood. He was alone.

Emily was gone.

Had he pressured her last night? He hadn't said anything about her staying. Maybe that was it—she thought now he didn't want her to?

No, how could she possibly think that after last night? She had to know how he felt about her after the way he'd held her and touched her. Made love to her like there was nothing in this universe but the two of them.

Was it possible he'd been too needy? He wished he'd told her there was no pressure, that she had as much time as she needed to make her decision, even while in his heart he wouldn't have meant it. He was only human, and that selfish niggling deep inside his gut could be silenced and ignored, but never truly eradicated. He wanted her for himself, dammit!

But even though that selfish part existed, he couldn't let it rule him. He had to explain.

Geoffrey rose and took a quick, cold shower. The frigid water helped clear his mind and wash away any fanciful feelings. He could be all business, and let his head do the talking while his heart waited in the sidelines.

Derek was still unconscious in the living room. Void of sympathy for his self-induced illness, Geoffrey happily ran the coffee grinder. He heard his brother grumble awake as he started the coffee maker.

"What time is it?" Derek croaked from the living room. He appeared at the steps to the kitchen, his hair tousled and his eyes bloodshot.

Geoffrey nearly laughed out loud at the sight of what he and Emily had done last night. Derek sat down at the kitchen table, smacking away the dryness in his mouth and looking utterly hilarious with that drawn-on curly-cue mustache.

The sight only made him ache more painfully for Emily. She was an enchantress he couldn't exist without.

"You were up late," he commented with a forced straight face. "What'd you watch?"

Derek shrugged. "Junk. Is that coffee ready yet?"

The pot was almost full. "I'll get you a cup," Geoffrey said cheerfully. He poured them each a steaming mug and watched Derek pad off to his room at the back of the house.

After only two mouthfuls, Geoffrey grabbed his keys and started toward the front door. Emily would be at the Mirthful Mermaid. He had to explain that he would give her whatever time she needed.

Derek's perturbed voice rang through the house. "What the—awww, man!"

Geoffrey laughed to himself as he stepped out into the misty morning. It felt good to have Derek more frustrated than him for once. Maybe he should have taken the permanent pen Emily offered, after all.

◆ ◆ ◆

Emily swallowed past the burning fear caught in her throat. "How did you find me?"

She was afraid to ask what Chelsie wanted, afraid to even look directly at the knife, afraid to acknowledge it in any way. *Ignore it, and maybe she'll change her mind and put it away.*

Unlikely.

"It wasn't easy." Chelsie's beautiful black hair swirled around her shoulders, rippling with the jerk of her arm as she thrust the knife forward. "They'd listed you as a traffic accident victim. A hacker I know gave me every drowning and Jane Doe record in Washington, Oregon, and California. I almost didn't come down here to check it out, but the Newport police were so secretive about your file, I knew something was strange. And low and behold, here you are."

Emily forced away the choking fear. "What do you want?"

Chelsie advanced, urging Emily toward the other side of the pier. "Get on the boat. Your new boyfriend won't mind."

How did she know it was Geoffrey's boat? Emily's mind whirled with confusion as she shuffled sideways, her gaze never leaving Chelsie's.

Chelsie glanced once over her shoulder. "Hurry it up!" She lunged forward, urging Emily on with threatening jabs. Once Emily mounted the dock step, Chelsie knelt and unraveled the mooring lines from their cleats.

"You just have to bat your little eyelashes and they come drooling at your heels, don't they?"

What was she talking about? Chelsie looked different than Emily had ever seen her. There was something in her eyes, something dark she'd never noticed before.

"What do you want, Chelsie?" she asked again, louder this time.

Chelsie stepped up onto *Penny Lane*'s deck, that knife thrust out the whole time. "Shout like that again, and I'll cut your tongue out. Now get down in the cabin. We're going for a little ride, you and me."

Chelsie shoved her when she was on the ladder, sending Emily staggering to her knees onto the small cabin's floor.

"The keys are in that drawer. Get up. I didn't push you that hard."

"Chelsie, whatever you want, we can talk this through—"

"Shut up! We're going to talk, all right. I just want to be sure we don't get interrupted."

"We can't take this boat out of the harbor!"

"Sure we can." Chelsie narrowed her eyes. "Keys are right there, in that drawer. Easy now. Don't try anything, or I'll cut that pretty face to ribbons."

She waited as Emily opened the drawer and retrieved the motor key. Geoffrey used a banana slug, the buoyant, yellow key fob that kept a sailor's keys from sinking if they fell in the water. Chelsie had obviously been in the boat before, and the key fob identified the motor key at first glance.

"Let's go. Up top."

Emily put the keys in her left hand and used her right to hold the ladder's rail on the way back up. Her mind raced with the possibilities. The night on the *Maraschino* was still murky, but now she remembered red-haired Sonja.

I'm pregnant...I'm pregnant.

Think! What else happened?

"Was it you in the beach house that morning?"

Chelsie laughed. "Start the motor." She kept a steely eye on Emily as she released the ropes from the deck cleats on *Penny Lane*'s starboard side. "Take us out."

"Chelsie, no, this is crazy—"

Chelsie's eyes blazed. She surged forward and lashed out, nicking Emily on the side of her jaw with the tip of the blade.

"Don't you dare talk to me like that! I've put up with your sanctimonious bullshit for long enough."

Emily winced and staggered back, but Chelsie gripped a fistful of her shirt and yanked her back to the wheel.

"Okay! Okay, Chelsie, take it easy."

Emily searched the pier, but no one else was around. Surely there must be people who lived on their boats. If she screamed, could someone get to her in time? Would anyone even hear? Or would it anger Chelsie into slashing her with the knife?

"I see you remember how to sail," Chelsie said as Emily backed *Penny Lane* out of the slip. "What else do you remember that you aren't telling me?"

"I don't know what you mean." Emily clawed at her memory. What had happened that stormy day on *Maraschino's* deck?

She had little time to remember. Chelsie stepped forward and reversed the throttle for her, and then gave the wheel a spin. *Penny Lane* started a slow trail out of the marina.

A sudden squall, pouring rain, waves topped with white caps. Seven seasick passengers, all of whom had drunk too much and loitered too long on Hutchison's Island. They were scared, nauseated, full of regret. But there was no danger; Maraschino could hold her own in a storm twice as fierce...

◆　◆　◆

Indecision rolled through Geoffrey as he drove, and he nearly turned around a dozen times. If she wanted to be alone, why was he crowding her?

He just wanted to explain that he *wouldn't* crowd her, and then he'd go home and find some cold cream to help Derek wash the ink off his face. He smiled again as he thought of that mustache.

He pulled his SUV into the Mermaid's lot and parked beside Emily's red Honda. He stepped out into the brisk morning and tried the front door. It was locked. Maybe she'd gone to sleep? She certainly hadn't gotten much sleep last night.

He grinned like a fool at his own reflection in the glass. Neither of them had gotten much sleep. He stepped back and looked up at the small, second-floor window. Maybe she was taking a bath in Gran Millie's old claw foot?

This was a mistake. He should leave her alone if that was what she wanted. He turned back to the SUV.

"Where's Emily?"

He recognized the demanding voice before he saw the stocky young man emerge through the mist.

Colin. The guy was like a gnat you couldn't get rid of. He made no effort to conceal his anger.

"She left her parents' house yesterday, but she's not answering her cell phone."

Above his annoyance, a pleasantly warm vapor crept over Geoffrey. Emily had turned off her phone so they wouldn't be disturbed.

"Was she with you last night?" Colin advanced steadily, trying to be intimidating. Geoffrey stood his ground, and the other man stopped a few paces away.

"You need to ask Emily where she stayed last night. If she wants you to know, she'll tell you."

"Why can't you back off, man? She's confused and you're making it worse."

Geoffrey said nothing.

Colin balled his hands into fists. "You're setting yourself up for a fall. Take the easy way out, dude. Trust me on that. You think you're the first guy to come sniffing around with an eye for Emily? There've been others, plenty others, but it's me she always stays with."

"If you're so confident, why are you here?"

Colin scowled and glanced away. Geoffrey could see he was teetering between worry and fury.

"It isn't the same this time. She was hurt, and still doesn't really know what happened—"

"What *did* happen, Colin?" Geoffrey advanced a step. "Why was she arguing with her best friend?"

Colin wouldn't meet his eyes. "I don't know."

"I don't believe you."

That got the other man's attention.

"You might as well come clean. She's going to remember, sooner or later."

Colin's scowl deepened. "Did you stop to think about what you're doing to Emily? Of what she's going through with you messing with her head?" He pointed a finger accusingly. "Just because you're rich doesn't mean you can give her a better life. She doesn't need to live in a glass house, she likes the life she had. Things were good in Astoria before she met you. The most expensive truck on the planet and a bigger diamond doesn't mean you're the better man for her."

Colin advanced, turning his jabbing finger to his own chest as he spoke. "I'm the one who stood by her after her old man started drinking. I'm the one who gave her the life she wants. Northern Expeditions was her family's before my father bought it, and it'll be hers again when we get married."

Geoffrey refused to be intimidated by an arrogant kid with a hot temper. Colin was burly, but he was too, and taller by at least four inches. "All right, I'll make you a deal. You look me straight in the eye and tell me everything was perfect with your relationship, and I'll step down." His heart leaped with his daring.

Colin's eyes narrowed and he stared hard for a long minute. Then he glanced away, a muscle working in his jaw.

"You wouldn't be here right now if there wasn't something in your past that might drive her away," Geoffrey continued before the other man could accept his foolish wager. "You're just hoping to convince her back to Astoria because you want me out of sight and out of mind. If there's one thing I've learned about Emily, she's smart. Do you really think she'd be happy to hear you're interfering with her decision?"

"You don't know what you're talking about. There's nothing."

"I think I do. In fact, I'll bet it's probably something you did, and you want to keep her from finding—"

Geoffrey froze. He stepped past Colin, staring through the fog. A small sloop with familiar lines motored slowly out of the marina. He strained to see the spot where *Penny Lane* was usually visible from the

Mirthful Mermaid's doorway, past the edge of the marina's cinderblock restrooms. He couldn't be sure, but the slip beside his neighbor's *Yankawa Express* looked empty.

"Oh no."

"What is it?" Colin's voice held a hint of alarm, as though he knew Geoffrey's trepidation concerned Emily.

He was right.

"My boat is leaving the marina."

◆　◆　◆

"Nice place your boyfriend's got. Were you going to string him along forever, like you've done to Colin all these years?"

"It *was* you that day."

"And it was me in the alley that night, too."

"Why, Chelsie?"

Why? Why, why, why...think, dammit! What happened between them that was so horrible Chelsie wanted to kill her?

In an instant, one thing was clear; she hadn't been afraid of the red-haired woman—Sonja—she'd been aghast. A glimpse of that night on *Maraschino* flashed through her mind.

"Why do you think?" Chelsie snapped, dragging her away from the memory she fought to reclaim.

"Colin?"

"Of course, Colin," Chelsie hissed. "It's always been Colin."

Colin! But how? When? Was it something so horrible she would never remember?

"*...Emily, help Sonja bring in the storm sail and batten 'er down. We'll motor the rest of the way. These kids are too sick for half-reefed sails. And could you* secure that loose winch? I should've had that thing fixed weeks ago."

"Sure, Graham. You've just got to be gentle with it. Let me get my lifejacket."

She'd gone up on deck. Joe was forward, Sonja at the mizzen. Her longtime friend looked up and saw her. She hesitated, tormented contemplation on her face, before she changed her mind and edged closer on the slippery deck.

"We need to talk."

"Sonja, what's been eating you these past few days?"

"I think you know."

"I don't. But I'm sick of this. Just say it, or get over it."

"I'm pregnant. It's Colin's. We were together the night of the Spring Fling."

Emily closed her eyes. Molten anguish flooded her gut as she relived it, exactly as it had that stormy afternoon on *Maraschino*. Sonja was pregnant, and the baby was Colin's.

Sonja, water streaming down her face, her red hair in soaking wet strands. "You don't want to marry him. If you did, you wouldn't have refused to set a date all these years. Let him go, so he can do right by this baby."

Emily hadn't known what to say.

"You don't love him, don't need him. Do the right thing and bow out."

The memory suddenly came clear. At that moment on deck, with the sea tossing and the sky growling, Emily had realized she knew exactly when Colin and Sonja had gone off together at Spring Fling.

"You wretched bitch. How could you do that to me? You're my best friend. And you're wrong, I do love him. But you can have him. You two deserve each other."

"*Emily, we didn't mean to—*"

"*Spare me the excuses. 2We didn't mean to.' Do you think I'm stupid?*"

"*I never wanted to hurt you.*"

"*Get out of my sight. I never want to see either of you again.*"

Emily stared into the milky whiteness in front of *Penny Lane* with unseeing eyes. She had taken off her engagement ring and dropped it in the electronics compartment. Warm drops mixed with the cold rain on her face as her tears gushed. She remembered wiping them away with the back of her hand, ashamed. Colin and Sonja had played her for a fool.

"Nice try." Chelsie shoved her aside. She adjusted the wheel and *Penny Lane* glided out of the path of a harbor buoy.

"You really don't remember, do you?"

Poor Sonja. Desperate, alone, pregnant. In the face of peril, Emily's anger toward her best friend suddenly vanished. None of that mattered now that she was staring down the pointed end of a hunting knife. She would never get the chance to tell her best friend she forgave her.

"You know they blamed Sonja, but the police didn't have anything to hold her on. Not yet, anyway."

She knew that much from what Colin had told her, only now she understood why he had believed Sonja responsible so intently.

Chelsie's words echoed in her mind and their deadly intent rang clear. *Not yet, anyway.*

Emily caught her breath as she steadied herself on *Penny Lane*'s lifeline. "What do you mean?"

"If you don't remember what happened..." Chelsie

looked her up and down with surprised disbelief. "And you clearly don't...then you haven't told anyone she didn't push you."

Emily swallowed. "I do remember. I told Geoffrey."

Chelsie laughed. "You always were a lousy liar."

"What are you going to do?" Emily finally found the courage to ask the question. She needed to know what was planned for her. It was obvious, but she wanted to hear Chelsie say it.

"I'm going to finish what I started that night, of course. You were supposed to drown."

Emily gasped and backed away. The backs of her knees collided with the low roof to the main cabin. There was no place to run, no place to hide. *Penny Lane*'s small dinghy was secured astern. Even if she could get to it, she'd never get it down with only one hand, and certainly not with a crazed slasher hot on her heels.

Chelsie only laughed. "Going to make it easy for me and jump?" She took a plastic ziplock baggie from her pocket and unsealed it. "This time they'll have the evidence they need to send Sonja away."

Emily watched in horror as she removed a small clump of red hair and jammed it into the crevasse under a bolt on the compass. Sonja's hair.

"She's pregnant, you know," Emily said. If she could convince Chelsie that Sonja was her biggest problem, she might let her go.

Chelsie seemed unimpressed. "Thanks to you, everyone knows that."

"You can't keep her from Colin if she's going to have his baby."

"Not for long, she isn't."

The breath rushed from her lungs. Chelsie only laughed at the horror on her face.

"She's driving into Seattle this morning to see a prenatal paternity specialist for an appointment I was helpful enough to set up for her...at an office that doesn't exist." Chelsie grinned wickedly. "When she finally gets home, there'll be nobody to back up her claim that she wasn't here, drowning you. But before she even learns you've died, I'll wager she helps herself to a big glass of milk. Calcium is good for the baby, you know. As soon as she drinks from the carton in her refrigerator, she won't be pregnant for long."

"You're a monster," Emily screamed. "Why?"

Chelsie's eyes gleamed, lit with fury. "Because Sonja isn't the only one your darling fiancé knocked up, but I aim to be the last one standing. It's me and *my* baby Colin's going to end up with."

Chapter Twenty-Six

Jose opened the Mirthful Mermaid's door behind them. "You looking for Gran Millie?"

"Where's Emily?" Geoffrey demanded.

"Miss August? She go to marina."

Geoffrey set off at a sprint across the road and down the ice plant covered hill to the marina's sidewalk. Colin stayed with him the whole way. The gate to pier fifteen sat ajar on its frame. He didn't need to enter his code.

"Why would she take your boat out?" Colin asked.

"She wouldn't. She couldn't, not alone."

He strained to see through the fog as he ran to the end of the pier. *Penny Lane*'s carved wooden nameplate disappeared into the fog-shrouded bay. He didn't need to read it to recognize his own boat, and the empty slip confirmed it beyond a doubt.

"There are two people on deck," Colin stated.

"I can see that," Geoffrey growled. As soon as he said it, *Penny Lane* was swallowed in the mist. Like a mournful farewell, the hum of her motor faded to nothingness.

Geoffrey turned around and started back up the pier. He took out his cell phone and dialed 911. "I need Coast Guard emergency services, fast."

He nearly barreled over Trenton Farwell on the

way up the steep ramp to the gate.

"Whoa, Geoffrey, where's the fire?"

The Coast Guard put him on hold. "Trenton, I need to borrow your boat. It's an emergency."

"Sure, sure thing. What's going on?"

Colin stomped up the pier behind him. "I'm going with you."

Geoffrey ignored him. There was no point arguing with him. "Emily may have been kidnapped."

"That cute little blond? I thought her name was—"

"Trent, we need to go now!"

Trenton was pushing eighty, but he kept pace with Geoffrey as they ran to gate nine. He leaped onto his boat as Geoffrey untied the lines port side and Colin unfastened starboard.

Feeling their urgency, Trenton wasted no time. His restored Seahawk roared to life. The old man reversed out of his slip and throttled out of the harbor at illegal speed, rocking sleeping boats with his wake.

"Is it this Sonja girl?" Geoffrey demanded as he settled into a seat across from Colin.

He shook his head, running his fingers through his hair. "I don't know how it could be. Her car was still in the driveway when I drove past her house before five this morning."

Coast Guard services finally greeted him on the line.

"This is an emergency," Geoffrey told them. "We have a small craft lost in a whiteout outside Newport Bay with a possible hostage situation on board." Jesus, it sounded like a low-budget TV movie.

"The nearest cutter is assisting a trawler run aground a few miles north," the operator responded.

He already knew air rescue couldn't do a thing in

this fog. "This is an emergency. A woman's life is at stake."

"We've got men in the water, sir. They'll be en route as soon as they can."

◆ ◆ ◆

"Cut the motor." Chelsie switched the knife to her left hand and flexed the fingers of her right.

"You'll never get away with this. You'll be caught, and you'll go to jail." Emily's teeth chattered with cold and fear. She didn't turn the motor off, hoping to distract her. The longer it ran, the more chances someone would hear it and find them. "They won't let you keep your baby in jail, Chelsie."

"Shut up! You stupid bitch, I'm sick of your superior attitude. You don't know anything."

"You still have the chance to change that, if you stop now."

Chelsie's expression remained stony. Emily's efforts weren't working.

"Nobody suspects me now, and nobody ever will. It's Sonja they'll lock up."

Emily closed her eyes. It was true; she'd told Geoffrey so many times it was a red-haired woman she suspected. She would die and poor Sonja would go to jail. And Colin would fall into Chelsie's trap. She would snare him, and he'd live out the rest of his life with a killer.

Regret crushed like a lead weight on her shoulders, but one thought soared above all the others: she would never see sweet Geoffrey again. Never tell him she loved him. Never get the chance to tell him she would have loved to marry him, make a little cousin for Jocelyn with him. Never look at his smiling face again, never receive his magical kisses again.

Her death would be too much for him. He couldn't endure the tragic loss of a second love and survive as the wonderful, kind man he was. She couldn't bear for him to be hurt this way.

This couldn't be happening!

"What are you going to do, bring *Penny Lane* back in by yourself? Someone will see you."

Chelsie shook her head. "I'm taking the dinghy."

"Your fingerprints are all over this boat. They'll check everything. Geoffrey will make them. He's too smart to fall for your manufactured evidence."

Chelsie's eyes narrowed. "We'll see."

The sneer on her face cast Emily back to that stormy afternoon when clouds as thick and black as industrial smoke had blocked out the sun. *Maraschino* tossed so violently she'd had to grab the fife rail to stay on her feet. In her distress, she'd forgotten to anchor to the jack line. She turned around to secure herself.

Chelsie stood at the main mast, staring at her with narrowed eyes and bared teeth. Her lips moved, the words snatched away by the howling wind. But Emily could see what had been said.

Goodbye, bitch.

She opened her hand and Emily saw the main sheet slip through. A flash of white came at her from the right, no time to block it.

"You let the boom swing free." Emily gulped back the hurt that was almost as intense as her fear. How could her friend betray her like this? "You knocked me overboard."

A sarcastic smile equally hateful replaced Chelsie's vicious sneer. "Congratulations. But a little too late to tell anyone."

"All for Colin?"

Chelsie flipped the knife in her hand so she was fisting the handle and punched Emily hard in the mouth.

She fell backward, across the low cabin roof and onto the narrow length of deck. Brilliant shards of ice splintered in her injured arm. One leg thrust out under the lifeline and she nearly went over.

The engine went silent. She looked up as Chelsie pulled the keys from the ignition and threw them into the water.

"You bitch!" she screamed through the sudden quiet. "You never appreciated him like you should have. You don't understand what it feels like to love him!"

Emily scrambled to her feet and backed away. Chelsie followed, the knife thrust out in front. Her eyes blazed with insane anger. "And you sure as hell don't know what it feels like to love someone who doesn't love you back."

The boat was small. Emily couldn't avoid her for long. "You think killing me will make him love you?" Her voice shook so badly she could hardly form coherent words.

"He'll never learn to love me with you around, even if I do have his baby," Chelsie spat back. "If you're dead and Sonja's in jail for killing you, he'll fall right into my arms." She laughed. "It's nothing personal, I just hate you."

"He'll never love you," Emily shouted back.

"Shut up!" Chelsie demanded. "Get in the water. I need to get back before this fog burns off."

"Chelsie, don't do this. You can stop this before you make the biggest mistake of your life!"

"Shut the hell up!" She jabbed with the knife. Emily continued backing away, around the bow and down the port side.

"I can swim back to shore. If you don't stop this now, I'll tell the authorities exactly what happened!"

Oh Geoffrey, if only I hadn't left you this morning! She longed to be in the safety of his arms, nestled comfortably in his warm embrace, buried under soft blankets. Instead, a cold, watery death waited.

She remembered the night when Geoffrey accepted his award and she'd first realized she'd fallen in love with him. She had suspected, even without her memory, that she had never loved another man the way she loved him.

She'd been right. Emily bit back a sob as she realized she would never see him again.

"Which way is shore, Emily? Swimming with that cast will be pretty tough. And this time, you're not wearing a lifejacket."

Somewhere in the fog, a speedboat approached. Chelsie glanced over her shoulder. It was the split second Emily needed. She wrenched open the cabin compartment and removed the flare gun. She looped the index finger of her left hand through the ring of the safety pin and wrenched the gun away with her right.

"Don't come any closer!"

Chelsie's eyes went wide as Emily pointed the flare gun at her.

The speedboat's roar faded to a dull hum. Emily's heart sank.

"You won't shoot me."

"Why wouldn't I?" Emily tried to sound resolute, but her voice still quavered. The truth was she would never be able to pull the trigger.

Voices carried through the fog—it was Geoffrey and Colin, and they were shouting for her!

"Over here!" she screamed.

Chelsie belted out an inhuman shriek. She threw the knife aside and lunged for Emily. Chelsie grabbed her wrist and forced it up as the flare gun went off. Chelsie crashed into her with the full weight of her body, and Emily's second shout for help was cut short as the breath was kicked from her lungs.

Ocean and sky twisted in a blur as they went overboard.

Chapter Twenty-Seven

Cold water closed over her head and the thunder of bubbles rushing to the surface was deafening. The frigid water instantly brought her senses alive.

I will get through this. Geoffrey is coming for me!

She kicked toward the surface, fighting against the sling still attached to her shoulder.

Out of nowhere, Chelsie came upon her, forcing her back down. Emily's lungs burned with the need for air. Chelsie had been a competitive swimmer in high school. Restrained by the body sling, Emily was as good as drowned.

She fought to the surface for a too-quick breath before Chelsie reared over her again, forcing her under. The crazed girl surged out of the water like a dolphin, heaving all her weight onto Emily's shoulders.

Panicked, Emily kicked, desperate for one more gulp of air. She managed to come above the surface in time to glimpse Chelsie's fury-filled face surging forward again. In the blurry distance, *Penny Lane* seemed miles away.

She tried to scream as she came above the surface again, but ended up with a mouthful of salty water that tumbled down her throat like a rock. Dark spots swam before her eyes as she choked underwater. Chelsie's kicking legs were closing fast.

Chelsie kicked above her and threw her weight onto Emily's shoulders again. Coherence slipped away and Emily wasn't sure which way was up.

Suddenly the Velcro tore free and her arm came free of the sling, but her vision was growing darker as her brain starved for oxygen. There was a pattern, she realized dimly. For every surge out of the water Chelsie managed, she then sank back under before she could kick back up again.

Emily kicked away, trying to get out from under the bigger girl. If Chelsie managed to get her balance above Emily's shoulders, there would be no escaping her.

She surged away, waiting through what seemed an eternity without air as Chelsie sank back under.

With the last of her strength, Emily kicked above the surface, drank in a beautiful mouthful of life-giving air, and fought against the pain to lift her arm above her head.

She slammed her cast against Chelsie's skull just as the girl came through the surface. There was a gurgled gulp and Chelsie disappeared back under. Emily brought her feet up and kicked out with the last remaining ounce of strength she possessed. Both feet hit something soft, and suddenly she was free, back paddling through the water. She drew in three, four, and five deep breaths. Air had never tasted so wonderful.

Penny Lane was far away and disappearing quickly in the mist. Emily's arm hurt like the devil, but she knew if she didn't make it back to the boat, she was as good as dead.

◆ ◆ ◆

Geoffrey's heart sank when he saw the empty deck of the drifting sailboat. The yellow key fob bobbed in the water nearby. Trenton angled the Seahawk around to the portside so they could board easily.

"Emily!"

The deck remained empty, no answering call from the boat.

Splashing called his attention. "Trent, there!"

Emily was in the water, dogpaddling awkwardly. She was struggling toward *Penny Lane* and didn't appear to see them.

Trent adjusted course and headed for her, reversing throttle perfectly to bring the Seahawk to a quick stop beside her, and then cut the motor.

"Colin!" She choked over a mouthful of water as she reached up.

Colin. Would it have hurt less if she'd simply punched him in the balls?

He and Colin leaned over the side and each took an arm. Emily cried out as Geoffrey pulled on her injured arm. A chunk of her cast came away in his hand. He released her and quickly grabbed the belt loop on her jeans. Soaking wet, she weighed nearly twice as much.

They hauled her on board and she collapsed on her knees. Colin maneuvered himself between them and gathered her into his arms.

"Jesus, Emily, I thought I'd lost you again."

Geoffrey backed away, feeling like an odd third wheel. It seemed the background would always be his place in life.

She burst into tears. "It was Chelsie! She's in the water."

Colin froze. "Chelsie?"

"Someone's in the water?" Trenton leaned over. He and Geoffrey scanned the glossy surface. It rippled gently, thick and silver like liquid mercury. The mournful wail of a seagull was the only sound in the deathly still morning.

Colin guided her to the Seahawk's rear seats and urged her to sit down. She was shivering, hugging her broken arm against her body. Geoffrey took off his jacket and draped it over her shoulders, and Colin pulled it closed around her.

"Geoffrey...I'm sorry." She looked up at him with shiny eyes, and his heart cracked in two.

"Don't apologize, Emily."

Colin dropped to his knees in front of her. "It's all right, Emily. You're safe now. Don't worry about a thing."

"You've got to call Sonja." Emily's voice, though soft, cut through the still morning. "Where's your phone?"

"What are you talking about?"

"Call Sonja now!" Emily burst into a fit of coughing. "Tell her not to drink the milk in her refrigerator. Chelsie's poisoned it."

When Colin brought his phone out, she snatched it from him and dialed. Trenton started the Seahawk's motor and throttled forward. They circled slowly, but there was no sign of anyone in the water.

"Bring us alongside *Penny Lane*," Geoffrey told him. "Maybe she got back on board."

"No!" Emily stopped dialing. "She's dangerous. She forced me onto the boat with a knife and I think she dropped it on deck before we fell into the water."

She brought the phone against her ear. "Sonja, it's Emily. Sonja? Are you there? Yes, I'm all right. No, Sonja, shhh."

Geoffrey leaned back against the front seat beside

Trenton. He felt so uncomfortable, he considered diving into the water himself. He could hear the voice buzzing through the phone. Sonja was sobbing.

"It's all right, everything is okay. Shhh, listen to me, Sonja. Don't drink the milk in your refrigerator. I'll explain later. Yes, go pour it out now, while we're on the phone, okay? No, honey, I'm fine. I'll be home soon. I love you, too. It's all over. It doesn't matter, just forget about all that. We'll be like we were before. Everything is going to be the way it was again."

That was all Geoffrey needed to know. She'd made her choice. She flipped the phone shut and stared up at Colin with wide eyes. Geoffrey turned around. She was in shock, and her true feelings were on her sleeve.

He had no doubt she truly cared for him and her decision had been difficult. But now, having faced another life-threatening event, whatever barrier in her mind that had prevented her from remembering her past—and deciding her future—had been broken.

"It was Chelsie," she said, rocking back and forth on the seat. "I remember now. She pulled the main sheet loose so the boom hit me and knocked me overboard. I saw her let it free." She covered her face with her good hand and cried. Colin sat on the edge of her seat and pulled her under his arm.

Geoffrey wanted to ask why this woman had tried to kill Emily, and he had a feeling Colin knew exactly why, but it was no longer his place to involve himself in Emily's life.

He turned around and helped Trenton scan the water. He didn't care to watch the other man tenderly embrace Emily. The soft sounds of her crying pulled at his heart, reminding him of what he'd lost.

A Coast Guard cutter slipped out of the fog and rumbled up beside them. "Did you call in an emergency?"

"There's a girl lost in the water," Trenton shouted across to the cutter. "Or she may be on board the sloop."

The harbor patrol drifted closer.

"She has a knife," Emily told them. "She was going to kill me."

The officers angled the cutter around so they could board *Penny Lane*. Two of them moved stealthily across her deck, guns drawn, and went below. They emerged a few moments later. "No one here," one of them called back.

Emily's features crumbled. "She's still in the water."

"Take me over to *Penny Lane*," Geoffrey told Trenton. "I'll bring her in." He had to get off this boat, and stop watching the two of them like the sorry loser of a reality TV show. *Most Pathetic Guy. Least Likely to Get the Girl.*

"You want someone to help you bring her in?" one of the officers who'd boarded *Penny Lane* asked him. Geoffrey shook his head. He needed to be alone right now. He started up *Penny*'s motor and cast a last look over his shoulder.

Emily had been wrapped in a silver survival blanket. She stood in the back of the cutter, still in Colin's ever protective embrace, speaking to the Coast Guard officers.

Rays of sunshine slipped through the evaporating fog, mocking him with its warmth and cheeriness. He didn't look back again, only forward to his bleak future, as he motored *Penny Lane* toward Newport Harbor.

It was over. Her attacker, like her past, was no

longer a mystery. Emily had remembered what happened that night on her fiancé's ship. She'd told her friend Sonja things would be back the way they were.

She was going home.

Ava Bradley

Chapter Twenty-Eight

"How's my favorite patient doing?"

Dr. Carlson hung his clipboard by the door and gave her a giant smile. Emily thought back to the first day she'd met him when he'd called her the very same thing, even though she'd never seen him before in her life.

"Well, Dr. Carlson, I've just had my first shower in three weeks. I'm peachy." She laughed at the same time hot tears stung. Her emotions were racing high, though she wasn't sure if she was happy or sad. Her laugh was dangerously close to turning into a gale of sobbing. Emily drew in a deep breath to force it away.

The Coast Guard had questioned them for what seemed like hours, yet in all that time, there had been no sign of Chelsie. Finally, they'd taken Emily and Colin back to the marina where an ambulance waited to carry her to the hospital. Her arm hurt terribly, and her cast was falling apart. She'd hit Chelsie hard enough to shatter it. Since they were going to replace it anyway, Emily had begged for a hot shower first.

It had felt like heaven.

"Your arm is fine. The bones are knitting nicely. You'll only have to wear a cast for another three weeks. Now, how about a different color this time? I have passionate pink or gruesome green."

Both were traffic-reflecting neon, but Emily thought

something bright would be good this time. She chose pink.

Colin walked in, strode over and kissed her on the cheek. "How's she doing, doc?"

"She'll be fine, but then I knew that when we met three weeks ago." Dr. Carlson winked and patted her on the knee. He stood and kicked his rolling stool away. "Nurse Thompson will be in to help in a moment." He made a hasty exit, as though he knew Emily wanted to be alone with Colin.

Colin moved to her right side to avoid bumping her exposed arm and gave her a quick hug. "You had me worried for a minute."

Emily leaned away. Colin's smile faded.

"Time for you to come clean." When he remained silent, she added, "I remember what happened that night."

He sighed and moved away. She stayed seated on the examination table and watched him pace the tiny room.

"Sonja is pregnant," she started for him.

He stopped and faced her.

"She told me that night on deck. She wanted me to break our engagement."

"I know." His voice was heavy with regret. Emily's irritation jumped. How dare he pout like a poor abused dog somebody had kicked! She remembered how angry she'd been that night, and took another deep breath to keep herself under control. Now was not the time to rehash all that. Terrible things had happened, but they'd survived them. Now was the time to heal, and rebuild.

"Were you going to tell me?"

"I should have, right away. I know that now."

"Chelsie said she was too."

He stopped, mouth agape. "Chelsie? No, I..." His shoulders slumped. "Jesus."

"How many times, Colin?"

He closed his eyes. Emily felt a twinge of pity for him, but then she remembered his cheating had nearly cost her her life.

His nostrils flared as he blasted a heated breath. "Twice with Sonja, once with Chelsie."

Emily felt as though a prizefighter had just punched her in the stomach. *This shouldn't surprise me*, she told herself. *I knew as much already.*

And now she knew how Geoffrey felt. Strangely, she hurt more for him, for enduring this pain, than she did for herself.

I'll make sure he never feels it again, she vowed silently.

"You wouldn't set a date. I felt like that meant I was free to do what I wanted. You have to understand—"

"*I* have to understand?" she repeated back, dumbstruck.

"I was wrong, I know that now." He shook his head and sighed. "I knew it then."

He crossed the tiny office and took her uninjured hand. Emily was too numb to stop him.

"I almost lost you, and I realize how stupid I was. If you can forgive me, we can come out of this stronger than ever before. I swear, I'll spend the rest of my life worshipping you. Marry me tomorrow, Emily. We can put all this behind us and have the life we deserve."

Emily gently pushed his hands back and tugged hers free. She shook her head. "No, Colin."

"Emily, don't do this." His expression crumbled.

"It's not meant to be."

He grasped her hand again. "Yes, it is. I love you. You have to believe that."

"I do," she told him, and she truly did believe it. "And I love you, too. I will always love you. But I don't want to marry you."

"Emily, no. Don't say that." For a moment, his eyes begged. Then, like a curtain being lifted, she saw his pained acceptance. "I can't believe I've lost you."

"You didn't lose me. I'm here, Colin. I survived, and I'll always be a part of your life. Just not as your wife."

She lifted her good arm, beckoning him. He wrapped his arms around her and cried silently, and her eyes burned, too. Not having the life she'd thought was hers with Colin would always hurt, but now she realized that life wasn't real to begin with.

Sheriff Gaffney stuck his head through the door. He knocked when he saw them together.

"Mike, hi. Come in." She motioned him inside.

Colin turned away and swiped a thumb across his eye.

"Heard you had a little scrape out on the ocean."

She nodded. "But I think I'm going to be okay."

"Glad to hear it." He shifted, turning his hat in his hand. "The body of a young woman was pulled from the water. They're bringing her into the morgue downstairs. We'll need you to make an identification."

Colin drove a hand through his hair. "Oh, Christ."

"You go. She was pregnant with your child." Emily swallowed, but couldn't stop the two fat tears that spilled over and rolled down her cheeks. She looked at Mike. "I have something important I have to do."

◆ ◆ ◆

Geoffrey slammed the front door and stalked to the kitchen. Derek sat at the table, eating a cheese sandwich. The ink mustache was faded and smeared, but still visible.

"What's up, bro? You look a little scruffy."

Geoffrey opened the cabinet where cookies and crackers were kept and reached behind a large box of Jocelyn's sugary cereal. He retrieved the airline-sized bottle of raspberry vodka hidden there and poured it into a glass.

"Dude, it's not even noon."

"So?" Geoffrey filled the rest with orange juice. "Those of us who don't have a problem can do this on occasion if we want to."

"Ouch."

He slugged a deep mouthful, refusing to let Derek make him feel guilty.

"So where's Emily? She was here last night, wasn't she?" He grinned and grunted out a ridiculous frat boy sound.

"She's gone back to Astoria."

"When's she...she's coming back, isn't she?"

"No. She isn't." He turned his back, taking another deep mouthful of his raspberry screwdriver.

Derek shifted behind him. "Oh. Sorry."

"So am I."

"No, really, I am, dude. I thought you two made a great couple."

Crap. Derek wanted to get sentimental. Geoffrey took a final mouthful and poured the rest down the sink.

Emily was gone. It would hurt like hell for a long time, but he would get over it.

No, he wouldn't. She was one in a million. He should

have been more ardent when he told her exactly how he felt about her. He should have done more.

Maybe he could. Did he dare? He had to.

He might look like a fool, and he'd probably have to do it in front of that cretin Colin, but he could make one last effort to tell her he was the man for her.

He strode out of the kitchen and reached for the doorknob before he fully acknowledged the glimpse of Mike's unmarked car through the narrow door-side window.

He yanked open the door, fishing his keys out of his pocket with the other hand.

Emily stood before him, wearing nothing more than a hospital gown, OR room shoe covers, and a new, hot pink cast on her left arm.

She smiled. "Hi."

He glanced over her shoulder. Mike leaned against the driver's door, grinning.

"Do you still want to marry me?" she asked.

He snapped his gaze back. Was that a trick question? Of course he wanted to marry her! He sought an answer, but couldn't manage a single word.

She stepped through the doorway. Geoffrey stood back and allowed her to take his hand. *Say something, numbskull.*

She knelt down on one knee. "Geoffrey Barthlow...uh oh." She pulled her hand free and reached behind herself to close her hospital gown. Mike laughed and turned away.

"Geoffrey Barthlow, will you marry me?"

"Say yes, dude."

He nearly jumped out of his skin when Derek spoke immediately behind him.

"Yes!" He pulled her to her feet and hugged her, picking her up to spin around. "I want nothing more in this life than to marry you, Emily Atkinson."

Happily Ever Later

Geoffrey leaned out of the hospital room's doorway at the sound of Jocelyn's voice. She saw him, gave a tiny squeal, and ran the rest of the way down the hall.

"Uncle G!" He scooped her up and she wrapped her arms around his neck. "It's a girl!"

"How did you know that?" He kissed her cheek.

"Mom told me."

Leah shrugged. "She promised she wouldn't tell, and she didn't, did she?"

"She sure didn't."

They had let Dr. Carlson—*Mrs.* Dr. Carlson—tell Leah the results of the ultrasound after she promised to keep it to herself. Emily wanted to be surprised, and so did he. Secretly he'd hoped for a girl, but being surprised had been wonderful.

"We brought flowers," Jocelyn announced.

"For me?"

"No!" She giggled. "For Emily."

They entered the recovery room. He set Jocelyn down and she tiptoed over to the bed. "Oooh! She's so pretty!"

"Just like her mother." Geoffrey returned to the seat he'd occupied for most of the morning on the other side of Emily's bed.

"You're glowing." Leah set the spring bouquet on the bedside table. "Six hours of labor wins the record for this family."

"It was tough." Emily smiled down at her tiny bundle, sleeping contentedly in the crook of her arm. "But worth it."

"So what-cha gonna name her?" Jocelyn asked.

Emily gazed at Geoffrey. "I don't know. We didn't even know she was a girl until this morning."

"Well, you could name her April, for her birthday," Jocelyn said. They all stared, and she giggled. "What? It's a name, you know."

About the author

Ava Bradley has a vivid imagination. As a teenager, she thought she'd write a book, have Stephen King-like fame, and buy a big house for her family in Woodside Hills (where today you can't find a fixer-upper for under a million dollars). Reality sank in fast, and today, Ava understands the term "starving artist." But even so, that doesn't stop her from writing the stories spinning through her imagination.

When asked why she writes romance, the answer is simple. There's too much violence, anger, and hatred in this world, and this is her way of bringing back a tiny bit of joy. Her favorite stories to write are about normal people like Emily Atkinson, who find themselves in dangerous situations but somehow manage to rise above the odds and triumph.

And always, with a happy ending.